Serpientes

Diney DeRuy

authorHOUSE™

1663 Liberty Drive, Suite 200
Bloomington, Indiana 47403
(800) 839-8640
www.AuthorHouse.com

First published by AuthorHouse 08/08/05

ISBN: 1-4208-7317-2 (sc)
ISBN: 1-4208-7316-4 (dj)

Printed in the United States of America
Bloomington, Indiana

This book is printed on acid-free paper.

Prologue

About a year ago, Mark Gordon, a small town high school biology teacher in Greenland, Kansas, began to question what makes professionals in seismology think that earthquakes only originate *naturally*, below the earth's surface. There had been some strange events lately that had taken place in his otherwise peaceful and quiet part of the world, making him think in a diverse way. He'd been doing his own research after school, at night and on the weekends enlisting his students to help.

Mark was starting to appreciate how our ancestors initially described these immeasurable shifts in the earth's crust and that it could, in all actuality, be the veracity.

Today, scientists believe earthquakes are caused either by explosive volcanic eruptions or by Tectonic activity associated with plate margins and faults. They explain these marvels as a sudden tremor or movement of the earth's crust. Mark agreed with the latter, but had his mind open to the former. He was on to a different enlightenment concerning the world under him and was out to prove it.

One reason Mark was skeptical was because the techniques used today were developed in the 1800's. Robert Mallet, who designed many of the London bridges, measured velocity of seismic waves in the earth using explosions of gunpowder. He looked for variations in the seismic velocity that would indicate variations in the properties of the earth. Mark thought this wasn't an explanation of reason; it was no more than a proven theory of underground motion.

During the same time period, Fusakichi Omori studied the rate of aftershock activity. His equations are still used presently. Although twentieth century exploration has increased, Mark thought the logic was profoundly outdated.

Before them, Aristotle was one of the first to even attempt an explanation of earthquakes based on *natural* phenomena. Prior to November 1, 1755, when a cataclysmic shock and tsunami that killed an estimated 70,000 people in Lisbon, Portugal, scholars looked almost exclusively to Aristotle for explanations.

Basically, the investigation into the origin of earthquakes is not as vastly developed as what people are led to believe. People accepted or accept the rational given, even though none of these experts were taken seriously until the 1900's when Seikei Seikiya, a Japanese researcher, became the first professor in seismology.

Seismologists analyze these two main causes instead of looking into other possibilities, such as deviations in the realm beneath us occurring, *before* a quake actually happens, perhaps by another life force. And they study the magnitude of the shockwaves as a rule, which determines the extent of damage and the focus point, or epicentre of the earthquake. Hardly viable in exposing anything new in Mark's opinion.

Typically, the great earthquakes are scrutinized, such as the 1783 Calabrian that killed 35,000 people and/or the 1822 and 1835 Chilean earthquakes. No one considers less significant ones that don't rate on the Mercalli or Richter Scales, or that aren't in California.

But they do happen and they happen everywhere, it's just that individuals are usually imperceptive of them.

This past year, where thirty year old Gordon grew up and made his livelihood, he began to notice weaknesses in the high school's foundational structure. Curious, he started looking into the entire town's construction and became concerned with the surmountable base fractures. He discovered these unusual ruptures were occurring at a phenomenal rate, according to what's considered normal.

There was no justification for this; the town was properly built, unless they were experiencing numerous vibrations from down below. And supposedly they were not located above a major fault and, of course, there were no volcanoes in Kansas. Underground springs, yes; however, Mark was fairly positive by now that wasn't the cause of this settlement's damage.

Having a degree in biology didn't exactly make Mark knowledgeable in the field of earth quaking, but he was intelligent and learned quickly. He also made phone calls asking questions to those who were experienced, concerned and perplexed by his bizarre unearthing. The ground under them was essentially fluctuating on a frequent basis. His mission was to find out why and what could be done. This was his home and he wanted to get married one day and have a great life here. Not see it sink into the earth's mantle.

This wasn't the only odd circumstance in Greenland, KS. that made Gordon believe his ancestor's theory; something unknown to man thriving submersed, being the real underpinning of the earth's trembling. Soon after he first suspected there was diminutive seismic activity taking place on a recurrent level, he began investigating stories of unusually large snakes terrorizing the few average citizens who claimed they saw one. Mark was the only biology authority in town. The folk called him for many things and these snakes happen to be one of them.

After seeing some of the strange, sizeable and countless holes created by these creatures, it was certainly reasonable for him to presume they could be the source of the rumblings under this town. Especially after his findings since the inception was proving the possibility.

Truthfully, it was beginning to scare the shit out of him. His alarm for the safety of his kin was lamentably on the rise.

Mark was beginning to grasp that no one really knows what lives deep inside of the earth or when and if a breed of whatever, possibly reptiles, will decide to surface. There's no guarantee that the human race will always be the controlling race. The dinosaurs did rule many years ago, after all, and they are extinct. Why wouldn't he suppose evolution could be throwing this planet into another loop?

Serpientes

Chapter one

Aɴɴ Roᴄᴋ ᴡᴀs ʜᴀᴘᴘʏ, smiling, gazing out her and her husband's 1987 black Chevy Blazer. Mitch was driving and they were equally relaxed, yet excited. It was a beautiful late afternoon in March and the couple was heading to their future destination; Greenland, Kansas. Ann couldn't decide if this was the best day in her life or not.

Everything was perfect in Mitch and Ann Rock's world. Newly wedded last week, they had just spent four glorious days in Bermuda on their honeymoon. They flew back to the city yesterday and stayed last night with family, saying their goodbyes, before leaving to start their new lives.

Mitch and Ann are both twenty-eight years old. They were childhood friends and high school sweethearts. They attended the same University and Mitch holds a masters degree in Mathematics, Ann in English. Mitch landed a job at the high school in Greenland weeks after graduation in December. Ann plans to look for work after they finish remodeling the old farmhouse they recently bought there.

It was a dream come true for this pair; owning their own home and the ten acres it sat on. They were smart about the decisions they made throughout their short lifetime, the first one being birth control and the next most important one, hoarding for their expectations in the future.

Ann had worked at the JC Penney store for the past six years and made decent money. Mitch did odd jobs in his spare time, a handy man of sorts, who always had plenty of employment. Since they lived together in a one bedroom flat during their college years and shared a car, they were able to save quite a bit of money, forever planning for this day.

"Oh look, Mitch, there it is!" Ann said, eagerly.

"Honey, we're home," Mitch sang, just as energized as his lovely wife. Grabbing her hand and giving her an adoring glance, he then asked, "Are you going to let me carry you across the threshold?"

"Yes, of course, my wonderful man." Ann was so much in love with Mitch it was almost pathetic. She'd always felt that way about him.

Mitch turned the wheel of the Chevy and pulled off the dirt road and onto the chat drive. There before them stood the fifty-something year old, worn out two-story house, with a detached garage that looked more like a shack, plus a very large dilapidated barn in the back, along with overgrown weeds beginning a new cycle. However, that's not what they saw. Mitch and Ann saw a beautiful freshly painted home with plenty of children running around and horses in an immaculate stable. Included would be a well-built wood privacy fence surrounding a manicured lawn, possibly cows covering the rest of their acreage, or something. They fancied a pool in due time, too.

Getting out of the car leisurely, taking in the karma of the land, Ann wandered over to Mitch and stood in front of him facing the property, leaning back on his chest. He put his arms around her. They admired their good fortune together.

"You ready to be an old farm woman?" he teased her.

"Oh, God yes! Look at how wonderful this country is," she said, gaping at the novel terrain, breathing in the fresh country air and becoming enveloped in the silence. "I **never** want to go back to the city."

"Me either." Mitch was awed by the remarkable as well.

Approximately two minutes later, Ann commented, "Actually sweetie, it's almost a little too quiet, don't you think?"

"I don't know. We do come from a long line of city dwellers. We'll just have to learn how to be simple folk and get used to what goes with it as we go." Mitch shrugged. "Shall we?"

Ann grinned at her husband.

Mitch let go of her, only for a second, while he pulled out a bottle of cheap champagne along with two plastic goblets, from a cooler in the backseat. Grinning in response to his charming partner in life, he quickly scooped her up into his arms and carried her to the front door.

Ann fumbled with the keys trying to unlock it in her awkward position. She couldn't really see that well since dusk was upon them. They giggled.

"Hurry up, you're getting heavy."

"Oh shush."

Mitch and Ann bought this house the same day he accepted the position at Greenland High School. It was a great deal, they thought. It hadn't been lived in for at least two years and there hadn't been any offers in that time, so the bank here was ready to let it go for next to nothing. The lady in charge was also willing to set up their loan with the best interest rates, without the additional standard fee. Lucky for the Rocks they spotted it, while driving around the day they visited for Mitch to sign the contract with the school board, discovering where they wanted to spend eternity.

The two knew they would have to put a lot of money and elbow grease into this old homestead, probably having to gut the entire place in order to fix it up. But, since Mitch knew how to do most construction – he was born a natural when it came to home repairs and Ann was a hard worker who figured she could learn to do anything – they went for broke. Hell, they were young.

Ann would oversee the renovations for as long as it took. There was plenty of cash on hand to hire out when they needed, plus Mitch's salary would be more than enough to make the meager house payments. It would be exciting and fun. The Rocks were more than ready to begin a life away from their norm.

Chapter two

"Oh boy," Ann said, a bit overwhelmed upon seeing the place in chaos and filth, instantly realizing the labor that needed to be done.

"You would think the bank could have sent someone out here to clean the place up a little. Gees."

"You sure you don't want to stay at a hotel for a while?"

"No...I'm positive. I don't want to waste any of our money. It'll be fine," she said, rather unconvincingly.

Mitch put her down and gawked about the joint. "Let's say we put the champagne on ice for another day and get busy cleaning this mess." He couldn't stand grime. Neat freak, actually.

"Yeah, I'm with you. I'll start getting the supplies out of the car." Ann was trying to sound cheerful and committed. She knew, well they both did, this was going to take time and effort. They were as prepared as they could be. Except, talking about it didn't seem as daunting as what they had in front of them now, especially after such a long car ride. It took close to seven hours to get here from St. Louis, MO. She was a little tired and it had been a long week.

"Okay, I'll get the coffee brewing. It looks like we're going to need plenty." Mitch acted optimistic. Ann knew he wanted to rent a place or something during the process of making this run down, aged house into a modernized, comfortable family home. She loved him for his grit and vowed right then and there that she would not grumble during this trial.

At least, they had all weekend to get it into a somewhat livable place, before Mitch started work on Monday.

"We can do this," Ann said, noticing her husband stare at the cobwebs overhead.

"I know. I know. I'm ready."

"Come on then." Ann punched his arm in a loving way, wanting him to follow her and help get what they needed out of the Blazer, including a crucial element; the coffee maker.

"We can always sleep in the car tonight."

"May have to," Mitch answered her, with a look of amazement, still staring up above.

As Ann bopped out onto the cement porch and proceeded down the steps, there was an abrupt rustling noise in the brush next to the house. It startled her and she let out a loud gasp, then yelled, "Mitch!" instantly frightened and immobilized.

He was by her side in a jiffy, his eyes wide. "What? What is it?"

Clinging on to him for dear life, Ann insisted, "There's something down there, in those bushes!" She pointed to where she heard the noise.

"Okay, calm down. We're in the country now. We need to get used to little varmints. *Unciticize* ourselves."

"Oh good one. *Unciticize*? Remind me to write it down."

Into her second year of school at Washington University, Ann became obsessively serious about her profession to be. It began with her correcting Mitch's language habits then quickly soared into a full blown neurosis. She would get outright agitated if Mitch used any kind of slang.

Soon, she was trying to fix anyone and everyone around her; the grocery store clerk, her friends, his friends, and even the professors at the university. Subsequently, Ann began studying so much when she wasn't working or at class, she wouldn't sleep for days on end. This went on for about six months. It was when the crying fits started that Mitch gave her an ultimatum.

He told her one night they were finished if she didn't seek help. And he meant it. He couldn't deal with "her problem" and the strain on their relationship. Thankfully, this had been a solitary episode and the only one that had ruined a period of time in their otherwise ideal life.

Ann did seek help, afraid of losing the man she loved. It took strength and persistence, but with medication and psychotherapy for about a year, she overcame her need to be faultless in speech.

It was during her counseling when they came up with the idea to make a slang dictionary. Since the creation, they had recorded every jargon or made-up word in a journal Mitch had bought for Ann. In fact, this helped Ann deal with her need to speak properly all the time, while she learned to ignore how other people chose to talk. They had a good time with these new and bold terminologies, and also with the idea of getting published one day.

Mitch bent over and peered into the bushes, getting as close as he could looking for the culprit. The porch light didn't give off enough light though, and since it was almost dark he couldn't really see anything.

"Holy shit!" he suddenly piped, clumsily jumping up and backwards just as the bushes rattled again. He stumbled into Ann, but was able to spread his arms out in front of her to protect her.

"What is it?" Ann tightened her grip on her husband, ready to climb on top of him if whatever it was were to attack. But the moving hedge began to quickly move away from them. They followed with their eyes, the creature they couldn't see via the dancing shrubs, all the way to the end of the house.

"Christ, that scared me to near death! What do you think it was?" a nervous Ann asked her hero, still clinging firmly to him.

Straightening his shoulders, wanting to be the man, Mitch answered her confidently, "Probably a rabbit."

"Oh."

Ann and Mitch looked around the twilight terra firma for a good long minute.

"I don't think I want to sleep in the car after all."

"No, me either. Let's get everything unloaded, pronto. Come on," Mitch said, taking a hold of her hand, guiding her to the Blazer. He was keeping his eyes open for any unwanted pests the whole time. The unexpected had flustered him, too.

Chapter three

Mitch and Ann cleaned until dawn on the first night in their brand new home. She batted down the dust and he scrubbed the floors. Surprisingly, everything was in working order. Of course the bank had reassured them there was nothing wrong with the place. The employee had explained it was merely that people couldn't envision what the house could be like with some tender loving care. The bank was more willing to tear it down than spend a dime on the remodeling, because they weren't positive it would sell compared to selling the land alone. Which would have been an even bigger loss for them, the reason they made this young couple such a good offer.

"I'm starving and in need of a decent meal," Mitch grunted, as he slowly got up off his knees and stretched.

"I'm sick of granola bars."

Laughing to herself, Ann replied, "Me too. Hey, let's go into town and eat, check things out. It's time we meet some people. We are citizens here now, you know." Her enthusiasm was catching.

"Alright. You've got yourself a date." He smiled dotingly at the wife with the dirty smudges on her cheeks.

"You want to clean up first?"

"No. I imagine I'm going to look this way for quite some time. No reason to take a shower when we're just coming back to sweat some more."

"Okay, but promise me you'll take one tonight." He winked and gave her a sexy grin. She got the message.

Ann Marie Rock was five-eight and weighed right at one-hundred thirty-five pounds. Not too thin, but not heavy. Healthy is how Mitch described her. She had dark brown curly hair she wore mostly tied up in a bun or under a baseball cap, which she had on now. Her eyes were a beautiful color of green with a touch of shimmering teal, and her smile was infectious. She was self confident, yet sassy with a good sense of humor type gal. And she looked great in jeans and a t-shirt, their wardrobe of the past six years.

Mitch Adam Rock already bought the necessary khaki pants and dress shirts along with two new sport coats that he would need to teach his classes in, forever and always organized. He was barely an inch taller than his wife and not much weightier. He had short, blondish brown hair he kept in a crew cut every three weeks and even though he was in jeans and a t-shirt, too, his were pressed, before putting them on. Mitch also wore glasses with a tint of blue in them, enhancing his already rich aqua eyes, emphasizing his intelligent look.

After they locked up their brand new domicile, the Rocks drove to town, about a five minute jaunt. Mitch and Ann knew the way around since they'd been down three times previously, locking in the job and then the house deal.

Deciding to eat at a cafe called The Diner, the Rocks ordered a massive amount of breakfast. The waitress, a Miss Charlotte, struck up a conversation as they ate. The three were discussing the town, job opportunities for Ann and who to call for help with their project on the previous Hammer home.

"So, you knew the Hammers?" Ann asked, interested in the history of the house.

"Sure did, kid. Actually, it was just old man Hammer that lived out there for about twenty years. Don't know what happened to his wife. It was way before my time." Charlotte played the part. She was pretty and friendly, around fifty and appeared to be well maintained under her uniform. She leaned on the back of the booth next to Mitch, not in a flirting manner, more like a small-town-knows-everybody way.

"I thought the bank told us a Miss Susan Hammer was the last owner?"

"That's right. Hank Hammer died going on about three years now, left the house to his daughter. She was a strange woman," the waitress mentioned, offhandedly.

"What do you mean *strange*?" She had Mitch's attention.

"It's like this," Charlotte explained, chomping on her gum throughout the small talk.

"No one who knew Hank ever remembered any visits his daughter might have made, while he was living, and he never mentioned her to anyone. But, low and behold, the day he passed on, suddenly here she was, and she moved right on into that house without a problem. Said she was going to fix the place up and sell it."

"Too bad she didn't," Mitch commented, deviously. Ann gave him one of her *stop it* looks.

"What happened to her?"

"You see, everyone around here knew and liked Hank so we all tried to help her, except we all knew she was money hungry and didn't care about her dad." Charlotte made a production out of rolling her eyes at the notion, before going on.

"Anyhow, soon after she got here, she started...babbling."

"Babbling?"

"Yeah, babbling. It was bizarre. She scared some of the folk here. Then, after a while, she quit coming around and one day she was just gone." She snapped her fingers. "Just like that.

"It's too bad, too. Her father didn't owe a lot of money on the house. Chicken farmer. He made a good income. She could have made a pretty nice profit had she kept her plans. Sorry kids, that's town gossip," she said, laughing at her blunder of disclosing information she shouldn't have repeated.

"Did anyone try to find her?" Mitch was behaving more sincere now asking this question.

"The bank did. Not a trace. The woman up and vanished. They repossessed the house.

"Hey kids, I've got to get back to work. Hope to see you two in here a lot." She gave them a big smile, while prancing off to take care of the three new customers who had just walked in.

"Well that's spooky," Ann told Mitch, the minute the waitress was gone, her face one of marvel.

"It's not spooky, Ann, it's just weird. What I'd like to know is what kind of profit the bank made. If old man Hammer didn't owe very much on his house, then..." he stopped and began doing the math in his head.

"Mitch, we got a hell of a buy and you know it. What I'm afraid of is that we're going to find her body or something when we start tearing up the place." She was serious, sitting there eye balling her husband.

"Oh for pity sake, Ann. That is sooo not going to happen. Sounds to me like the woman was plain ol' crazy. She probably escaped a mental institution and they probably found her and locked her back up."

"You think?"

"Yes. What do you think...that it was her in the bushes last night?" he said, sarcastically, then chuckled at his own joke.

"No...Mitch..." Ann realized she was being silly and smirked at his comment.

"Come on, Mr. Funny guy. Let's get back to work, you ready?"

"I don't think I have a choice, do I *sweetums*?" (That word was already in the journal.)

"I think you're loopy from lack of sleep." Ann shook her head.

"Great food, huh?" Mitch grinned at her as he pulled out his wallet to pay the bill. "Cheap too."

Chapter **four**

IT WAS LATE SUNDAY NIGHT and the duo had worked nonstop the entire weekend. Mitch and Ann had the place fit for human habitation, aside from the fact they had zero furniture. What they owned was everything they could get in the Blazer; clothes and toiletries, their computer, a few personal mementos such as pictures, and lots of cleaning supplies.

They took turns running into town to the hardware store and for food or whatever else. On one of Mitch's turns, he bumped into a man and started a conversation with him. As luck would have it, he just happened to be the bug guy in this small town. Mitch slipped him a couple twenties to come out on Sunday morning to spray for creepy-crawlies, the reason being more important than the money. Ann had been pretty jumpy. There were so many spiders and roaches in the house, along with ants and you name it, she couldn't function without shrieking every other minute or shouting for Mitch to, "Come and kill this monster".

Thank God there hadn't been anything worse – like a body.

Anyway, they could now assess what specifically needed to be done in order to make this house a true home. At this point, they were both particularly thrilled about their decision to buy and fix up the place. They felt they had indeed made another right choice, in their already precise life.

With the dust gone and the windows cleaned, which took a lot of muscle to do these large old fashioned panes, Mitch and Ann could finally see what this place had to offer. They had been so wound for the count when buying this land, especially right before the wedding, that neither had really been able to picture anything.

The rooms were enormous, making it fun to think about what kind of furniture they would buy. No need to knock out any walls. The wood flooring would need refinishing, the woodwork, too, but they weren't going to have to go the extremes they originally anticipated. The newlyweds were overjoyed by that prospect.

Resting on the floor in what would be the family room, Mitch and Ann sat facing each other talking, both worn to a frazzle, but showered. They were wrapped in separate blankets and Mitch had found enough kindling for a fire. It crackled, illuminating the two.

"Everything seems sturdy enough, Ann. The foundation, the walls, floors...I think we got more than an exceptional deal on this place after all." He stopped to reflect for a moment, then continued, "The front porch needs to be completely torn off and rebuilt, and the paint job on the outside isn't going to be cheap, but I couldn't find a thing wrong structurally. We're not going to need to replace much at all, including the windows. Cleaned up nice, didn't it?"

Sipping her champagne, Ann watched her husband's thought process working. They had been over the same things for two days now. He just liked to talk their judgments through to the bone to be absolutely positive they were making the best choices.

"I'm happy, Mitch. And the windows are fine with me **if** the wasp can't fly through them. That man did take care of those, too, didn't he?"

"Yes, Ann." He winked at her. Guess they were going to end up spending a lot of money on insect detail.

"Good, I still feel like I have spiders crawling all over me. Ooo." She shuddered at the notion.

"I can tell." He quickly remembered her sleeping on top of him last night.

Wasn't all bad.

"When I was at the hardware store, I priced paint and varnish and what it would cost to rent the equipment to re-do these floors. If I do it all myself and you help when you can, we can save a ton of money. Before that, all we have to do is scrape off this ungodly wallpaper, prep and paint. Of course, the woodwork will be harder to refinish and will probably take forever, but still...we have the rest of our lives.

"Mitch, I was thinking about starting a retirement account with the left over money." Ann did her share of planning their future.

"Whoa, slow down...a retirement account? I'm not old enough."

"Sure you are, silly. Why shouldn't we? It doesn't have to be traditional. We can call it a savings account or whatever you want. I just think it's time we invest and besides, we'll have it for emergencies and when the babies start arriving we'll have extra money...you know." She grinned coyly.

"Yeah, I get it." He smiled back. "You're a thinker aren't you? I'm going to call you my little *braineator*."

"Oh, another good one for the book. You're on a roll this week."

"Hey, wait till you see what's all in the barn. When I was going through it..."

"Cripes, I will never go in there!" Ann interrupted, quivering again.

"I should have figured, anyway just listen. I found an old riding lawn mower and some tools. I think I can get it running without a problem. I'll be able to cut the grass after school tomorrow or the next day."

"I didn't think about that. Gees, do we have to cut the whole ten acres?" Ann was a little worried here.

"Hell no. We need to get some kind of a fence up, though. We could earn extra money renting the land to cattle owners who have nowhere to put their herds in the winter. It's a big business. I read that it's more expensive to harbor the animals in the winter, so most land owners don't do it. But there is still a profit to be made."

"Oh, okay. I'm game to try anything and everything," Ann said, sounding encouraging. "And I really do want horses. I know I would love to ride and I want to learn. I mean, who wouldn't in this beautiful countryside?"

"Well then, you better get used to bugs and rodents and crawly things."

"I know. I can't help it. There were so many! Jesus, just thinking about them gives me the heebie jeebies."

"You're so cute. Come on over here to *the man* of the house." Mitch patted the floor in front of him.

"I'll protect you my lovely wife." Ann quickly scooted over to him. She turned and faced the fireplace, snuggling up to her savior.

"This is nice." They sat mesmerized by the sparkles, Mitch holding the stressed out Ann.

Eventually they fell asleep.

Chapter five

THE NEXT MORNING, dressed in his new khakis and a white dress shirt, sporting a colorful tie adorned with one of his sport coats, Mitch was ready to go to work on his first day at the school. It was the end of the year, that's true, but the woman who had the job for the past thirty years was retiring and he would be learning her curriculum. Mitch would take over the classroom, teaching his own students starting with summer school in June.

"Wake up, sunshine," he softly whispered in Ann's ear, bending over her.

Instead of the sleeping beauty's eyes slowly opening in a lady like manner, Ann bound up off the floor with a squeal, knocking Mitch to the ground on the way. She immediately began rubbing her body feeling for possible creatures.

A bit flabbergasted, "Ann, for crying-out-loud, nothing is on you," Mitch said, rather callous, looking up at her from his position on the floor.

"Oh, Mitch...I must have been dreaming," Ann responded, diffident, gaining her senses back somewhat.

Then, realizing she was the reason he was on the ground, she hurriedly said, "I'm sorry, sweetie. Are you okay? You look nice," while smiling her innocent smile and melting his anger.

Shaking his head, getting up and brushing himself off, Mitch smiled back at her reluctantly, wishing he could resist her charm once in awhile. "I'm fine. I need you to drive me to work if you want the car today, nightmare queen."

"Yeah, sure. Coffee made?" Ann was slowly waking up, trying to remember what day it was, pretending to be alert, and ignoring her new nickname.

"Yep, got a cup ready for ya in the kitchen, beautiful."

"Right, beautiful. I'll bet I am."

Ann had worn her white Russell sweat pants and her new Kansas sunflower t-shirt to sleep in. All she needed was her ball cap and thongs to drive him up to the high school. She rushed to get her purse and while grabbing her coffee, said cheerfully, acting bright eyed and bushy tailed for her day, "Okay, I'm ready, let's go.

"I can't believe I didn't hear you get up."

On the drive there, Ann asked Mitch if he was excited about work. They hadn't really talked about it since their routines were changing so radically and rapidly. He was. He said it was a great opportunity for his very first job as a teacher and that it seemed to be a great town to live in and raise a family. Everything was great. The new life, just everything.

Mitch kissed her goodbye as he enthusiastically got out of the car, ready. Then he strutted off waving at his wife as he went. Ann sat there for a time staring after him, foolishly grinning, proud of her husband, happy that he was happy, before driving back to the farm.

Ann was exhausted and more than sore from the weekend chores, but couldn't wait to begin her day's projects. Arranging to get a phone hooked up was her number one priority. Then off to the bank to open a new checking account and probably the grocery store for a few pantry items. After that, she was going to look for a real bed. They'd slept on the floor the past two nights and on only a mattress the past six years. This was going to be a huge treat for them.

As she pulled into their driveway, her mind was spinning with how well things were going for her and Mitch. They had been smart in the past concerning the choices they made for themselves. The future looked to be bright. She was imagining children when suddenly she spotted something out of her peripheral vision, causing her to slam on the brakes and spill the rest of her coffee.

"Oh…my…God!"

Ann's eyes were as big as they could get. Blinking a few times to make sure she was seeing what she thought she was seeing, her entire body immediately tensed with panic.

Smack dab in the middle of the porch, by the front door to the house, was the longest, blackest, nastiest snake she'd ever seen in her life, not that she'd normally ever encountered snakes in the city. It had to be at least fifteen to twenty feet long, she speculated and it appeared to be fat, like it weighed a ton. Its shiny, slick, shimmering body was slithering from the top of its head to the bottom of its tail, back and forth, in a slanting, gyrating motion. However, it wasn't going anywhere. Ann could see its head rise when she hit the breaks, which caused chat to fly everywhere, throwing a smoky dust into the air.

"Jesus Christ...what am I going to do? Well shit. Shit. Shit. Shit. Oh God!" Her skin became cold and instantaneously tingled to the beat of the snake's movements. The back of her throat closed, while her jaws clenched, along with her hands wrapped tightly around the steering wheel. Her heart pounded. Ann couldn't take her eyes off the damn thing. The tears began to well up.

"Don't cry, Ann," she demanded of herself, unclenching her right hand and quickly fanning her face. She wouldn't be able to see it if her sight was blurred. The tormenter could possibly slide over and swallow the car for all she knew. She shouldn't take her eyes off of it for this very reason.

Concentrating for a second, "Come on, Ann, think of something. You can handle this..." Mitch's words about them being farm people now and learning how to live around varmints, rang through her head.

"Fuck. Yeah right. This is one hell of a varmint! This is just great." Her hands were sweating and she began shaking uncontrollably, sitting in the car alone, talking to herself. Fear loomed inside of her. Ann was filled with terror and couldn't help it. The enormous reptile was extremely intimidating and incredibly gross to her, ugly and uncommon. Shocking!

"God, I have to do something. There's no way I can drive back into town and bother Mitch his first day at the school.

"Good Lord, it's so disgusting! Please make it go away!

"Think, just think of anything." Ann nervously scanned the area for a weapon as she sat there stupidly trying to think of how to get rid of this unwanted surprise.

Rocks. Nothing but rocks around her.

What was she supposed to do, beat it to death? No way could she even get close to it. What if it touched her? What if it tried to kill her?

The snake's head stayed higher than the rest of it. The beast kept shifting its glossy, repulsive body up and down, back and forth, side to side, endlessly. Ann knew it was watching her. *Does it know I'm afraid? Will it hurt me if it thinks I'm afraid?*

"How in the world am I supposed to get used to something like this? It's so big! Damn it!"

After a few minutes of desperately trying to compose herself and be a mature adult, Ann found some tenacity and slowly put the car in park. With conscious effort, she reached for the door handle and cracked it open an inch. Ann decided she was approximately thirty feet from the black, hideous, never ceasing in motion real life evil, but she'd played softball in high school and thought maybe she could scare it away if she hit it with one of the rocks.

"All you have to do is pick up a rock and throw it," she whispered now, so as the snake wouldn't hear her.

Surveying it closely, Ann sucked up her dread and slid her left leg out of the barely opened car door. Breathing shallow and forcefully, she noticed the mammoth snake didn't make any progress towards her.

That was a good sign.

With a careful watch on the creature from hell and while leaving the engine running, Ann very gradually pushed the door open a little more and stood on the one leg, gaining the courage to ease the rest of her body out of the car, very cautiously.

Trembling with the notion of actually doing something about the unbelievable, Ann kept saying to herself, "Be tough". Calling on rationalization to get her through this, Ann focused on her nerve. The time ticked by as she beckoned her valor to get herself out of the freaking car.

"One good chuck is all it's going to take. You can do this Ann. You have to get used to this."

But, the insurmountable amount of anxiety rising in her was undeniable and taking over her very soul.

She immediately popped back into the vehicle with a groan and locked it. Ann couldn't stand being eye level with the gruesome atrocity on her porch, out here, in the middle of nowhere.

"Shit! Damn it! Oh God, please help me," she wailed, hugging herself, giving in to the tears.

Ann sat in the car staring at the snake, the snake staring at her, for almost an hour. She had an inkling the damn thing wasn't going anywhere. She needed more coffee, she needed to pee and she needed to get busy. Christ Almighty, this was getting ridiculous.

Summoning all her audacity and telling herself this was ludicrous, she couldn't be such a ninny if they were going to make this their home, Ann spontaneously threw the car into drive and stepped on the gas. Once again chat was thrown into the atmosphere, and she purposely did not look in the direction of the snake finally, her gaze focused on her goal instead.

Without delay, she was parked by the side door, in between the house and the garage that hadn't been cleaned yet. Ann flew out of the Blazer with flamboyant velocity. Struggling with the keys and fighting her urge to run, she managed to unlock the door and get herself safely inside within seconds, shutting and locking it behind her.

Ann almost collapsed with the fright taking over her total being. She burst into tears once again as she leaned on the door, feeling every beat of her heart. She couldn't remember ever being this scared of anything. She was practically paralyzed, except she began running her hands up and down her body and started to scream between sobs.

The feeling of helplessness took over.

Chapter six

ALL ANN COULD DO THE rest of the morning was watch the grandiose ophidia through the window, next to the front entrance. She kept crying, cursing and praying, wishing the overgrown life form would move, go away or be a dream. She also kept trying to talk herself into getting used to it, because maybe if she accepted the monster as part of her new world, she wouldn't be this scared of it.

Every time it changed positions her own skin crawled, though. Ann would automatically jerk and start frantically looking around inside the house to make sure nothing was in there that might harm her.

Before settling in this spot, she'd managed to run up the steps two at a time and fish out a pack of cigarettes she had hidden. Mitch didn't like her to smoke and she was almost off the cancer sticks for good, but now wasn't the time to worry about a nicotine addiction. Ann smoked one after the other, agitatedly. However, there was no way she could stomach another cup of coffee.

Ann felt immeasurably forlorn. Her mother warned her she wouldn't be happy in the country. Now, she wished she had listened. She honestly didn't think she wanted to make it here anymore. This was too much.

"Oh God, Mitch is going to kill me," she moaned.

Around noon, Ann forced herself to take a shower. She dragged her feet warily up the steps, her eyes glancing worriedly from left to right, checking out everything in site. She thoroughly inspected the bathroom and secured the door and window, before stripping and carefully climbing into the soothing, hot running water. Unfortunately, by now she'd had time to imagine all kinds of critters that could get into the house.

"You're safe, Ann. Quit being absurd, nothing is going to get you. It's just a dumb snake," she kept repeating to herself. But when she closed her eyes to relax, all she could see was the mental image of the gruesome snake's devil eyes watching her.

"Ooo!" Ann began washing as fast as possible, the urge to check on her visitor overpowering. It was the fastest shower in the west, before she hurriedly hopped back out, after quickly rinsing her hair, drying off rapidly.

Spying the hallway first, making sure it was clear, Ann made a mad dash for the suitcase in the bedroom. Feeling vulnerable bare, she speedily dressed in clean sweats and a T in record time. She tucked her wet hair up into the same ball cap and jogged back down the steps, skipping the rest of her normal grooming habits, such as putting on some facial cream. At least, she had taken the initiative to brush her teeth in the shower.

Holding her breath, she peeked out the front door window. Closing her eyes tightly at first, she let them open gradually, all the while praying to God, "Please let it be gone."

When she finally found the courage to look, there was nothing there. Just the weeds trying to grow through the cracks in the cement. The strange annoying had vanished. Ann breathed a sigh of relief and tears of gratitude began falling.

In that same instant, the thought that it had to have gone somewhere, entered her head. She quickly wiped the moisture in her eyes with her hands and strained her neck to get a good glimpse of the yard, searching hard for the unwanted.

She didn't see any sign of the bad snake, but started to wonder where the darn thing came from in the first place. *Does it live close by?* She ran from one window to the next and up the steps to each room, gawking out of every one, looking for the large creepy reptile.

It probably does live around here. That's why there weren't any mice, suddenly dawned on her. Mitch made a comment last night that it was funny they hadn't seen any. An empty house like this would have attracted them. At the time, she was glad there weren't, but now...

With every window she peeked out of and saw nothing, Ann felt a bit better, while questioning what was worse, a snake or mice. She wasn't sure if it was such an awful being to have living outside, compared to mice on the inside. It's not as if it tried to attack her or even tried to get in the house. It didn't do anything really, except sun itself, staring back at her with those haunting, oblong shaped eyeballs.

"Yuck!" The thought of it alone made her sick no matter what she told herself. Nevertheless, Ann was beginning to feel thankful, thinking the thing was gone, because it was nowhere to be found. She went to look out of the last window, the one in the side door off the kitchen, praying emphatically that she could get on with her day. That this episode was over.

"No!" she let out a thunderous cry. "Oh God, no, no, no!" The hysteria was back. Ann gave in to the upset, falling to the floor and hugging her knees as she wept passionately. The snake had skimmed its way up on top of the Chevy and was basking in its glory.

"Why didn't I...get the...hell out of here...when I had a chance?" she bawled.

Ann sat with her arms tightly wrapped around her as hour after hour passed. Every so often she'd slowly sneak her head up, peering out the small window to check and see if the unreal was still there. It looked like it was in love with their car. The snake boogied continually, kinking itself and unlinking itself, in constant bizarre action.

It was simply implausible.

Chapter seven

Mitch Rock waited on his wife to pick him up, sitting on the hard cold steps in front of the school. He felt somewhat embarrassed as all the kids and the teachers left. He kept glancing at his watch, wondering what happened to Ann, frustrated *and* worried.

About 4:00, he decided to go ahead and walk home. Mitch figured he would see her if she was on her way and vice versa.

Mitch reminisced about his first day on the job as he trekked down the street saying *hello* to whomever he passed, until he hit the dirt road that led out of town. The five miles wouldn't kill him, it was just that he didn't have on tennis shoes and he was in his dress attire. He didn't want to get them grungy. He was also carrying a file of important information with him, from Mrs. Weaver, the instructor he was replacing, and didn't want it to get crumpled or bent.

Mitch didn't like surprises or things out of the ordinary, but he kept moving, having no other choice and tried to remain positive, hoping like hell he would see the Blazer any minute. Luckily, it was a sunny, yet cool afternoon and he would do his best to make the best of it, deciding without a doubt that he was going to purchase a mountain bike. He bet Ann would love riding around this breath taking territory, too. Hiking, possibly camping.

All in all, he thought the day went well. Everyone was really nice and he was introduced to most of the other teachers. Mrs. Weaver was pleasant and obliging in explaining her methods and helping him get accustomed to the classroom, but he pondered if he would actually use her syllabuses. She was old and they were outdated.

Almost an hour and a half later, Mitch finally arrived at home. Coming around the corner and making his way to the drive, he calculated in his head the pace of his hike. He figured the appropriate mileage divided into the time would mean he walked at about 4.4 miles per hour. Not bad, considering he had on the wrong shoes and the extra clothing.

Mitch was starving, a little sweaty and tired; however, glad to be home, anxious to see Ann. Hauling his ass up the driveway, he noticed the Chevy parked right next to the house. It seemed odd to him, but he had no idea of what all Ann might have bought today. She may have needed it to be close if there was something heavy she had to unload. It wasn't exactly strange. He peeked into the window on the passenger's side. It looked like she got whatever out.

Surely my wife has a good reason for not picking me up, he thought.

When Mitch went to turn the knob on the back door to go inside, it was locked. He gazed in through the window, cupping his hand around his eyebrows. He couldn't really see anything, so he knocked and yelled, "Ann? Let me in."

He waited and watched for her to come through the kitchen, but instead her head came popping up from what appeared to be out of nowhere. Mitch let out a startled yap of his own and gauchely two-stepped away from the scare.

"Christ, Ann! What the hell are you doing?"

Seeing her gawk around the yard and not open the door Mitch hollered again, "Let me in, Ann."

"Do you see anything out there?" she questioned, through the window, glancing downward to see if anything was at his feet.

"What do you mean, do I see anything?" Mitch became instantly troubled thinking someone might have been here and could have tried to attack his wife. He started furiously looking all over for any sign of trespassing.

"Are you okay? Did someone hurt you?" he asked, nervously.

24

"Do you see anything, Mitch?"

"No, it's okay. Let me in," he pleaded, frightened for her. *What could have transpired out here*? He had a desperate need to touch his wife.

"Please, Ann," he begged.

She hastily, in one motion, opened the door yanking his arm to pull him inside then slammed the door shut and locked it in tempo. All the while instructing him to, "Hurry!"

When Mitch saw his wife's puffy eyes and red face, her in complete disarray, his heart skipped a beat. He tossed his file to the ground, uncaring of the consequence at the moment and took the love of his life into his arms. Trepidation for her instantly consumed him.

Ann said nothing for a short time, as she cried softly, burying her head into his shoulder. Mitch was almost afraid to ask, uncertain he wanted to find out what had destroyed this beautiful woman.

"Ann, honey, have you eaten today? Can I get you something?" He didn't know what else to say.

Loosening her grip on him, Ann wiped the tears from her swollen face. Without looking him directly in the eye, she answered forcibly through her sobs, "I want to go home, Mitch.

"I hate it here."

"Okay, sweet pea, we can go home. It's all right. I'm here now. I won't leave you again." Mitch spoke fast. He thought the worst; that Ann had been raped. His crushed heart and weight of the sympathy he had for his wife was turning to anger and hate for the culprit. He wanted to get her into the car and to the Sheriff's station as fast as possible. Mitch had an insurmountable need to find the animal that harmed his wife and *kill him.*

"I'll do anything you want, Ann, as long as you're..." his words trailed off. He was sick to his stomach. What were they going to do? How would they get through this?

"I'm sorry, Ann. Do you feel like telling me anything? I'm not sure what to do for you, sweetheart...I..." He was almost in tears.

"There was a snake, Mitch!" she suddenly blurted. She was weeping some more, the dam had been opened.

"It was monstrous! I swear it was huge...at least twenty feet!

"When I got home it was blocking the front door. I couldn't do anything, because it was so gross and oh God, so big." She gestured emphatically with her hands. Her stormy eyes also told the story.

"It was watching me!"

Stunned, a shell shocked Mitch said quietly, in disbelief, "a... snake?"

A freaking snake?

"I managed to get in the back door and then that awful thing got on the car. It was there the whole day!" Ann was about as dramatic as she'd ever been. She articulated between blubbering.

"I couldn't do anything.

"I couldn't leave the house.

"It was black and slimy! And so big!

"Every time I looked at it, it was looking back at me, like it wanted to hurt me.

"I was so scared. The eyes were...were...

"I can't do this, Mitch. I can't!

"I want to go home!"

"A snake, Ann?"

Chapter eight

M ITCH WAS STUNNED, BUT HOLDING in his shock for the moment, trying to settle down his wife of a week and two days. They had no furniture to maybe sit on and discuss this matter and he thought she probably needed something stellar to drink. Hell, if he had some bourbon right now he would have downed it. This was very confusing for Mitch, especially after he thought she'd been manhandled or worse. He didn't understand how his wife could fall apart, all over a brainless reptile. He wasn't sure what this meant.

"Ann, calm down. There is nothing out there. I just walked up the drive and didn't see hide nor hair of anything. Whatever it was, it's gone, okay? Please honey, stop and think for a minute."

"No! I want out of here, Mitch! Get me out of here!"

"Okay, okay." *Oh man.* Thinking as fast as he could, still staring at Ann in awe, he came up with, "Let's get our clothes and go to a hotel. Can you help me get our stuff?" They weren't actually unpacked, but Mitch had hung up a few things in the closet and had most of his bathroom articles in the cabinets.

At last, Ann stopped with the tears; however, her breathing continued to be erratic. Drying her eyes, while enduring the shakes, she took a quick look out the window at the Blazer. It was getting dark. If they were going to make a run for it she needed to move her butt. She would have to be able to see if the awful was nearby and she needed light to do that.

Pulling him along with her she urged, "Hurry up, Mitch. We have to hurry!"

"Alright. I'm right behind you," he said, doing his best to stay calm and soothing. He raced up the steps with her to gather their things. Ann simply shut one of the suitcases and zipped it, instructing Mitch to get the bathroom bag, too. He abided by Ann's orders, even though he was completely bewildered as to why they couldn't take a few minutes to pack their clothes neatly or make sure they had everything they needed for a couple nights.

The newlyweds high-tailed it back down the steps and directly to the back door.

"Okay, go check the car," Ann told him, on the alert for any signs of invasion.

Picking up his folder first, Mitch carried the bags out to the Chevy in haste. Opening the door he threw them in, then turned to see if Ann was coming. She had the kitchen door closed the instant he went through it and was anxiously awaiting him to search the Blazer, inside pantomiming to him. He obliged her. At least, she was functioning to some extent.

Mitch knew he had to get her out of here, so they could talk about this, rationally. But he thought it was foolish for her to be consequently out of control over an asinine snake. Actually, he hoped it was just everything else taking its toll, like them both graduating, the wedding, the honeymoon, moving and deciding to live in the country. Instead of the other thought he had; that she was having another nervous breakdown.

Mitch had gone through a whorl of emotions, too, lately. Worse, was the upset he just suffered, while unknowing of what might have happened to Ann a few minutes earlier. He was still wavering himself, but ignoring his own feelings. He had to think about her and the situation at hand.

Mitch made an ordeal out of his mission to find something intimidating inside the Blazer, wanting Ann to feel safe. He went as far as to crawl underneath the vehicle to make sure the snake wasn't high-jacking them from down under. He found nothing. Including

28

any kind of trajectory that might be left by such a considerable beast his wife described.

"You satisfied?" he hollered.

"I guess," she answered, using her vocal cords to penetrate the glass window.

"Can you please pull the car closer? I don't want to walk on the ground, and watch out! That thing could be anywhere!"

This was crazy. It was late, Mitch was worn-out, hungry and getting stiff from his unexpected and long walk today, let alone being tender from all the work they had done over the weekend. He wanted a shower, some food and a TV wouldn't hurt either.

Aiming to please her, he rashly maneuvered the vehicle as close as he could, turning the ride around, so the passenger side was closer. When he reached over the seats to open the door, she yelled again.

"No! Don't open the door." Ann was still frantically looking about.

"Roll down the window, I'll crawl in."

Mitch wouldn't do it. Enough was enough. He got out, shutting the car door behind him and determinedly walked over to her. He insisted Ann open the back door she was hiding behind, using a stern voice. When she did as he wanted, Mitch quickly picked her up and carried her the two shanks to the passenger side, opening the door and shoving her in. He then shut the door once more and stepped sideways to lock the house. With the job done, he hastily walked around the car one more time and opened the door, got in and slammed the door shut as quickly as he could. Without a word, he thrust the gear into drive and tore out of there as if the hills were on fire.

Nervously, Ann watched the house as they rode out of site. Once it was out of view, she couldn't exactly relax in the car. The thought of that real life, gargantuan snake on top of the ride was controlling. Her skin was tickly with the memory. She also scoped the inside of the auto continuously.

They didn't talk on the trip into town where the one and only hotel was. The place consisted of rows of small cabins spaced apart by rows of individual driveways. This was a hunter's dream haven, especially since they were located in the center of western Kansas.

As soon as they were checked into their own small cabin, Mitch left to get dinner, leaving Ann to run a hot bath. She feebly said she would be fine for a few minutes. There was a small eating joint next door, so Mitch would only need to jog over, first letting Ann know he wouldn't be gone long.

Striding into the Hamburger Inn, Mitch thought about what he would do if Ann refused to go back to their new home. What if she went back to St. Louis? He rejected the concept, because it didn't matter. Mitch was staying here. He liked his new job. He and Ann would have to work things out or they would be married living in two separate states.

Trudging across the parking lot with two incredibly large double cheeseburgers and about a pound of fries, Mitch noticed a liquor store across the street. What luck. He chose that route next and purchased expensive beer, Fosters to be specific. Then Mitch made his way over to their temporary living quarters.

"It's me, Ann, don't be alarmed," he said, walking into their room, making sure to lock it up for the night. He threw all but two of the beers in the small fridge that was opposite of the bed and underneath the television set, and stripped out of his clothes in record time.

Naked, he carried the deluxe meal to his wife.

"Hey, this is nice," he said, observing Ann in a comfortable, oversized Jacuzzi, bubbles and all. He handed her the food and climbed in excitedly, opened the beers and gave her one.

In a mouse-like voice, Ann said, "Thank you."

She then asked sheepishly, "Do you hate me?" keeping her eyes down, not looking at him, gulping the ice cold beer the second the words were out.

"I don't *hate you*, Ann. What a crazy thing to ask. Eat your food. It cost ten bucks for 'the best cheeseburgers in these parts'." Mitch thought he saw a hint of a smile for his talented imitation.

He watched her take a bite, before digging in himself. Ann was eating and that's all he really cared about. He kept his eyes on her, knowing she wasn't at fault for scaring him the way she did. He figured there was no reason to say anything to her, just let it go.

It appeared she hadn't had a thing all day as fast as she ate. He was famished, too. They conversed with their mouths full. It wasn't like anyone was around.

"Big snake, huh?" Mitch did hope Ann would recognize her irrational behavior, though.

"Mitch, I'm telling you the thing was **colossal**. And that's not what even frightened me the most. I swear to you it was watching me the whole time. Its eyes were an eerie yellow with black slits." She shuddered.

"Ann, sweetie, I would think that's probably not true. Snakes use their tongues to detect what's around them. It might have just seemed as if it was watching you, when it was essentially sensing you."

"Oh shut up! You don't know any more than I do about snakes, Mitch Rock. Those intense eyes followed my every move! It was totally unnerving. I won't go back." Ann downed the rest of her beer. She got out stark and went after two more, letting the floor get soaked in her footsteps. Too much of a bad day to care about anything.

Upon returning, Ann handed her husband one, taking a deep breath, before sliding back into the suds and apologizing, "I'm sorry I took your head off. I'm just so upset. I don't know what's wrong with me. Can't we think of something? Maybe there is someone who gets rid of snakes that large around, 'these parts'."

Mitch smiled at her. Her dry humor was one of the reasons he loved her so much. She seemed much more coherent. It was her first day alone, he should cut her some slack. Besides, he hadn't seen the perilous reptilian.

"I'll tell you what, tomorrow I'll ask the biology teacher if he can help. If anything, he would certainly know if anyone takes care of these kinds of pest." He nodded his head in agreement of his idea, thankful he had one, while polishing off his deluxe burger.

"Boy, that was good," he said, as he breathed, perfectly satisfied with the food.

"It's wonderful. I didn't know I was this hungry." Ann enjoyed the meal, too.

"Mitch...honey...thank you for rescuing me today. Really." She batted her baby greens.

"No way cupcake, I'm way too tired tonight," Mitch informed her, immediately, interpreting her to want sex. His eyelids were already incredibly heavy and he could hardly keep them open as it was.

"Mitch! Oh my gosh...I'm sorry! How was your first day?

"Oh no, did you walk home?" Ann asked, mortified, finally getting her wits about her.

Chapter nine

Mɪᴛᴄʜ ᴡᴇɴᴛ ᴛᴏ Gʀᴇᴇɴʟᴀɴᴅ Hɪɢʜ almost an hour premature the next morning. He was slow and practically limping, but walked to school anyway, so Ann could have the car and sleep in. It wasn't as long of a hike today since he was already in town. He took a gander at the immaculate surroundings, while climbing the steps to the main entrance. He really did feel *at home* here.

Rounding the corner on the third floor of the 1920's building, Mitch bumped into the teacher he had come early to see. They were dressed identical since the school had a dress code for the adults as well as the kids.

"Mr. Gordon? Hi, I'm Mitch Rock, the new mathematics instructor." He held out his right hand to shake the guy's, holding his folder under his left arm.

"Yeah, nice to meet you. Call me Mark, Mitch. How ya doing?"

"Good, thanks Mark. I'm really impressed with this old school."

Mark was about six feet tall, with an athletic build, in which, Mitch had to look slightly up to him when speaking. His face was friendly, his hand shake strong and he looked Mitch in the eye when he talked to him. Mitch felt as if they would become good friends. He also suspected they were about the same age.

"Me too. I love it here. Hope you do.

"Come on in and check out my classroom. You caught me at a good time. I have to be here ahead of classes, so I can feed my specimens." He laughed at himself as he unlocked the door and flipped a switch to turn on the lights. The men casually wandered in.

"Holy...cow," Mitch yelped, upon seeing the numerous caged animals.

"You have a zoo in here," he was saying, taking a long look around when a large blacksnake in the corner towards the back caught his attention. He ambled over to the enclose and peered in, bending slightly forward to get a good look at it.

The snake immediately lifted its head and showed Mitch it's yellow, surefire oblong eyes. He flinched and stuttered, "Whoa, what kind...of snake is...this?"

"The infamous black rat," Mark reported, as he prepared his collection of creatures for the day. He explained that the students did a lot of the work during classes, but a few of the pets, such as the cat, needed tending to early every morning.

Not really listening, "I've never seen one up close," Mitch mumbled, inching away from the seven foot beauty, while his gaze was strangely locked with the mesmerizing eyes of the carnivore.

"It's disturbing if you ask me."

Glancing over at Mitch, Mark replied, "Yes it is, and you won't see many like that one there. It's a mutant."

"What?"

"Its genes have been altered."

Turning to look at Mark directly, breaking the standoff with the beast, a bit confused, Mitch asked, "What happened to it?"

Giving him his full attention now, Mark answered with a question, "I'll bet you didn't come in here on your second day to hear my theories regarding a defected black rat snake, ump?"

"Well, not exactly. I am fascinated though, and would like to know." Mitch sat down in one of the many student desks and stared at Mr. Gordon, his face innocent, eager to know more, waiting patiently to be informed. He was sincere.

Mark Gordon avoided discussing his theories to regular folk. And he was well aware Mitch was new to town and the area. He didn't want to scare the guy for that matter or anyone else. He kept his private research to himself, along with the handful of students that were interested and donated their time. Although, none of them knew to what extent Mark perceived the snakes to be dangerous; a potential threat to the town's construction.

In this small of a settlement, he also knew Mitch and his wife bought the old Hammer place. Mark would have bet money the reason the man was here was because they'd caught a glimpse of one or more large snakes out there. Then again, the sightings were rare and unusual. These snakes seemed to know what they were doing, how to hide that is. It was pure luck he caught the one he did about six months ago.

Mark eyed Mitch suspiciously. He wanted to be absolutely, one hundred percent positive, before telling anyone his true qualms about these earth dwellers. He wasn't the kind of guy to distress anyone if there wasn't evidence. However, he figured he had plenty of data to prove these tainted snakes were causing the minute earthquakes here that were destroying the buildings and...

"Okay, I'll tell you what I came in to talk to you about," Mitch broke the silence, after feeling a bit weird. Mark seemed to be looking at him strangely.

"My wife swears she saw a ten foot blacksnake out at our farmhouse, uh the old Hammer residence. Well, she said twenty feet, I just thought half that size might be more believable," he chuckled, mostly to ease his own tension.

Mark raised his eyebrows. "Go on."

Feeling goofy for sure, Mitch went ahead and told Mark the whole sordid story, anyway. About how much his wife freaked out, everything she'd said about the experience and the truth of why he was here, leading him to asking for aid in the situation.

"She doesn't want to go back. I don't know anything about blacksnakes, but I have to tell you, spotting that one over there..." he turned and pointed at the limbless amphibian with the curling tail and peculiar eyes, which was still watching him, or so it appeared, "...I sure wouldn't want to run into one double its size." He laughed timidly.

"No, nor would I," Mark said, smiling oddly.

"Say, Mark, can you and your students help out?"

"We'll be glad to take a look for you." He paused to think about the meaning, before he went on.

"Mitch, that place has been empty for two years. I would venture to say you do have plenty of snakes around there. I'm not saying that something can't be done, just kind of wanting to let you know, so you're not surprised."

With his face sagging, Mitch replied, "Okay, I understand."

"An empty house like that surrounded by all that land is heaven for the normal black rat snake. And they get mighty big, Mitch, close to ten feet like your wife said. They also climb trees and probably really love the old barn out back." Mark sounded casual.

"They're part of the Colubrid snake family, Elaphe Obsoleta Obsoleta. It's one of the largest snake species there is and they like to be around other reptiles their size. The black rat can lay as many as thirty eggs at a time, which in turn, hatch in seven to fifteen weeks. The young stay close to home, unlike the myths you've probably heard; that they don't live within twenty feet of one another." Mitch's expression turned to one of doom and gloom. Mark didn't pay attention. He was too busy informing his new colleague of what he knew.

"Now farmers like to have a few of these around, because they control the mice population. Do you have mice out there?"

"No."

"Well, that's a strong indicator.

"Nevertheless, the rat snake is not afraid of humans. They're used to living around them, actually. And they're harmless, unless you scare one or surprise it. The black rat will shake its tail into whatever surrounds it and can sound like a rattlesnake when it gets spooked. Or it will strike with its tail if it thinks it's in trouble. Their bite is nasty, but they won't hurt you if you don't bother them.

"They're neat snakes, really. They kill their prey by constriction, suffocating it by encircling its victim's head, wrapping it in one or more coils. Good size food, too, and they'll also eat other kinds of snakes. Another reason the farmers around here like them."

Seeing Mitch's concerned look at last, Mark asked, "Mitch, something wrong?"

"I'm a little worried," he half heartedly joked.

"When can you come out?" He was trying to act like a man, but after hearing so much information on the supposedly Not Dangerous If You Don't Surprise Them Snakes, he was a bit vexed. Along with the fact, that his house was probably invaded by thousands, or so it sounded, and that they most likely were all gigantic. He didn't think he wanted to go back to the farm as much as Ann didn't want to. He decided on the spot, he wouldn't tell her any of this. In fact, he was positive he wouldn't tell.

"I can come today, after classes."

"Great.

"Thanks."

"Don't mention it, this is what I do. Hey Mitch, try not to worry. I'll know right away if there is a problem. Meet me here when school lets out."

"Can do." Mitch wasn't positive he wanted to go with him, but he guessed he was. He stood up and started to back out of the room as he courteously told him, "I better let you get back to your animals. I'll see you later."

"Yeah, sure. Nice to meet you."

"Likewise." Mitch took one last look at the unbelievably spooky snake, before heading down the hallway.

Mark could hardly wait. He hadn't thought about this abandoned place being a refuge for these transformed snakes. But as he talked, it dawned on him it was a certain prospect. He knew they were out there and more of them were surfacing, he simply hadn't been able to find them. They were tricky to track, especially in Kansas with the winds erasing any kind of earth trail. And they weren't leaving skins behind. Another reason he was obsessed with these mutants.

The one he had managed to capture was purely by coincidence. Out hiking around the high school one morning, a little after dawn, he stepped on the slippery reptile. Fortunately, the tail. It reached around and did bite him, but got its fangs stuck in his boot. He acted fast, without fear, grabbing the neck and pinching down, so he could control it.

Mark quickly carried it into the building, up the stairs and down the hall to his classroom. He'd had to hold the snake as far out to his side as possible, all the while the thing struggling to break free as it dangled to his feet. It was stronger than a typical blacksnake and he had to put much effort into this normally easy task. This one was obviously different from the get go, because he'd done this several times before. Black rats typically become docile when confined.

Mark had to find a sturdy cage, while combating to keep his grip on its rubbery head and this particular blacksnake didn't make the chore easy. But he managed. It was only after the completed seizure, he realized the eyes were abnormal. That's what led him to modify his conclusion on what specifically was happening to this small town and possibly all over the world.

Chapter ten

MARK GORDON'S SHREWDNESS, EYE for detail, his imagination and education is what led him to his assumptions that connected the black rat snake with the town's building deterioration. To the investigation of the how and why. To the research he'd worked night and day on for close to a year. Recently, he was on the verge of believing this could be a problem on a large scale. Possibly, a 24,901.55 square mile scale.

Mark was a history buff, more specifically, an architectural history buff. He loved to learn about building structures and study the construction as a hobby. He often walked around the small downtown to admire the work done in the twenties and then deduce where their ideas came from, with the knowledge and equipment they had back then.

When Mark first realized he was seeing new cracks in the foundation of the school a year ago, it definitely caught his attention, leading him to note the downtown harm as well. Maybe he wasn't educated in the field of formation, but he knew enough at that point to be bothered.

He began studying diligently, contacting people conversant in this area of expertise. This led to his belief that the damage done here was identical to that of an earthquake damaged building, unless the structure had been built with this type of concern. In Greenland it wasn't a concern.

Using his mind's eye, Mark began making rough, crude instruments to measure the earth's movement in and around Greenland. He didn't actually put together a seismograph, but an eclectic tape measure of sorts. He then positioned them in the ground about town and in the surrounding country, if the resident didn't mind him coming and going all the time.

He called his devices *crust sticks.* They were ten feet long with claws on one end that opened when pulling upwards. This was to make sure they did not move unless he moved them, very important. The sticks were electrically magnetized in three strategic places. When and if the earth beneath them did move, he would witness the variations according to what his sticks recorded. Mark waited thirty days, before removing his crust sticks and photocopying the information, then replacing them.

Each month there was a disparity. At first, Mark assumed he hadn't made the design of his contraptions precise, because of the notable measure. And he couldn't actually feel the ground tremble. But after careful and thorough examination and testing of his invention, in a controlled environment, Mark was positive they were correct. After that, he and his students became aware at all times to be sensitive to the floor underneath their feet.

Next, he began to investigate the earth's layers and causes of earth quaking activity. Major vaults and volcanoes did not exist in this part of the world as far as he could determine. There had to be another reason. He had thought underground springs could be the adversary, in the beginning...

One day, while searching the internet in the town's library, Mark came across an article. It told how the ancient ones believed large snakes lived under the earth's surface, and when angry, they used their grandness and power forcing the earth to move.

This struck a cord with Mark. He began remembering some of his grandfather's tales and other people's over the years, about the "largest snake they'd ever seen". In fact, it was like those "biggest fish stories". Mark hadn't given these a second thought, until he came across this enlightening news piece. Sitting there that day something in his head snapped. There had been more sightings in the near past than what he knew to be regular.

Mark stared at the computer screen for hours, pondering the prospect. In particular, that large snakes lived in the ground and were causing the earth to thunder, therefore, causing the recent distress on the town's construction. The underground springs throughout all of Kansas would be a perfect place for snakes to live. It wasn't precisely a reflection based on naught.

The word *recent* is what triggered his brain to delve deeper into the idea. The damage was newer than forty, thirty or twenty years ago. What this meant to Mark was that these snakes either did not always live beneath Greenland or that they had grown. His assumptions were the earth's crust could have shifted normally years ago and brought with it an opening to the creatures that lived without the sun.

The second concept was today's pesticides, particularly here in God's farming land, could have soaked deep down into the soil and into the streams for years and years, bringing about a change to these natural, probably common biological phenomenon of undreamt nature.

Mark somehow knew that day he had to look into this possibility, seriously and with alacrity.

Mark and his students began testing the dirt around Greenland as far down as they could without delay, to evaluate any large levels of something. They also searched for snake holes and charted where there may have been many or larger than what they thought was ordinary. It wasn't like anyone had a yearly graphic representation of snake habitats.

Ultimately, what they found was excessive herbionon in the earth. It was banned on the use of produce, but not before it had been used for years and years, by farmers around here and the world. It was suppose to control the Chinch population from eating the corn crops, as well as other bugs from destroying many other crops, which didn't work. It was marketing propaganda.

Mark realized how green the human race really was, when finding out we use chemicals as soon as invented, before ever considering the harm it could do to Mother Nature.

Or to humans.

Or to animals.

One problem they had though, was finding the unusually large snakes, until Mark literally stumbled upon the young one that morning, before class began. Only then could he essentially put his theory to testing, by drawing blood from the mutant animal and comparing it to a normal one. It was dumb luck that he had a black rat snake, from when he was a kid. He didn't fool himself into thinking his old snake didn't have variations, but at least he could compare about ten years of change. It proved to be enough, when the results were in. Almost fifty percent of the tests he'd done proved a difference.

It seemed like every day since that one, Mark learned something new about the now defunct rat population. Of course, these snakes normally live out in the open, in cliffs, even barns, so Mark hadn't even expected the black rat Order, before catching the one he did. The newer, improved snake was just that. For example, one thing he noticed about the fresh catch after a couple of months, was the snake did not shed its skin. Normally they do two to three times a year to keep their outer layer smooth for tunneling.

Also, the hovels they looked for and charted seemed to disappear this last half of the year. They had found a couple of places where the ground looked to be pierced with giant bullet holes. In reality, it was damn right scary to be in the midst of a find such as this. But they never saw the snakes. They would take pictures of the ground and keep constant vigil, until the weather conditions eventually covered them up. This was curious, because it was as if the snakes moved whenever Mark and the students uncovered, what they thought to be, a living area.

He had to constantly keep in check his perspective and not let his imagination run rampant.

In addition, the snake he had was growing rapidly, further promoting his theory about pesticide use. But, Mark couldn't be absolute if it was because of the effects of the herbionon or not. Or if hundreds or thousands of snakes, probably more, were all growing so fast that they were running out of room in the land underneath and if that were the explanation to the increased surfacing and sightings.

Nonetheless, the normal rats are a marvel of nature, without help from the agricultural industry. They typically can climb a tree lightening fast and are known to hang from the branches forty feet high. They can also scale someone's house just as easily and can be found sunbathing on top. The normal rats can live twenty years and are the most adaptable snake in the Colubrid family. Which, made sense that they could live strictly submerged, especially if by underground springs.

Mark often wondered what else lived deep down inside the earth, below humans, growing, mutated or not.

But, when thinking about regular snakes and understanding what they can do, Mark's ideas were logical. The black rat doesn't have eyelids or outer ears. Sunlight isn't necessary, although they like it. They flick their forked tongue picking up chemicals left by other animals, including humans. They can hunt, follow their own kind or find their way to where they made their home using this method. The smooth skin makes it easy for them to slide through the earth, one reason they shed it so often. And their agility to squeeze through the smallest aperture when they are five or six feet long is amazing, really.

He paid attention to the capture in his room. There was another reason Mark kept a close vigil on the improved species. He suspected these snakes could pose a threat to people in another way, because of how this enhanced reptile ate the other blacksnake and how fast it digested it. He had put them together just to see what would happen. A big mistake. Although now, because of the incident, he was pretty sure the faster these things grew and surfaced, the faster they would need bigger food.

Chapter eleven

Aɴɴ ɢᴏᴛ ᴜᴘ ᴀɴᴅ ᴡᴇɴᴛ for a jog soon after Mitch left for work. She didn't sleep especially well, the snake's image burned into her brain. Every time she did doze off, she woke having a recollection of the animal. It was as if those eyes had penetrated her very core.

The exercise around town did her good and she felt much better after her shower. From the motel's room phone, she called her sister to see how things were back home and also to tell her about her day yesterday. Ann and Meg were about as close as two sisters could get and they told each other everything, even though they were nine years apart. Meg was there for Ann during her counseling days, supporting and encouraging her through the entire ordeal.

Turned out to be, Ann was worried she was relapsing, the real reason for the call.

"I'm scared, sis. I don't want to have these kinds of problems my whole life. It's stupid what that snake did to me yesterday. I couldn't do anything. My heart was pounding and I was practically frozen in fear, fixated with the dumb thing."

"I would have been the same way, Ann. Don't beat yourself up. Look at what you've accomplished in two weeks. You're probably just exhausted and no one can deal with life's pressures when they're tired.

"And another thing, it takes time to adjust to living in a new town. I'm really proud of you. I don't think I could make that many changes in such a short period. It's okay to cry once in a while. I'm sure you're fine."

"I know, it's just that this was different then being tired, or having pre-menstrual syndrome. It consumed me. Just like when..."

Meg cut her off, before she could say it. "Ann, that was four years ago! Leave it in the past. I'm telling you it's normal to be afraid of snakes. Now, you made a big life change. Give yourself a break, huh?

"By the way, are you getting ready to start your period?"

"Yes, in a couple days. You think that's what's wrong?"

"You do get cranky, sis. Yeah, it's possible."

While listening to her sister, Ann thought of something. "Meg, I know what I can do," she said, with a more upbeat tone. "I can go to the library and research these large blacksnakes. Maybe, if I know everything about them, I won't be frightened. Besides, the waitress over at The Diner said they were nothing to be scared of."

"The waitress at *the diner?*"

"Yeah, I stopped for some coffee after I ran and the same lady that waited on us the first morning was there. I sat and visited for a few minutes. She knows a lot about this town. I really like her."

"What's her name?"

"I don't know, I forget. Oh man, goes to show you what a mess I am."

"No you're not, Ann. I think learning all you can is the smartest way to go about this. To tell you the truth, I hope you find out how to get rid of that snake, before I visit. I certainly don't want to see one."

"Oh, Charlotte is her name!" Ann felt better that she did remember. *Whew.*

They ended the conversation deciding Meg would visit as soon as her classes were out for the summer. She was in her freshman year of college. When Ann hung up, she simply pushed the little button down on the phone where the receiver goes and released it, dialing the phone company next. Luckily, they could meet her at the house at 1:00 this afternoon, which worked out perfectly for Ann. She was having lunch with Mitch and this gave her the rest of the morning for the library duty.

Glad she called her sister, feeling almost good, Ann went into the bathroom to take her birth control before leaving. She searched through her suitcase and found the little plastic box that marked the days for each pill. She'd taken the same birth control since she was a sophomore in high school.

This thought momentarily made Ann think she should most likely come off them, sooner rather than later. Particularly since she was a smoker.

Ann's face gave way to surprise when she realized she was on the wrong day, popping out Friday's supposed to be pill.

"Oh no, how could this have happened?" she asked herself, trying to remember when she missed the dosages. Four to be exact. She had been extremely busy lately and there had been a lot going on, but Ann didn't recall missing any daily pill. She'd been so faithful over the years. It was a habit to take these. How could she have missed four freaking days? Or not notice the discrepancy before?

Sure, she wanted kids, but not at this time in their youthful lives. She wanted to plan their family. So did Mitch, entered her mind and she immediately felt panicky. He didn't like bombshells. They did everything in life according to preparation and arrangement. It was Mitch's safety net, so to speak, and hers, too, she judged briefly. They simply weren't ready. And the fact that his health insurance with the new job wouldn't even cover her for three months, hit her hard.

Ann wasn't sure what to do. If she were already pregnant, no way should she take another pill. But if she wasn't, she certainly should. If she could only remember the days she missed then she would know.

"Ann, I can't believe you are this stupid!" She threw the pills across the bathroom on impulse. All she could do was wait it out and she knew it. Hopefully, with luck or God's will she would start her period early. She would have to feign a headache if Mitch wanted sex, something she'd never done before.

"This is just dandy," Ann scolded herself, pissed.

Ann picked up the hamburgers a few minutes before noon and headed over to the school. They were identical to the ones they had last night, given that she got them from the same place. She wanted to get there early, so she could go in and see her husband's working character. *Surprise him.* How ironic she thought, rolling her eyes at herself.

Climbing the steps to the front entrance, Ann was intrigued with the quaintness of the building, hoping she would be working here one day as well. Then the idea that her child would attend school here walloped her. She could only pray she would be planning that day a few years in the future, instead of in eight or nine months.

Ann had her large tote bag she carried for a purse, slung over her shoulder and a smile on her face, peering into classroom 306. Mitch sat in his own desk adjacent to Mrs. Weaver's as the woman was dismissing the students for lunch. She was profoundly proud of her mate.

Unexpectedly, as the bell rang, the boys and girls darted out of the room like a herd of elephants, causing Ann to have to step back swiftly, before getting trampled. She nearly fell over. She'd have to get used to high school students, she determined, composing herself.

When the chaotic crowd dispersed she strolled into the room and greeted her husband and other teacher.

"Nice to meet you. Mitch has said nothing but kind words about you."

"You, too, Ann. I want to tell you I'm relieved that I have such an excellent man to replace me. I worried about who would be taking care of my kids. That's the hardest part about retiring."

"I'll bet."

When the formalities were over, Mitch walked Ann to a spot behind the school to have lunch privately.

"Boy, this place is manicured. Really nice," Ann commented, glancing around the lawn.

"I know. The school takes a lot of pride in its appearance. I really like it here."

"I'm glad, Mitch." She gave him a look of meaning, hiding her secret from him. No reason to tell him, until she knew for sure.

Sitting down next to a large oak tree, Mitch asked, "How do you feel today?"

"Better, really." She smiled her charming smile.

"I talked with Meg this morning and decided to research these standard and astounding blacksnakes around here. Look." She was excited about her discoveries at the library, handing Mitch a picture of a black rat she copied.

"Wow."

"I have pages of information on this species. I think I can learn to appreciate them. You see, they are very common around here. Sometimes people misunderstand them, like me I guess." Ann made a face of inanity.

"But the farmers like them, because they control the small rodent population and other critters. They don't kill these kinds of snakes and that's why they get so big." Ann had made the decision to give this her all. She spoke confident and unwavering.

Mitch got a kick out of her willingness and fortitude. "I found out some things, too. I talked with Mark Gordon, the biology teacher. He's going out to the house with me after school to look around, make sure we don't have a problem," he said, causally, enjoying his wife and his lunch.

"Why would we have a problem?" Ann asked, alarmed that he used the word *problem*.

"I don't know."

"Yes you do."

Mitch knew he couldn't get away with that gaffe. He unenthusiastically told her, "Because the house has been empty for two years."

"Oh.

"Well, that's right." Remaining optimistic, she went on, "They live in abandoned places. And, I found out they hunt at night, not during the day. So my snake was just sunbathing. They're harmless. I mean, if you leave them alone. If they do bite, they're not poisonous. I wouldn't want to get bit, don't get me wrong..." she laughed stupidly. "...but they can't kill you. All I need to do is stay out of their way." Taking a bite of her burger Ann was quiet, while she chewed. She continued informing her husband about her day after she swallowed.

"This says people are only panicky of snakes if they don't know enough. So you see, I can be taught to not be afraid." She was happy with herself. It showed.

"I'm impressed. You going to study herpetology now?" Mitch wisecracked.

"No, not exactly. Umm...you could call me a *snakeapist*," she said, her grin becoming broad with her new slang word.

"Good one! That's the Ann I know and love. Don't forget to write it down. And you have to have the definition."

"I know."

"What is it then?"

Ann spoke slowly, while attempting to get this straight. "Let's see, a *snakeapist* is someone who learns about snakes and who gets over their fear of them." She was really pleased with herself and went on with a somewhat cocky attitude.

"Some people think that being terrified of snakes and spiders stems back down the evolutionary channel. That we inherit the apprehension from our ancestors."

"Interesting."

"It has been and I've been staring at those pictures, getting used to how they look. I want to get used to them.

"By the way, I'll be waiting on you and Mark today," Ann said, as an afterthought.

Instantly worried, "Oh no, you don't have to. In fact, don't. Go shopping or something." Mitch didn't think Ann should be around Mark, not today anyhow. He stared at her with anticipation that she would listen to him.

"Mitch, I'm fine. Besides, I'm meeting the phone company out there at 1:00, so I'll just wait. I want to. I want to meet this Mark guy and talk to him. He can help me learn."

Mitch's thoughts went to this morning and he was pretty sure he didn't want his wife talking to Mark Gordon about snakes. Mainly how he describes every detail, no one needs or wants to know. But, he could see her mind was made up.

Maybe he could tell Mark on the way out to the farm today, not to scare his wife?

Chapter twelve

Aɴɴ sᴀᴛ ɪɴ ᴛʜᴇ Bʟᴀᴢᴇʀ at the end of the drive, fighting back the feeling of – *something might attack her at any given moment.* She was waiting on a guy named Jeff to install the phone lines. Her watch read 1:10. He was late and the past ten minutes seemed like ten years. Her eyes continuously scanned the area for signs of the menacing bother that terrorized her yesterday, and today, although she couldn't see it anywhere in the present. (The memory.)

A honk from behind, jolted her out of her intense search. Ann jumped and at the same time looked into the rearview mirror. Spotting the company truck, she breathed a sigh of relief, "Thank God." He was finally here.

Ann waved to him, as she swiftly climbed out of the Chevy, carefully spying the ground. Suddenly, chills went up her spine. She realized she was standing in Snake Territory. Ann tried to mask her feeling of pure terror.

"Ma'am, could you move your car, so I can drive closer to the house?" Jeff yelled, from the driver's seat of his truck. However politely he said it, Ann flinched anyway.

"Oh, sure, yeah, sorry," Ann uttered, uneasy, feeling absurdly idiotic. She promptly got back in the Blazer and drove up to the house as requested, hating the fact that she felt fretful of her own home.

Getting out again, while trying to act nonchalant, she asked, "Are you Jeff?" She smiled sweetly, hiding her nervousness.

"Sure am, you Ann Rock?"

"Yes, pleased to meet you. Come on in and I'll show you where we want the phones." She opened the door for him without delay, her heart pounding, doing all she could to hold back from telling him to move his slow ass.

Quickly shutting the door, she asked, "You do know we want two lines?"

"Yep, got it right here in my orders."

"Good. We need one for our computer, in there," ...she pointed to the other room, "...and I want the line in the kitchen and our bedroom upstairs to have the main number."

"You got it." Jeff grabbed a couple of tools from his utility belt and promptly started to work.

Ann followed him around like a lost puppy, chatting about anything that came to mind. He wasn't much of a talker, so she had to do most of the thinking and questioning, which wasn't easy, staying as close to him as she possibly could, while constantly on alert.

"Do you have a wife?"

"Sure do."

"Oh, well what's her name?"

"Becky."

"How nice. I hope to meet her one day. We're new to town." Jeff glanced up and gave her a courteous nod.

Smiling back, she asked, "Um, how did you two meet?"

"Man never kisses and tells, miss."

"Oh, right.

"So, do you have any kids?"

"No, not yet."

"Are you from here?"

"Born and raised."

"Big family?"

"No, just me and my brother."

"I see..."

Before Jeff left, he wrote down the new numbers and told her to call the office if she had any problems. Ann thanked the stranger, staying on his heels as they walked out the door. She hopped into her car in a flash, remaining vigilant in her task of scouting the area. The entire hour and twenty minutes it took for Jeff to do his work was extremely nerve-racking for Ann. She shivered with the extra adrenalin pulsing through her body.

Ann reversed the car to the end of the drive again to wait on Mitch and Mark Gordon. She tried to concentrate on the material on the blacksnake population, as the seconds slowly ticked by. Checking her watch periodically, she kept telling herself, "Shouldn't be too long."

Mark and Mitch met after school as planned. Mark introduced Mitch to two of his students that were going along for the hunt.

"David is a senior this year. We're going to miss him," he said warmly, patting the boy on the back.

"Luke is a junior."

"Hey guys, thanks for helping today."

They drove Mark's beat up old truck with the ugly, what Mitch thought the color to be rusty red, camper, appearing to be out of the sixties. Mitch sat up front. The conversation was light.

Rounding the corner, Mitch cracked a grin when he saw his wife sitting in their vehicle at the very edge of the driveway, the engine running and her relentlessly gaping about the place. He knew she must be terrified to be here alone. But at least the phone lines were in.

"Let me out here, Mark. I'll drive my wife up to the house. Uh, she's a little apprehensive of snakes' guys, if you could, please don't say anything to scare her more than she already is."

"Understood," Mark replied, genuinely, whereas David and Luke both snickered.

"Hey sweet pea, you okay?" Mitch couldn't help but grin at her. Ann glided over to the passenger seat.

"Hi! I'm so glad you're here." She was dramatic.

"Everything go okay today?"

"Yes. The phones are charging now. One thing done."

"Good," he said, slowly maneuvering the Chevy up to the house.

Getting out of the car and staying within an inch of Mitch, Ann introduced herself to Mark and the boys. After the hellos, the three of them went directly to the back of the pickup to fish out flashlights and binoculars, stuff. Ann and Mitch stood behind them taking a gander at what all Mark had inside the truck, while they casually visited.

"What we're going to do first, Ann, is check around the house and barn, the foundation and in the yard, looking for any signs of infestation," Mark told her, while he pocketed a couple screwdrivers.

"Infestation?"

"Yeah, uh...of that big snake you saw yesterday." Mark shot Mitch a glance.

"Sure sweetie, they'd like to trap it and take it to the school to study," Mitch added, prudently.

"Oh, okay good."

"It was on your front porch first?" Mark hurriedly asked, to change the subject err.

"Uh-uh, over there."

"And about what time?"

"Let's see, seven-thirtyish." Ann shrugged her shoulders.

"We'll start there. Come on, guys," Mark told the helpers, as he headed that way. The newlyweds stayed on their rear.

Pointing the beams of light at every crook and cranny, the team of snake seekers calculated, very seriously, the Rock's home. They moved slowly and cautiously around the house, using their binoculars to spy the roof and gutters. No one said much. Ann fidgeted and kept check behind them in case something was to approach, without sound. The longer they took the more optimistic she was, seeing as they weren't finding anything.

Walking around to the back side of the house, the boys were bent over analyzing the ground, while Mark was using his latest eyewear to scrutinize the roof. Ann and Mitch were heedlessly watching the students when Mark suddenly yelled, "Look out!" surprising everyone.

They all heard the rumble from up above and simultaneously the foursome gazed upward at the same time. Unable to move, because they all had to look to see what Mark was bothered about, everyone took an unexpected blow. It happened so fast they were caught unaware.

Ann's snake came tumbling off the top of the house in a dead heap. And it was big enough to collide with all five of them.

Screaming crazily for Mitch, Ann fell to the ground. She began batting the air with her fist and kicked at the dirt with her feet in a rage of panic, as the part of the reptile that battered her snaked off her body.

Mitch managed to push the slippery beast away jabbing at it with both hands, taking a couple staggered steps backwards, keeping himself from getting the brunt of the rap. He was freaked out and stunned, powerless to utter a word.

Luke was swatted in the cranium with the snake's tail as he tried to react. He went down to the dirt faster than anticipated, letting out a wail.

Mark and David were flattened with the chief section of the snake ending up on top of them. It landed on the two square in the chest, taking them to their backsides.

"Jesus Christ!"

"Holy shit!"

"What the hell!"

"Help me!" Ann's voice was heard above all.

"Hold on to it!" Mark was the only rational one.

"Don't let it go! Ugh!" As Mark wrapped his arms around the giant amorphous, it twisted its head around with great speed and bit him. He took the teeth in his left elbow, crying out in pain.

"What are we supposed to do, Mark?" David yelled, above the commotion, fighting to get a grip on the creature on top of him. The large reptile was wiggling and slashing to get free.

Ann continued to scream her lungs out, helplessly backing up, still on her bottom.

Luke was hollering, too, about what exactly he should do.

Mitch stood, unmoving, in shock of what he was seeing.

"Get its neck, get its neck!"

"How?"

"Mitch! Get a rope!

"Come on guys, hold on to it!" Scared as he was, Luke dove for the head hoping and praying they could control the monstrous thing. The snake held its fangs in Mark's arm and was not letting go. He had to do something for his teacher. He was bleeding.

Everyone was aghast by the snake's size. It was hard to do anything, but the biology teacher and his students didn't give in to their fear. All three fought to get control of the giant animal.

Coming out of his daze, Mitch moved with audacity for the truck on tenterhooks, to find a damn rope. He didn't want something this size being loose around HIS house.

"Ann, get up!" Showing neither pity nor patience for her fit, Mitch seized her arm and pulled her off the ground with one heave, dragging her with him. All she could do was stumble and continue to howl in high pitch.

Mitch thrust her into the vehicle powerfully the instant they reached it, then jumped in next to her, starting the engine pronto. He knocked the gear shift with force and sped to the other side of the house through the yard, where Mark and the boys were struggling with the atrocity. He was reacting despite the fact that he was stumped out of his reason.

But when they reached Mark, he, David and Luke were on foot chasing the mammoth black rat snake into the countryside. The huge reptile was gliding away at remarkable pace, moving its large body in a jerking, yet decisive and persistent motion.

"Damn it! Shit!" Mitch wasn't sure what action to take. Should he stop for the running men or chase the speeding snake? Without further judgment he went with his gut impulse, stomped on the gas and kept driving, passing the boys and the injured Mark.

"What are you doing?" Ann shrieked.

"I'm not going to lose this thing to the wilderness! I'm going to kill it if I have to!" He gunned the truck keeping his eyes steadfast on the expeditious, slippery orphiormorpha.

"No! Let me out!"

Mitch didn't listen to her. He was on a mission of the most important kind.

The large snake seemed to sashay with the wind, making it a difficult opponent. Mitch had the used pickup going sixty miles per hour in a matter of seconds, trying to catch up to it. He and Ann were being tussled all over the place, hitting bump after bump in the rough terrain. Ann's ear-piercing scream never ending.

Just as the truck was on the monster's tail and Mitch thought he could run over it, the snake curled sideways and slung itself upwards. Before he could blink an eye, the massive amphibian was thrusting itself up a giant oak, its ability awesome. Mitch slammed on the breaks coming within inches of the bark.

"No, don't kill it! We want it alive!" Mark was bellowing, as he and his companions gradually caught up to the Rocks and the tree. The three of them were panting heavily when Mitch flew out of the motor vehicle, his eyes on the snake's tight corner security shelter.

"Did you see that?" he asked, amazed. "How in the hell is that possible?"

"Turn the truck around, David!" Mark was giving orders, wanting to get this situation in control, ignoring Mitch. David did what he was told immediately.

"Luke, get the camper opened! Now!" In the glint it took David to get the truck backed up to the tree, Luke had the tailgate down and the camper hood hiked in the air.

"Okay, get ready boys," Mark instructed, as he hastily pulled a gun from the backend. He cocked the hammer and aimed it at the snake, which was hanging in the branches a good twelve feet high. He only had two rounds, so he would have to make this attempt to bring the outrageous down, a faultless one.

The men were staring upwards when Mark fired the blasts, one after the other, wasting no time. His aim was perfect. He hit the snake in the mid section on the first try and in the head the second.

The snake coiled and fought to climb higher, but in a matter of minutes it became lethargic. The long, fat body went lifeless and slowly began to roll downwards, in a straight, immobile manner. Its weight propelled it through the limbs and it hit the top of the camper with a loud thud. The black, inert reptile slid with half its body ending up on the tailgate and the other half dangling to the ground.

"Help me get it in the truck," Mark grunted, trying to push the heavy creature into the bed." Mitch, David and Luke rushed to his aid, tugging and shoving the sedated creature, before the tranquilizer wore off.

"Damn, this thing must weigh a ton." The four strong healthy men were using all their might to move the carnivore.

"I can't believe I'm actually touching something like this," Mitch groused, grossed out, yet determined the snake wasn't going to terrorize their farm. They heaved and hoed until the unanticipated was in the bed of the truck, in entirety. Mark rapidly locked it up.

There was an eerie silence in God's country, except of the four men trying to catch their breath. What just happened was hard to come to terms with, for each of them.

David broke the quiet, "What are we going to do with it, teach?"

"I'm not sure," an exhausted biology professor replied. With the fiend finally secured, he held onto the bleeding elbow. They gawked at each other in total wonder.

"Is everyone alright?"

A horrified and unnerved Ann came squealing out of the cab about this time.

"Mitch!" She ran to her husband.

"Its okay, Ann. Calm down, we got it." He reached for her to comfort her, but she jumped full force on him, clutching her arms and legs tightly around his body. He almost fell over, but managed to maintain his mannish stance.

"Get me out of here!"

Chapter thirteen

Aɴɴ ᴀɴᴅ Mɪᴛᴄʜ Rᴏᴄᴋ ᴡᴇʀᴇ taking pleasure in a can of beer, as well as its medicinal purposes, sitting on the bed of their comfortable and safe hotel room about eight, when there was a knock on the door. Mitch got up quickly to answer it. They had been waiting on news from Mark Gordon.

Spying through the peephole, before opening the door, Mitch greeted the guy, "Come on in, you okay?" he asked, concerned, observing his bandaged arm.

"Yeah, sort of. Those fangs went pretty deep. Had to have twelve stitches. Can you believe that?" Mark answered, shaking his head at the mishap.

"Wow.

"Want a beer?"

"I would love one." Mark sauntered in and sat down in one of two chairs, putting his injured arm up on the small table in between them.

"You doing alright, Ann?"

"Now," she said, with a flare of melodrama, rolling her eyes.

"Sorry I was such a mess. I was just terrified of that snake. Oh God, I can't stand even thinking about it." Ann sat on the double bed in her pj's, clutching the covers as they visited.

"It's understandable. I was, too, to tell you the truth. I've never seen a black rat that size. To even think they could exist around here is frightening.

"Thanks," he told Mitch, accepting the frosty cold Fosters. He took a large gulp. Mark was a bit dazed by the afternoon incident as well.

He didn't bother to tell them it was another mutant.

"So, what did you do with it?"

"Called over to Lawrence. The professor in charge of the science department with the university, is coming after it in the morning." He took another swig and feeling the effect commented, "This sure hits the spot."

"Where is it for the time being, Mark?" a skeptical Mitch asked, again, wanting a more specific answer.

"In the truck. No where else to put it."

Awkwardly opening the curtain, Mitch took a fleeting glance outside.

Laughing at him, "I didn't drive it over here. The boys are watching it. I parked it at the sheriff's station, just to be careful. We don't have to worry, though. Once the news got out, I think the whole town showed up to keep an eye on our aloof visitor. There's quite a crowd. Everyone wants to see it."

"I don't ever want to see it again," Ann piped in.

"Don't worry," Mark comforted her. "And don't worry about there being any more that size either. I think this is probably a freak of nature," he lied.

"Thank God. I'm just glad you captured it and didn't kill it. I feel sorry for it. I can't help it. I'm scared, but it's not that snake's fault. Maybe this guy can give it a good home. I hope so."

"Woman."

"Oh, well maybe she can give it a good home."

Mark maintained a closet for his true suspicions. Still, he was going to have to check out their place again tomorrow. Find out if they had more than one of these sizeable, transformed rats slinking around.

He was afraid that there could be a den close by the Rocks and the mysterious organisms could be emerging from this particular hideout.

He had expected there would be additional snakes creeping up all along. He just couldn't be sure of where and when or of how many. However, he had a geographical record of the sightings from the past year and the land around the Rock farm was a likely bet for a lair.

If the reptiles below the ground were growing at a rapid rate due to pesticide use and for so many years, Mark figured they were getting crowded out of their murky and customary habitat. There could be hundreds or thousands of these larger than life snakes around the state or around the world if his theories were correct. It would only be a matter of time he bet, before he started hearing about other towns' distress...

"Mark?" Mitch said, wondering what the guy was thinking about, again.

"Yeah?"

"What's up?"

"Nothing. I wanted to make sure you two were okay, that's all."

Giving him a curious look first, then blowing off the man's remoteness, "Once my wife quit screaming I was fine," Mitch said, in jest. Mark chuckled. Ann could certainly be heard earlier today.

"I was wondering if I can go back out to your place and look around some more. Maybe do some experiments, involve my classes. Would you two mind?"

"No, I would love the company," Ann immediately replied. The thought of being out there alone was daunting, especially now. But she figured after some time went by, she'd be okay. She and Mitch had discussed the situation and decided to move forward as planned. The snake was gone and they honestly didn't expect another one that big to be lurking in the bushes any time soon.

"What kind of experiments?" Mitch asked.

"For one, we'd like to try and find that large snake's true haunt and examine it. I would also like to put in some of my crust sticks around your property, to measure any kind of underground activity in the territory."

"What do you mean by *activity*?" This made Mitch suspicious.

"I keep track of any depressed developments. We do have springs deep in the earth that cause sink holes. It's no big deal, it's a hobby really." He shrugged his shoulders acting nonchalant.

"We'd be out there from time to time over the months."

"Sure, okay. I guess it wouldn't hurt," Mitch gradually agreed, then asked Ann if she wanted another beer.

"No thanks, I'm fine." Ann was only pretending to drink the one she had. She kept quiet about her mistake and would, unless she didn't start her period. For the time being, she was going to be careful about what she put into her system.

"Mark, maybe you and your class can teach me about all the snakes around here. Other things, too. I don't want to be petrified every time I go outside."

"That would be great, Ann. I love talking about the creatures. They're a fascinating phenomenon of the cosmos.

"By the way, tell me what your plans are."

"We're going back tomorrow, after Mitch is done with school. Hopefully, we'll have a bed and dresser by then, maybe a kitchen table, too," Ann explained.

"You guys into antiques? There's a great shop down the way, out on Highway 10. Lots of great buys."

"What's it called?"

"Helpers. Mr. and Mrs. Smith run the place and have ever since I can remember."

The threesome chatted another thirty minutes, before Mark announced he was going home. It had been such an adrenalin rush day that he was exhausted. And he had to get up early to meet with this professor, Barbara someone.

Ann and Mitch went straight to bed the minute he left, feeling the identical mode of fatigue. It had been quite a day!

Chapter fourteen

Ann was refreshed this glorious Wednesday morning and ready to get on with life. Yesterday seemed like a dream to her since she had slept exceptionally well last night. The emotional roller coaster had really worn her out. Today she wanted to get up and get things done, feeling like she'd wasted two days of precious time.

Ann fixed herself up with a modest amount of make-up and styled her thick, silky hair, putting on a nice pair of jeans and a cute purple tank with matching sandals. Going to Helpers to get them a bed was her main objective. They wanted to spend the night at their farm, on a new mattress. Besides, furniture was bound to make the new purchase homey.

Hurrying from one place to another in the modest accommodations, grabbing her things, Ann ultimately pulled out another pack of cigarettes from her luggage. Mitch hadn't said a thing about her smoking the other day. She knew he had to have spotted the styrofoam coffee cup she was using for the butts when she was chain smoking by the front door, ogling the vertebrate. She hoped he'd stay quiet about it, too, because now wasn't the time to give it up. Her nerves were on edge with the unexpected life events.

Lighting up and puffing her smoke, Ann Rock closed the cabin door behind her. She glanced about the parking lot, before scooting into the Blazer and then looked around once again to be sure she hadn't missed anything. She deduced this would be a bad habit for a while, hunting for sneaky fauna.

She relaxed some with puff after puff and the fact she hadn't seen anything. Putting the car in reverse, she backed up and then pulled out onto Main street. She checked out the town as she drove, memorizing the stores and street names. Mark said if she went west to the end of this road, she would eventually wind up at her target.

This was definitely more like it, she thought to herself. Shopping, running errands and then working on the house. In her mind she went over her list of supplies she would need, before *going home.*

Several hours later, Ann picked Mitch up with the car loaded to the brim, filled with all sorts of brilliant treasures.

"Wow, you do all this today?" A stunned Mitch Rock asked his wife, upon seeing all the great buys she had.

"Are we broke yet?" He jokingly made the remark. Mitch knew Ann would never purchase anything, unless it was a good deal.

"Almost," she quipped, grinning at her husband, teasing him.

"What all did you get?" Mitch turned around in the car and started rummaging through sacks.

"I had a great day at Helpers. The delivery guys are bringing our bed as soon as we get home. It's wonderful, Mitch. I can't wait for you to see it. I also bought a family room set out there. It's beautiful and in excellent condition. Oh, and I found the perfect kitchen table with fabulous chairs to go with it. I could have bought everything at that place. But I didn't," she declared, with a giggle and continued to rave.

"Then I went to Sears. I got the biggest kick out of shopping there. You know, I felt like I had to buy everything at Penney's all these years. Look in that sack." Ann pointed to one. "It's a barbeque grill. We can cook out every night!" She was so excited.

"This is great!" Mitch was serious and just as giddy as his wife. They waited and saved long enough to have all this stuff, going without cool things in the past. Nope, Mitch had never had an outdoor grill before. He was feeling every bit of joy his wife must have felt when buying it.

"Thanks, Ann. I think I have a new toy." Mitch beamed.

"Hey, did you get anything for us to cook this evening?" He looked like a little boy with his first new bike, gaping at his woman.

Barely able to contain her glee she answered with a, "Yes, chicken. And I will put the leftovers in our brand new Frigidaire!"

"Alright, give me some of that." Mitch high-fived his wife.

"Tell me about your day at school, Mitch."

Unloading the car took quite a bit of time and exertion, but the duo didn't care about the extra work. This was incredibly thrilling and absolutely satisfying for them. They giggled and chatted the whole time, while going back and forth to the Blazer and the house.

Right about the time they were finished, Helpers and the Sears delivery trucks arrived with the bed, sofa and chairs, refrigerator, along with the sharp coffee and end tables. Mitch couldn't wait to get a good look at their new furnishings. He was practically hyper waiting on the moving guys to uncover the stuff.

"Ann, I love this couch," he told her, theatrically, sitting down carefully on it and feeling the cloth with his hand. Ann stood in the room smiling from ear to ear with her hands clasped in front of her face.

"Really? You do? I knew you would. The minute I laid my eyes on this, I was one hundred percent positive it should belong to us. I love it, too. Look at the intricate thread work. Isn't it great?"

"Yes, it's breathtaking, sweetie. You did fantastic. Well, I think you did. How much did it cost?" He whispered the last part not wanting the movers to hear him.

"That's the best news!" Ann walked flighty into the kitchen to get her purse. On her way back she was pulling out the receipts from the day, then she handed the wad over. Mitch went through the numbers rapidly, calculating them in his virtuoso mind.

Mitch and Ann were both subsequently engrossed in the great finds, so much so, that neither one noticed the movers had left the front door wide open.

For anything to come through it.

After much ado over the new arrivals and after they arranged it exactly how they thought it should go, Ann made the bed with the new sheets and comforter. White on white and that's how everything would be. White walls, white throw carpets, white furnishings. Ann wanted to add color with pictures and pillows, probably dazzling curtains. Something that could be changed for a new look if they ever desired and without excessive spending.

She and Mitch had planned for years how they would decorate the right place. When they saw the dark red, cherry finish on the floors and woodwork in this house, even though it needed to be re-done, they both realized how perfect white would brighten up the rooms. The big windows would let plenty of light in, too, making this house seem bigger than it actually was.

When the moving men left, Mitch went straight to work putting his grill together, which was a man's grill to die for. It had all the latest gadgets and extra burners on the side to please any outdoorsman. He worked outside the sliding glass door off the kitchen that led to a decrepit cement patio. He noted both porches would have to be fixed, but for now it was great. Nothing could ruin this day.

Chapter fifteen

IT WAS 1:00 IN THE MORNING, before the Rocks stopped to take a breather. Realizing how late it was they went straight to bed. The contemporary couple fell fast asleep as soon as their heads hit the pillow.

Mitch didn't wake Ann again the next morning. He knew she had to be as tired as he was. They'd had a blast last night going through all the new goodies and getting all of it in the right places, though. Taking a good look at the farmhouse, before leaving for work, he felt they were well on their way to making this the ideal home. Undoubtedly, it was the right decision to stay.

They were going to love it here.

Dressed in his dress code khakis and navy sport coat, Mitch made sure to lock the back door. Then he hiked all the way around the entire house looking for the unexpected or the out of the ordinary. When he was absolutely sure there wasn't some kind of fiend or ogre skulking in the yard or nearby, he fired up the Blazer and proceeded to work. Ann had a phone and her computer hooked up on the coolest little antique table she'd found with the neatest chair, so he was positive she would be fine. He would bring her the car at lunch if she wanted it, then again, she had plenty of work to do in the house and he doubted she would.

Ann's eyes popped opened about nine. She laid motionless in the king size, hand crafted, four posted bed, cradled in the overstuffed comforter and cotton sheets, staring intently at the ceiling, barely breathing. There was a strange noise coming from the attic. A weird, rustling type sound was reverberating through the floor above.

Ann's heart began to race. She didn't dare move, endeavoring to determine what could be causing the faint dragging sound. Was this normal? Had she heard this last night and wasn't aware of it? She held her breath willing her ears to be the better sense. *What could it be? Leaves blowing around up there?* Ann glanced out the window at the tree tops to see if the wind was gusting.

It wasn't.

Spying the alarm clock they had brought with them from St. Louie and the phone next to it, Ann reached for it.

She paused.

She couldn't call Mitch now.

"Damn it," she whispered. Ann didn't want whatever it was to hear her. She didn't know why. Her thoughts began running unchecked.

I know it's another freaking snake.
God, why is this happening to me?
What am I going to do?
This sucks.
This just fucking sucks!
Oh, wait.
What if its baby snakes?
Maybe they lost their mother yesterday and have no food.
They're probably on the way down here.
Could be hundreds of them!

Ann clung to her bedding in sheer panic listening to the outlandish, while imagining all kinds of scenarios. Her face was pallid and skin clammy. She was on the verge of another out of control fit. Her heart pounded in her throat and she felt a need to puke.

Miraculously, she heard a car pull into their driveway and honk its horn.

Flying up off the bed in a split instant, throwing the covers off her, Ann ran to the window. It was Mark.

"Thank God!" Ann's total body quaked with fear. She moved fast with major endorphins vibrating through her, snatching her robe from the closet and hauling her ass down the steps, almost falling, scaring her even more. She had the front door open in the next second and was waving titanic at the teacher and students, welcoming them into her home, thrilled there were other people here.

Over Zealous, "Hi! Come on in. Can I get you something? Coffee? Tea? I went to the store yesterday, it's no problem."

"Hey, Ann. We're not here to bother you. We'll be working outside, thanks though," Mark said, rather peculiarly, unknowing if she was okay or not.

"No please, I insist, come on in. Work in here today. I want your opinion on something." She was aggressive.

Mark couldn't be sure of what to do. It wasn't as if he knew the new couple well. He gawked at her stupefied. She was fidgeting with her housecoat and brushing her hair away from her face.

Was she coming on to him?

Ann waited anxiously for Mark to hurry up and walk through the door already. When he didn't and only stood there staring at her strangely, she finally grasped what he may be thinking and immediately decided to be honest with him, instead of embarrassed. Although, she was embarrassed to be honest.

Fumbling for her words, she stuttered, "Mark, I think...I heard snakes...in the attic. Please check it out for me, I beg you. I can't...help it, I'm alarmed." Ann came off desperate. Mark could see that she was, relieved she was only nervous.

"Ann, you don't have to pretend with me, **ever**. I know you're frightened of snakes and after the one we caught yesterday, I would think you have a right to be." He turned to his three collaborators. "Come on guys, let's see what's up there for the lady." Mark then faced Ann and smiled, attempting to comfort her.

"Oh thank you, Mark. I really am sorry about this. I woke to this strange noise and I'm really freaked out."

"Its okay, Ann, don't worry about it. The black rat snake is the largest in its Order and can..." Mark started in on his lecture. Ann listened to every single word in hopes of being taught all she could about the reptiles, wanting to not be afraid any longer. They ended up at the kitchen table drinking coffee and chatting up a storm while the kids did the digging around.

"...you see snakes are misunderstood. They are very important to our ecological system. Been around for billions of years.

"Did you know you can tame a snake?"

"No."

"Most people don't know anything about the reptiles. Twenty percent of the population is scared of them and I hear, 'the only good snake is a dead snake' from people all the time. It's not true. In fact, they're considered non-game by the wildlife conservation groups, meaning it's unlawful to kill one.

"Hell, they run from ya most of the time.

"You know it's not like we caught an Anaconda yesterday." Mark laughed at his own yarn.

"I know, but if you find more, what can we do?"

"Suppose we could let loose a couple red-tailed hawks out here."

"Huh?"

Chapter sixteen

BEFORE GOING TO ANN'S, Mark had met up with Dr. Barbara James at seven this cock-crow. She was the professor in biology at the University of Kansas, in charge of confiscating the unusual amphibian and returning with it. The department was definitely interested when he called and Mark knew it the minute she announced she would be here "first thing in the morning". He couldn't help but wonder why. The thought that this wasn't their first call concerning snakes of this size, flashed through his mind.

He didn't say a word about it being a mutant over the phone. He wanted to wait and see the reaction on the expert's face. You could easily tell it was different by the eyes since a normal rat's eyes were round. Of course, the vivid yellow coloring was a dead-give-a-way.

Miss James looked to be in her early forties. She was an attractive woman with short blonde hair and dark brown eyes. She wore jeans and a t-shirt for the trip down, which showed the detail that she was certainly well endowed; however, Mark got the impression she dressed her part when at the school.

Barbara was professional, introducing herself with confident eye contact and shaking Mark's hand with vivacity, letting him know it was fine to use a first name basis. She had a couple of gents with her he guessed were lab assistants who were just as polite.

Mark and the overnight deputy stood in front of his truck, eye balling the large cargo van the team from Lawrence drove. Wasn't exactly what he had pictured. No separation between the backend and them. Kind of dangerous he thought, especially since the damn creature was rowdy, making his own ride dance from side to side.

"Nice to meet you, too, doctor."

"Thank you. Can you show us the...problem?" She hesitated, noticing his truck sway, uncertain of what to call whatever it was he had.

"Right here in the back of the pick-up." Mark patted the vehicle. "Can't open the camper though, unless you want to tranq it."

"I'll take that under advisement," Barbara said, thinking about the situation, watching the unseen struggle from within. Then looking to her assistants, she nodded. One of the men opened the side doors to the van and pulled out two poles. Mark and the deputy could see the big plastic cage they had to put the snake in, but neither knew how that was going to happen with those measly rods.

The guy handed the second pole to the other chap and they bravely strutted over to the back of Mark's ingenious entrapment. Barbara moved to where she could observe. Mark and the deputy simply glanced at each other, a knowing smirk in their eyes.

"You ready?"

"Ready."

In the snap of a finger, the camper was open and both men were poking at the snake with the aluminum staffs. Each had a round clasp at the end supposedly to grab a hold of the beast. The men's eyes were bugged and the look of angst covered their faces with the very first glance they caught of the enormous rarity. They struggled to do their job in light of this unpredicted terror.

Mark and the deputy watched with amusement at the shocked expressions of the mod squad as they got their first glimpse of his find, even though they kept up the pretense of being professional-rodeo-snake-lassoing-cowboys, or something.

"Holy cow!"

"Son of a..."

"How on earth did you encapsulate this thing?" Barbara asked, astonished, while the two assistants tried in vain to get a grip on the unhappy rat snake. It was obvious they were in awe of it. Mark chuckled. It was also obvious the specialized, high-tech-snake-handlers were not going to be able to do the job.

Abruptly and with velocity, the snake came elevating out of the vehicle, its strong massive body in full view now, causing the three outsiders to move fleetingly backwards. The two men with the flimsy shafts started fidgeting and shimming around the quick moving, large, shiny black aberrant spirit, unsure of how to approach it or even if they still wanted to confine the surprise.

Barbara started shouting orders, although she wasn't getting any closer to it.

"Pin its head!

"Stay in front of it!

"Look out!"

In the next time frame, one rapid movement from the snake's tail took out the tallest man knocking him to the ground, just like that. He fell hard, hitting his head on the cement. Barbara reacted instantaneously when she saw one of her assistants hurt and went for the stick. She appeared as if she was on an obstacle course trying to maneuver by the uninterrupted shifting and abhorrent reptile to get to his tool. They looked like the three stooges, really.

Mark was prepared.

Picking up the tranquilizer gun off the top of his hood, he quickly and instantly delivered two darts to the fast traveling carnivore, which was about to get away. Naturally, the deputy had his gun drawn, but wasn't as expeditious as Mark, thankfully. They wanted this thing alive.

As the snake went limp once more, the now winded out-of-towners all turned to stare at Mark in disbelief.

He stared back at the threesome and cockily stated, "The effect won't last long. If you want it, you better move it, now," folding his arms in front of him.

This time they listened to him and scurried to get the snake in the cage, before it woke. The man who took the fall seemed to be fine, except Mark knew damn good and well you don't feel pain with an energy serge such as this. He rubbed his elbow, while keeping his eye on the woman of the group, remembering.

When the task was accomplished, after much grunting and struggling, Barbara brushed her hair out of her eyes and wiped the sweat from her brow, then looked at Mark. Walking over to him in a decisive fashion, composing herself, she asked candidly, "Did you know it was mutated, Mr. Gordon?" rather pissed.

"Yes."

"Why didn't you say anything?"

"Because I wanted to know if it surprised you."

She gazed at him curiously, before replying with, "What do you know, Mark?"

He gave her a canny look, raising his eyebrows. "Enough to know that we have a problem."

"Okay, you're right."

"I could see that."

Barbara smiled coy at him understanding his gist and said, "I guess we share notes."

Then she eyed him carefully. "I don't need to tell you to keep this under wraps."

"No, you don't."

"Well then, shall we?"

"Come on Doc, I'll buy you some coffee."

Mark took the beautiful biologist to The Diner across the street. They chatted nonstop for almost an hour, before she thought her and the entourage should get on the road. She promised to keep him informed, and vice versa, about anything new either found out.

Miss James didn't seem to have as much to go on as Mark. She told him this was her third call, but that this one was by far the most interesting. Basically, the other two calls were about curt infestation. And both were on farms not far away from Greenland.

Barbara had gone to trap the snakes, but hadn't had any luck. She told Mark that each time it seemed as if the preposterous vanished. She said she keeps in touch with the people who made the calls and as of today there wasn't any further news. She didn't go as far to say the snakes were thinking or acting in packs, but her linger proposed the intention. Mark matter of factly confirmed the same suspicion.

Mark also explained to her the theory about pesticide use, he'd been mulling around in his head. That it could be it was triggering the growth of the reptiles and that he suspected there were huge numbers of them. He hinted they could be dangerous to people in groups since after yesterday this thought had been nagging him. What he didn't tell her was his belief that they could be coming out in groves in the near future or that they were causing his town's underground disturbance.

Barbara agreed there was reason for alarm, because of the black rat's killing method. "This large of a snake could indeed kill a person," she told him, "but we can't exactly send people into frenzy. Our ecosystem needs these Elaphe. People would panic and be out to kill. The normal ones would probably be slaughtered instead, I'm afraid."

"I know. That's why I've kept quiet, so far." Then he made his thoughts perfectly clear.

"Barbara, if this starts happening on a frequent basis we're going to have to do something. It may come to killing them and the other typical blacksnakes if this gets out of hand. I can't be sure at this point in time if they will hurt anyone, outside of the fact, they scare people to near death, because of their size. But the point is; we can't let an individual life come to an end, because we're worried about planet earth. If I see any kind of possible threat to humankind, I'll be heard."

"I understand."

Chapter seventeen

Aɴɴ ᴄʜᴇʀɪsʜᴇᴅ ʜᴇʀ ᴄᴏᴍᴘᴀɴʏ ᴛᴏᴅᴀʏ, and truthfully, she enjoyed the conversation with Mark. He was very informative and made her feel at ease. There was no reason for her to be scared. Knowledge was the answer. More importantly, she wasn't alone.

Mark and the students worked outside after their long visit. Ann labored on the kitchen walls, scraping and steaming, tearing down the outdated wallpaper. They would have to resize before painting, but she was almost done with this part. Every so often she stopped and listened to the ceiling; however, she heard no other mysterious or forbidding clamor. It was peculiar to Ann that the noise up there this morning had stopped when she had company. And she was absolutely going to take note tonight, before going to sleep.

Mark said they didn't find any evidence of snakes being in the house or in the attic. "Could be the plumbing," he had told her. She calmed down after that and actually had fun getting her chores done, working hard to make up time. This is what she wanted to do, fix up this old house and live in the country, raise a family.

Ann put her cigarettes in the cupboard and decided to quit smoking, until she started her period. If she started. This was the second conscious day off the pills and there was no sign of the normal pre-menstrual syndrome. Which was one reason for taking the birth control to begin with; it made the symptoms less severe. Thing is, if she missed four days then she could already be late.

Ann deliberated the concept as she piddled and waited on Mitch – Mark and his helpers were long gone. She had thought her cycle would come early at first, but now she was a little confused on the precise timing.

Going over her list of to do things, Ann pushed aside her concern, thinking she needed to put the new expenses in her Quicken program, before any more purchasing. In which, that list was categorically long. She needed a physical break anyway and worrying about something she couldn't do anything about was a waste of time. Marching over to her new/antique desk with the adorning chair, Ann commanded the computer via the keyboard.

The Rocks were assiduous with the charting of their money and prudent in the way they handled it. They knew exactly what they needed and what it would cost or what they were willing to spend on each item. Ann also kept track of the balance in her head. So did Mitch. They discussed in great detail their finances over the years, one area the couple were exactly alike.

"Oh yeah." One more thing to write down. Out of the blue, Ann remembered she needed to call the utilities and put them in their name. Getting up to get her pad and pen in the kitchen, she just happened to notice Mitch sitting at the end of the driveway as she passed by the large bay window. *Wonder what he's doing?*

She skipped writing down what she needed to and instead, skipped out the front door to go see what it was he was up to.

Gleeful, she signaled him as she pranced outside barefoot and began walking to meet her handsome hubby. Ann could tell that Mitch didn't see her. He was staring out the driver's side window at something. At something on the ground, Ann suddenly realized after she was about halfway down the long drive.

Freezing in her tracks, she became crushingly worried. What could have Mitch so engrossed, or be so interesting that he wasn't coming up to the house? He's just sitting there. Why is he so occupied that he doesn't even see me, raced through her mind.

He must be staring at another snake, filled her heart in totality, which again began to beat rapidly.

Unable to move further, she hollered, "Mitch," while waving frantically. She did not get his attention, though. *What is he looking at?*

Getting incredibly scared and feeling the fear mound in her soul, Ann decided to make a bee line back to the house. She felt naked and alone standing in the chat out here in the middle of God's country, even though Mitch wasn't far away.

As Ann reversed, she saw it straight away. A large black rat snake, as big as the one yesterday, was slithering in the grass to her left and behind her. She hadn't heard anything and the shocker was certainly terrific.

Ann let out a harrowing scream. She wanted to run back into the house, but she perceived the snake to move with her when she tried to backtrack, preventing her from taking that route. Its head was up emulating her change in stance. The powerful body bent and bowed, the eyes focused on her.

"No! Stop it!

"Mitch!" Ann twisted and ran as fast as she could towards the vehicle and her husband. She could feel the amphibian's breath on her heels as she forced her stride to the max, in full blown madness. The last thing on her mind was that she didn't have shoes on.

Mitch heard Ann's deafening howl, couldn't help but, and swiftly looked out the front windshield. "Shit!" What the hell is she doing? He punched the horn letting Ann know he was coming to her rescue, from what he didn't know. He frantically searched the land with his eyes as he stepped on the gas to meet his flailing wife.

It was only a matter of seconds, but seemed an eternity, before Mitch reached Ann. Just as he slid to a stop, thrusting the gear into park and scrambling to get out of the cab as fast as he could, he caught his petrified, agitated wife in his arms.

"Ann! What's going on...are you alright?" he shouted at her, in his state of confusion and alarm.

"Get it off of me! Get it off of me!" She wiggled and fought him from stopping her.

"Get what off of you?" Mitch yelled, almost as loud as his hysterical spouse, exploring her full body, wondering what could possibly be on her.

"Oh God Mitch, it's another giant snake! It's chasing me! Ahg!" Ann clawed loose of Mitch's grip and climbed into the Blazer, leaving Mitch to witlessly hunt the ground alone.

"I don't see anything, Ann, where? Show me where!" He looked like a fool with his hands up and knees bent ready for combat, spinning in circles. He just couldn't find the enemy no matter how hard he tried.

Ann was as raucous as ever, "I'm going to be ill! Why is this happening to us? What are we going to do?" The whole time she was groping her body, incredibly freaked out by the grotesque, but looking wildly for the snake, too.

Mitch was incredulous. He couldn't believe this.

"Ann, there is nothing out here! Are you sure you saw something?" he questioned, getting a bit irate at her antics. And she was exceptionally shrill, grating on his nerves.

"It's probably the mate of yesterday's snake. It's mad at us and trying to kill us! I know it is! We have to get out of here!"

"Damn it, Ann!" Mitch glared at his wife through the glass.

"We are not going anywhere! Come on and help me find the villain and prove you didn't imagine it! If it is as big as yesterday's snake, I would have seen something."

"Oh fuck you!" Ann began bawling incessantly.

Feeling bad, yet extremely goaded, Mitch marched over to the window and rested his arms on the door. In a stern, yet unconvincing voice, he declared flatly, "I'm sorry, Ann…" then impatiently, "…but Jesus Christ, there is nothing out here. I think it's all in your head. See for yourself, will ya? Get out of the damn car."

"Fine!" In between sobs, "I'll get out…and look for it…if that's what you want." Swinging the passenger side door open with force, Ann stumbled out, her shoulders carrying the weight of the world, huffing up and down. Ann's fear gave way to anger and hurt. She stomped down the driveway, trying to catch her breath, looking seriously at anything that moved. She scoped the tree tops, the rooftop, the ground and the front door, she just happened to detect wasn't closed.

Oh no! What if it got in without us seeing it? she panicked in her own mind.

Now what am I suppose to do?

There's no way I'm gong to talk to Mitch after how he treated me. Practically calling me a liar.

I hate this. I hate this!

He's such a prick. There could be a Bigfoot in our house and he wouldn't care. That monster of a snake could be anywhere, but he probably won't see it.

I can't believe he said that to me!

Ann's heart was pounding and she was feeling more alone than ever. She heard Mitch driving the Blazer slowly, directly behind her, following her. Like that made a freaking difference.

That thing could kill me, before he could say boo, but he's letting me walk by myself anyway.

He doesn't love me.

I hope it does get me. Show him.

Ann's thoughts were incoherent, she couldn't control them. Her breathing was irregular and the tears dropped off her cheeks. She kept blinking them away, so she could see what was in her path, her gate awkward and hurried. She felt as if she were having an out of body experience.

With every step, Mitch felt worse and worse. *I know Ann is scared to death, but this is beyond ridiculous.*

He continued to explore the land for any kind of sign of them being invaded, but there wasn't a clue. He really did think Ann imagined it.

Mitch understood yesterday and the day before had been traumatizing for her and he too, was nervous that there could be another giant reptile like the one he helped restrict. Except the idea of them being plentiful was ludicrous. Sure, he was only a mathematician, but he was also reasonable.

Mark said it was highly unlikely there would be another snake that size. Hell, I talked with him, before I came home, just as he was getting back to the school this afternoon. He swore to me there wasn't a reason to believe there was a snake infestation out here. *"Just a fluke,"* is how he worded it.

I don't know what to do. We can't live here if Ann freaks out every single time she goes outdoors. She has to learn not to be afraid. Period. As he thought about this, he noticed she stopped short of entering the house. He put the car in park, rolled the window up that he'd been hanging out of, got out, locked it and quickly jogged over to her.

"Look Ann, even if there is another snake you can't become this panic-stricken over it. They won't hurt you. This is our home, not theirs." When he reached to touch her, she shied away. Mitch retracted and shook his head, gazing down to the ground.

"What are we going to do, stand here all night?"

No answer.

He waited for a bout, before moving around her and going on into their new home. After about a minute, "It's clear Ann, nothing got in," he hollered, once he had taken a good look around.

Compelling her self-control, Ann forced herself inside and then ran up the steps. She was high on adrenaline. It took every ounce of her rationale to make that climb. When she got into their room, she summoned all of her might and rapidly checked under the bed. With her gape wild, she began inspecting every corner of the room as speedily as possible, her lunch in the back of her throat.

When Ann finally convinced herself all was safe, she instantly secured the bedroom door. No way was Mitch sleeping with her tonight. She never wanted to talk to him again.

Chapter eighteen

Mitch Rock scrutinized the house and surrounding land thoroughly for about an hour. He wasn't sure what to do about his wife. He briefly thought about phoning Gordon, but he didn't know him that well. Mark would probably think they were both crazy people if he did. But maybe he should?

Thinking about whether or not to make the call, Mitch went upstairs and knocked lightly on the bedroom door. In a gentle voice he said, "Sweetie, open up, please. Let's make something to eat, huh? We can sit on the patio out back and hunt for *manators*. That's what we'll name these things. It'll be fun. Come on, we need to talk." He hung his head on the door.

Nothing.

Mitch made another attempt to persuade her to come out or speak to him. "Ann, think about this. If we have a problem, are you going to let it scare you off? Wouldn't you rather fight? You said you were going to learn all that you could, remember? I want to know what you know. Please can we talk?"

He waited. Still no reply.

Mitch gave in.

"Ann, I'm sorry I said you imagined the snake. I'm sure you didn't. I should have never challenged you to get out and look for it. Please, I was tired and hungry. I wasn't thinking clearly. I'm truly sorry. I can't stand to see you this upset. Please, let me make it up to you. Sugar pie, please?" he begged.

He heard her get up.

Ann had been sitting on the bed holding herself, watching intently for anything unusual to come through the door, when Mitch knocked. Thank God he finally did. She was wounded beyond belief.

Ann was certain she did not imagine that snake and had been racking her brain as to where it could have gone. All she could come up with is that there had to be a hole in the yard somewhere and they couldn't see it, because of all the weeds.

She listened half heartedly to Mitch's apology. Ann recognized she was off the wall with her fright and needed to be in command of it. That Mitch was right. She couldn't continue to get spooked every time she saw something. One reason foremost on her mind, was that it wasn't good for her health or the baby's.

Ann opened the door. She was still angry, but pretended to ignore her upset. "Can you get the lawn mower running?"

Relieved she was talking to him, yet confused as to where this came from, Mitch asked bluntly, "What?"

"Can you fix the lawn mower? That's all I want to know. Just answer the question." She had her arms crossed. A clear sign she wasn't getting over this mess-up any time soon. Mitch figured he'd better play it cool.

"Yes." Observing her demeanor, he then asked, "You mean right now?" She nodded her head.

"Okay, I can do that." He would do anything seeing Ann in such a state. She was mad at him and he was sorry or he knew he would be if he weren't. He could tell he was in big trouble. What was he thinking earlier?

"Then do it. I'll fix dinner," Ann stated, coldly and heatedly tramped down the steps, giving him a look of grief as she passed him. Mitch followed; the whipped pup that he was.

Ann began throwing things around the kitchen getting dinner ready, so Mitch high-tailed it to the old barn without another word. She was making Mitch two ham and cheese sandwiches and that was it. He could have a glass of water to go with them for all she cared.

Chapter nineteen

Mark Gordon couldn't sleep. He lay in his bed, eyes glued, focused on the ceiling, thinking. Could there have been a black rat or two in Ann Rock's attic? They were certainly capable of being slippery, ghost-like creatures. Rat snakes can go unnoticed, lurking near or sneaking quietly about, able to disappear in a snap of a finger or easily blend in with its surroundings. It wasn't likely to hear a snake coming or going, one of their self protection weapons God built into them.

All snakes were cunning, except the rattler, which does like to live among the black rats. Copperheads do too, but don't make the clatter noise. The blacks only imitate it by shaking their tails in the brush. Mark temporarily wondered if they adapted that trick from being around the rattlesnake.

Anyway, people knew when there was a rattlesnake near, unlike the rats.

That's what made these new mutants precarious. He went over what he already knew. They didn't shed their skin, leaving no visible trace and finding a trail was damn near impossible. Mark was more than aware they grew rapidly.

He suspected these snakes traveled in dens, moving their habitat whenever they felt threatened. How they knew they were threatened, he couldn't fathom. To think they were thinking as a group was too much of a premature variable to consider this early into the research, even though he did think that.

Mark was beginning to lean towards the idea that these rats were a form from beneath the earth's surface and this was the first time the beings were seeing the light of day, so to speak. This could explain the confident and inquisitive behavior. According to all of the sightings recorded thus far, the person or persons who had made the report had said the snake hadn't appeared alarmed or distressed. That it seemed to be watching them, curiously, until something or someone new approached. This was unusual for a typical rat snake.

He'd observed the same conduct in the one he captured. Mark's genetically deformed friend seemed to not only watch him, but it behaved as if to study his proceedings. That sounded stupid and Mark hadn't really given it a second thought until after today, when the large beast tried to escape from the KU team. He was probably the only one who observed the way its eyes followed the actions of the ecological science specialists.

That was an odd characteristic. If you've ever been around snakes, you know they don't really look at you and normally get out of your way or just ignore you. Unless these new defunct rats were preying upon humans, the only logical conclusion was that they could use their optical sense better than the archetypal.

The one they found at the Rocks was undoubtedly big enough to strangle a man. But would it?

There were a lot of unanswered questions going through this high school biologist's mind. If he could be positive about the severity of the problem his theories were leading to, then he'd warn the Rocks and the town. But he couldn't be absolute. Maybe this Doctor Barbara could be the person to help him in his discoveries.

Mark debated silently on what he would do tomorrow, unable to get the rest he needed. He was going back to Mitch and Ann's house for sure, but couldn't decide whether to explore the underneath of the house or try to find some kind of a hint leading to the large ophidian's warren. Each day that passed only made any kind of pathway less viable.

He and his students scoped out the Rock's foundation well enough, making sure there weren't any kind of openings a snake could flatten out its body to get through. There weren't any visible, but they didn't actually have the time they needed to go through every cavity under the house, let alone even begin to look at every blade of grass hoping to find a drag. It was more important the couple was at least safe inside the house, rather than find another snake, initially. Of course they did get interrupted and didn't finish the job. Today all they managed was to place the crust sticks in two calculated locations.

It was also time to pull some of the other devices around town and record the underground evolution. He supposed him and the students could split up tomorrow, allowing them to get more work done.

Deep into his thoughts, Mark was startled to say the least, when the phone rang. Hell, it was 2:00 in the morning. Who would be calling at this hour?

Reaching swiftly for the phone, an emergency of some sort keyed into his brain as he answered with an abrupt, "Mark Gordon here."

"Mark? This is Barbara James. I'm sorry to bother you and I know it's late, but there's something I think you ought to know."

"No, it's no bother. Please, go on."

"Mark, I've been fascinated with our bizarre and overgrown reptilian and that's why I'm still at my lab at this ungodly hour, pestering you. You see, I extracted DNA from the animal and have been running it through the GNOME computer database to label the defected genes and verify the derivation of source; I'll send you a copy."

"Alright, but I can come there. I would love to see your fancy shop, Doc."

"Anytime Mark, but that's not why I called." Her voice was excited and Mark could tell she obviously discovered something important. If she was calling him at this hour it must be consequently beguiling. He sat up, interested in her tenacity.

"Why did you call?"

"We made a makeshift habitat for this exceedingly large and by the way, very unsociable animal. When my associates completed it a couple hours ago, we transferred the snake to the more natural environment with plenty of food and water."

"Don't tell me it found a way out."

"No, it's still there, but Mark...it has company. There are almost fifty babies roaming around the apparent mother."

"That's impossible." Mark's brain went into overtime. "Black rats lay eggs."

"Not this one. They were born alive and there's something else you should know."

"Other than fifty live baby blacks being born?"

"Yes. They are all at least four feet long. And that would be the smallest. Mark, we have a real problem. The babies appear to be more aggressive."

As Mark let this soak in, he offhandedly asked, "What did you mean when you said *apparent mother*?" Not sure if he really wanted to know.

"The snake we got from you is Asexual. The babies are clones."

Mark let out a deep sigh, trying to grapple the implication. She didn't say hermaphrodite; an animal with male and female sex organs that need to mate to reproduce. She purposely used the term Asexual, meaning the snakes did not need to mate. Along with the other news this was incredibly weird to hear.

Without hesitation, he asked for a favor, "Barbara, I need you here along with whatever other experts are willing to come, to help me look for the dens. I would venture to say we need a geophysicist here." Mark was worried about how easy these reptiles could reproduce. He thought maybe this was turning into more of an emergency situation. He wanted to know everything he could as soon as possible.

"I'm sorry Mark, but I'm all you've got. Until we prove there is a danger in concrete data, I can't ask for help."

Chapter twenty

Mɪᴛᴄʜ ᴘᴀɪᴅ ᴀ ʜᴇꜰᴛʏ ᴘʀɪᴄᴇ for upsetting Ann. He ended up cutting grass for about two hours last night, taking out three acres around their home. He didn't actually hate the labor in the great outdoors, but he had wanted to spend time with his wife, make up to her. However, she insisted and specifically told him to look for snake pits.

He'd fixed the mower without a damper. Mr. Hammer had kept it in good condition; it was simply hard to start since it hadn't been used in two years. All it needed was new gasoline and oil, then he jumped the battery.

Mitch rode the John Deere in slow gear, because of the height of the weeds and unevenness of the property, keeping an eye out for intruders of any kind. That's why it took so long. He didn't see anything unusual, though.

He for sure did not enjoy the cold sandwiches his wife fixed and left out for him when he was finally done. Ann had gone directly back to bed after giving him instructions, locking the bedroom door for the night. Mitch ended up eating dry ham and cheese, then sleeping on the new fancy couch that wasn't as comfortable as it looked.

Fortunately, he had a built in alarm clock in his head, because Mitch would never be late for work. Plus the fact that he did not sleep well and knew what time it was the entire night. He got up ahead of schedule and took a long hot shower in the spare bathroom. Then, clad only in a towel, he made coffee, bacon, eggs and toast. Found a crude T.V. tray – the side of a box wrapped in foil – and humbly carried it upstairs, thumping delicately on the bedroom door.

"Ann? Sweet cakes? Please open up. I have a surprise for you." He waited a moment, before repeating the process. After a brief gap in time, he heard her get up and trudge over to the door. He hoped she slept well or else today wouldn't be any better.

Ann slowly opened the barrier between them. There before him stood a woman with her normally curly hair standing on end, frizzed to the max. Her eyes had dark circles underneath and were nearly swollen shut. She was in dire need of a facial and tender loving care. Mitch felt like a complete ass.

"From the bottom of my heart, Ann, I'm sorry. Please forgive me. I think all these changes in our lives have gotten the better of me, sweetie. I was a true fool for taking out my frustrations on you, the only woman I've ever loved." She stood there staring not uttering a word, silence loomed down the hallway.

At least she was listening.

Mitch was humbled. "I guess I don't want there to be any problems. I *wanted* everything to be paradigmatic, like our life has been so far. You know my need, I mean my fault, for orderliness and minimalism. Maybe I'm not going to make a good husband and father after all. That's all I could think about all night. If I can't learn to deal with adversity, Ann, I'm worthless to you." He was serious. The luggage under his eyes wasn't much better than hers.

Ann softened. "Good thing you brought food, Mitch. I'm starving," she said, giving up the anger and hurt.

"I knew that was the way to your heart." Mitch made an attempt to be light hearted, but his heart still felt heavy.

Ann could see his pain. She most certainly understood his impatience with any kind of hullabaloo. Or was it annoyance? Heck, she'd been with the guy for eons. She knew well enough this was going to be an obstacle, before she married him, but she thought she could deal with it.

She stumbled over to the bed, the sheets in chaos from her tossing and turning throughout the night, motioning for him to follow.

"Looks like you made enough eggs for an army," she emphasized, sounding very groggy.

"Yeah, I'm hungry, too."

Getting situated, each digging into the breakfast, they talked through yesterday's awful fight. Their first since the wedding.

"Mitch, you have to know our life is not always going to be perfect or run smoothly. I'm worried about your reaction, mostly because you took it out on me when we're supposed to be in this together."

"Do you think I need counseling?"

"I don't know. When I went through it, I gained the ability to basically change my attitude and way of thinking. It wasn't easy, but I did it. At that time, I figured out that the world, and the people in it, is limited. I can remember the revelation when it finally hit. From then on it has been less important for me to expect idealism.

"You were there, Mitch. Don't you remember all the discussions we had on the subject?"

"Yes, it's just that we plan everything and we make it happen according to our goals. We've both worked so damn hard to get here that I don't want to lose our dreams. I believe if we continue to be good people and do the right things, then we can have everything we want or desire."

"I understand, but Mitch, do you honestly believe if we have kids, they'll never get sick or have an accident? Would you expect them to never have a problem?"

"Well, no."

"What then?"

"Maybe I need time to adjust to our new life. The new job, having a house, living away from family."

"Do you miss your family, Mitch?"

"Yeah, and yours, too. And our friends."

Ann caressed his face. "You know what I thought about all night?"

"What?"

"We designed our future for so long that now that it's here, we don't know how to cope with it. Especially since there's a few glitches in it. Maybe we should both learn to live day to day and practice relishing each one? No matter what happens next." Ann wasn't about to tell Mitch she thought she was pregnant. Not now. She decided she was going to have to ease him into the idea. Might take some time.

"I kind of miss our old life, Ann. We had so much fun getting ready for this day. I don't know if I really want to be this age or be ready for all the responsibilities ahead."

"Oh, now you tell me." She made fun of the remark. It was the first time the newlyweds cracked a smile.

"I'm going to go to school early today and visit with Mark. Find out what we can do about these snakes."

Ann wanted to be sarcastic about him believing her this morning when he didn't yesterday, but held in the need. She sipped her coffee and thought about what they were going to do. About her own advice and how she was going to cherish every day even if she ended up having the KING of unwanted varmints spending time with her. That would be a hell of feat.

Mitch leaned over instinctively and kissed her. Ann became immobilized, doing some quick thinking on how to get out of having sex. She wanted it and needed the closeness it brought, particularly at this moment, but had to refuse, just in case. The thought that she should be forthright crossed her mind, except her heart said no.

"I'm sorry, Mitch, I have a splitting headache. Another reason I couldn't sleep last night was because I kept hearing noises outside. I think I need one of those big old fans in here to block out that kind of riff-raff." She gave him an innocent look hoping he fell for this and didn't get cranky with her again.

"It's alright, *sweetums*. I'm sorry, I should have been sleeping next to you. I'll tell you what, tonight I'm going to make you a special dinner and I'll even stop and get some expensive wine. I'll give you a back rub and spoil you. Then you'll feel better." He winked at her and touched her lips with his hand. Ann held her breath. It was pretty hard to resist him. Her heart skipped a beat, longing to be in his arms.

"Do you want to drive me to school so you can have the car?"

"Yeah, sure. Let me get dressed." Ann had no problem getting her ass out of that bed, before she became weak.

"Mitch, what were you looking at in the driveway yesterday, anyway?"

"A deer."

"Umm."

Chapter twenty one

Mitch sauntered into Mark's classroom about seven fifteen. He was feeding and nurturing his brood, as expected.

"Morning, Mark. How are you today?" Mark glanced up from his task.

"Hey Mitch, good, and you?" he fibbed.

"I hate to say this and hate to keep bugging you, but, well, I'm not so good. Ann saw another one of those large snakes."

"When?" he didn't act surprised. Mitch noted the mendaciousness.

"Yesterday, about the time I got home. She said it chased her, Mark. Is that possible? Would these kinds of snakes hurt people?" He leaned against the door, his expression one of concern, exhaustion showing in his attitude.

Mark studied the new mathematics' teacher. Without answering him, he strolled over to spy the roguish snake he had imprisoned. The carnivore had been watching him as usual. He gazed into the yellowish and unnatural eyes.

"I don't know, Mitch. The professor from K.U. is going to be here in a little while and we'll be heading out to your place. I'll find out, I promise."

Mitch walked over to him and stared at the impious confined blacksnake with him. "Want to tell me everything you do know, Mark? Like was Ann's snake also a mutant?"

He slowly nodded his head yes. "I can't confirm anything specific. I have no reason to think the misshapen rats will harm anyone. There have been other sightings and no one has been hurt. As far as I do know, where there's one, well then there's two. But they don't stay in any one place for long. They move on. I don't know why or how many. That's it."

Mitch thought about this critically for a minute, before asking meditatively, "You said you didn't find a trace of invasion at our place, so why are you going back?"

"To look for a beaten path." Mark never did look at the man.

"Is this serious or not Mark? To have a race of mutant snakes? Doesn't this sort of thing happen naturally and more frequent than anyone's willing to let on? What about those frogs a few years back? For the world and it's species to change isn't abnormal. It's part of evolution, isn't it?"

Taking a deep breath, "Yes and no, Mitch. Let's sit down." Mark ushered him over to his desk and motioned for him to sit at one of the students. Relaxing in his own chair he looked long and hard at the guy now, deciding to be upfront, to a degree.

"I thought the snake I caught over there was deformed, because of excessive pesticide use, spoiling our earth's natural resources by sinking deep down into the planet's crust. That these snakes's origin was from below the surface and they survived around the underground springs. I figured there is a reason they've decided to change territory..."

"Whoa...wait a minute, Mark. Why would you surmise they came from beneath the ground to begin with?"

Ann was dressed in her typical sleeping sweats with a different t-shirt on, orange in color. She had her favorite ball cap in place and wore her corresponding orange thongs. Not exactly a fashion diva, but she did match.

She made a snap judgment to go to The Diner and visit with Charlotte, pretty sure she worked every day. Upon flopping in, Ann spotted her right away chatting up a storm with another customer. She waved, then sauntered to the bar and sat down.

The waitress ended her conversation and bounced over to the newest town member.

"Hi ya kid, how are you?" She smiled sympathetically at Ann, yet warm, making her feel welcome.

"I'm good. A little tired from all the work I'm doing in the house, but other than that I'm okay. How about you?" she asked, pleasantly knowing that's not what the woman really meant when she asked the question.

"Couldn't be better. What are ya having?"

"The usual," Ann teased, and then said, "Coffee, black, thanks."

"Coming right up." As Charlotte moved around the island she asked her question differently, "You here to tell me about that big blacksnake they found on your land? Everyone has been talking about it and those who got to see it were adamant it was the largest reptile they'd ever seen." Charlotte couldn't wait to hear about it straight from the victim's mouth.

"It was really big, that's for sure. Slimy too. I can't even describe how scared I was, but it wasn't threatening or anything, it's just that the size of it is what really threw me into shock." Ann didn't want to come off as a wuss. She wasn't planning to tell anyone she'd seen another one either. No, her mission was to find out something.

"I'll bet.

"You know, Ann, snakes aren't really *slimy*. People describe them that way, but they're not." She smiled, setting the coffee down in front of her.

"Really?

"Oh.

"Thanks." Ann took a sip from the mug.

"You're welcome."

"Charlotte, what I want to talk to you about is Susan Hammer." The waitress gave her a perplexed look and her undivided attention.

Ann continued with her inquiry, concentrating on stifling any kind of mental health negatives. She didn't want Charlotte to spread word she was crazy, too, or something.

"When you said she babbled, can you be more specific?"

"Well that was a couple years ago, but let me think." She glanced to the ceiling focusing on her memory. Suddenly, her face became intense and her eyes bulged as she looked back at her new friend.

"Ann, she ranted about 'copious beast' taking over the universe and 'giant nebulous amphibians' trying to kill her. Something like that. But I do remember those were the words she used. She would hang on people and mumble more than anything about the world coming to an end, being taken over by celestial beings." Charlotte quickly put her hand over her mouth and gave Ann the *I'm sorry* gaze.

"It's okay, it's just snakes. And probably just the one. Go on, tell me more about her." Ann hid her incredulity.

Chapter twenty two

A SHELL SHOCKED MITCH ROCK left Mark's classroom the minute Doctor Barbara James arrived. Mark didn't tell him the whole supposition and kept light what he did say, but he could tell the new instructor was worried. He guessed he would be, too, if he didn't know much about snakes. Fear wasn't a factor for him, when dealing with the normal ones that is.

"Thanks for making the drive again, Barbara," he said, respectfully.

"I wanted to, Mark. Are you ready? Might as well get out there and get dirty."

Mark stood there temporarily toying with the idea of getting dirty with her. She was a looker. She had on some fairly tight jeans with a skimpy shirt, showing off her figure. Nice.

Mark surprised himself, suddenly realizing he was attracted to her. She was quite a bit older then he was.

"Mark, are you coming?" she asked, wondering why he was eyeballing her and not budging.

"Uh...yeah, ready." Recognizing he was in a trance, he moved his ass following her out of the room, staring at her posterior. Mark could tell she was on a mission by the way she strutted, taking long strides down the hallway, her rock solid hips swaying side to side. They didn't talk as they descended the steps and trucked outside. Suited him. He enjoyed visualizing possible developments.

"Your ride or mine?" Mark asked, once they reached the parking lot.

"Yours. I had to bring my own car today."

"Why?"

"Because I didn't tell anyone at the university what we suspect is going on. I took personal days for this trip." Barbara remembered which vehicle Mark drove and kept walking towards it as she spoke.

"Okay." Mark hurried to get in front of her and opened the passenger door. Miss James stopped in her tracks and gave the teacher an odd look. Then she brazenly grabbed the keys that were dangling from his other hand.

Marching to the other side of the car, leaving Mark to stand and gap at his mistake, she said, "I guess you want me to drive. That's fine. Just show me which way to go." Without missing a beat she was in the driver's seat, starting up the old jalopy, before Mark could get into the passenger seat of his overused, but faithful old truck.

A little singed, "Take a left out of here, then turn right at the four way stop sign. It's about five miles out of town," he instructed her.

Driving a little too fast for Mark's comfort, although he would never say it, Barbara stated bluntly, "Want to tell me everything you suspect, Mr. Gordon. **As a woman**, not as a biologist, I know you're not being totally upfront with me."

This broad was amazing. Mark could only stare at her taking control of her destiny behind the wheel and by calling the kettle. He felt limp all over.

"Well, I'm waiting." She flashed him a look.

"Alright. I think these snakes are in massive amounts, utterly under our noses. I think they're originally grotto dwellers that for some reason are growing rapidly and running out of room in the unbeknownst underneath us. I think they're the reason my town is seeing major structural damage. Because they're surfacing and because there are so many and of such great size, they're causing the ground to literally move," Mark told her, soberly.

He barely got those words out when Barbara started with her insights.

"They are not the same genetically as the black rat snake. I got the computer results back. We're looking at a different Phylum, Mark. They have been altered, but without data on the original, we can't guess at what or if any pesticide is the cause. Too bad, too. I'd like nothing more than to stop our agricultural engineers from using anything except natural means.

"At any rate, we know nothing about this Genus of snakes. Except that they are a large breed that bares countless broods at a single time. They come from the underground yeah, but I'm leaning more towards the concept that they live closer to the earth's mantle, which would explain the durable skin and why they don't shed it. However, I can't guess at why they appear to be observing us."

Mark was stunned and also awed with her overnight research. He wished he had all the latest technology at his disposal. Mark comprehended what she was saying, but he also understood the connotation of discovering a new classification of Colubrids. This would be her claim to fame in the herpetology world.

"Impressive, Doctor James. I suppose I should congratulate you.

"That's it, turn here," he quickly added, indicating which homestead.

Pulling into the drive and parking the truck, Miss James got out brash without responding to Mark's implication. It ticked her off, actually. Mark also climbed out, clear his comment disturbed her.

Catching up to Barbara, he grabbed her by the arm and spun her around. Mark decided he was going to find out what she knew. He was tired of her standoffish attitude and suspected she had more information than what she was letting on.

"Want to tell me what it is you're keeping secret, Missy? **As a man...** I can tell you're hiding something."

Surprised by his assertiveness, yet appreciative of his candor, Barbara answered him as one professional to another. "Recordings of seismic waves have been popping up all over the four state area, Mr. Gordon, and there is no rationalization for these events. But there is covert research going on." As Mark let go of her she said, "Friend of a friend.

"The concept is this; the center of our United States, us here, is in an isostatic rebound. The lithosphere is essentially done rising from the asthenosphere. A mountain range predicted to have sunk thousands of years ago is the 'guess'." She used her hands to make quotation marks as she said the word *guess*. "I'm sure you're aware of the speculation."

Finishing with what she had concluded, Barbara's eyes never left Mark's. "No one will come right out and say that something we know nothing about has been unleashed in the process. Which Mark, I believe is our snakes.

"As far as having a claim to fame, Mr. Gordon, is seriously absurd to me. My interest here is to find out if the human race is in danger and that's it."

Mark was pretty sure he was in love. Figures it would finally happen when the world was coming to an end. Oh, he'd dated plenty of women his age and some a few years younger, but never had he had a woman with her intelligence level and spirit. He couldn't help but ogle her mind through her eyes.

"Don't you have anything to say?" she demanded.

"Want to stay at my place, while you're in town, Doctor James?"

Barbara gave him a stupefied look, blinking a couple times, trying to hide her wonder.

Chapter twenty three

Aɴɴ ᴘᴜʟʟᴇᴅ ɪɴᴛᴏ ʜᴇʀ ᴅʀɪᴠᴇᴡᴀʏ to see Mark Gordon standing with an unidentified woman. She didn't care as long as she didn't have to be alone out here. She smiled and waved large at the two.

"Hi, Mark!" she said, parking behind his truck and getting out.

"Hey, Ann, how are you today?"

She shrugged her shoulders. "I'm okay. I'm glad you're here," she confessed, walking over to the duo.

"Barbara, this is Ann Rock. Ann, Doctor Barbara James. She's head honcho for the science department at K.U."

"Impressive, nice to meet you."

"You too." They shook hands.

"Ann was chased by one of the rats yesterday."

Barbara shot Mark a perturbed look. "Ann, tell me what happened," she immediately asked, while thinking Mark must have forgotten to tell her this tidbit. Barbara didn't like that. She needed to know everything.

"Would you like to come in?"

Mark butted in here, "No, I want you to reenact and show us exactly where you were when the snake chased you. And tell us everything, like what time it was when you first saw it, etc."

"Sure, come this way." Ann guided them to the end of the drive close to the house. Barbara kept her mouth shut following Mark, letting him do the surmising.

Mark, Ann and Barbara were unaware of the gargantuan, camouflaged reptile prowling in the large oak tree on the other side of the small garage, watching them. The snake was suspended in the dark twisted branches about ten feet up, its body coiled around one of the huge limbs five or six times. Its head dangled lower as it peered through the leaves with its penetrating deviant eyes. The blackened skin of the carnivore crept in steady motion as it studied the prey.

"Mitch was at the end of the drive looking at something when I saw him, well a deer, he said. That was about forty minutes after you left. I came out the front door..." she pointed, "...and came this way. I traipsed down to here." She began parading to the exact place, the other two retracing the steps with her, both scanning the ground.

Ann left out the part about getting spooked. "I stopped here. Mitch didn't see me, so I decided to go back in the house, because I was barefoot."

"You were barefoot?" Barbara inquired, this striking her as intriguing. The strong chemicals possibly emanating from this part of the body could be reason for the snake following her.

"Yes, well I had been standing on the cabinets most the day tearing down wallpaper and..." She quit with that line of the story since she could tell they weren't interested by the way they stared vacantly at her.

"Anyhow, when I turned around it was there, in the grass." Everyone looked over to the vicinity.

"How big?"

"I think it was bigger than the other one, Mark, but I can't be sure. I panicked," Ann came clean. "Its head was up and I swear it was looking at me as if I was its next meal. The entire thing went this far." She showed them an outline of its presence. Simply talking about this was making Ann feel squeamish.

"I told you, Ann, it's alright to be scared. Go on, what happened?" Mark calmed her, shrewdly detecting her discomfort.

"Well, I ran. I tried to dodge it and get back to the house through the overgrown weeds, Mitch cut the yard last night. They were pretty tall. But the snake moved the same way I did, blocking me from getting past it. I turned and ran my fastest down the rest of the driveway to Mitch.

"I swear it was on my heels, Mark, chasing me. Mitch didn't see it, though. Now I can't be sure. I mean, I didn't look back. I was terrified out of my wits, but I could feel it. Oh. This really gives me the creeps."

Barbara was extremely interested in the account. "What did your husband do, Ann?"

"When he heard me screaming he raced down the drive to meet me."

"On foot or in the car?"

"In the car. He screeched to a stop, jumped out and grabbed me."

"And you were screaming pretty loud?"

"Yes, very." Ann glanced at Mark and gave him a deliberate look.

"She can do some high pitched, incredibly vociferous roaring," Mark told Barbara colorfully, lightening the mood for Ann. "Why?"

She didn't answer him, but Barbara was thinking that she liked the way Mark Gordon dealt with Ann. And she'd been well aware of how nicely he was built and of his dark sexy looks. She hadn't really given him a good going over until she realized he was interested in her, after he asked her to stay with him. Barbara was considering the possibility.

"Please finish your story, Ann."

"Well, I got my butt in the car ASAP and never did turn around. Mitch didn't. He searched for it. Thing is, it was nowhere and it was so big it couldn't have just disappeared without a trace. That's why Mitch cut the grass, to see if he could find any holes in the yard. He didn't.

"To be honest, Mark, Mitch thinks I imagined it." Ann hated confessing this, but thought she should.

The biology specialists didn't know what to say to that. There was an awkward hush as they tried to ignore the remark, looking about the land, wanting to see something that could explain the snake's disappearance, still ignorant they were being spied upon by one of the large.

Mark broke the silence, "Ann, Mitch was in my office first thing this morning. He's very worried about you being out here alone and he certainly didn't tell me you imagined anything."

"Thanks, Mark. It's okay, because I really don't know anymore."

"Look, that giant snake we seized is enough to send anyone's imagination into overdrive, but for the record, it's highly unlikely your mind conjured it up. Usually they travel in pairs. That's why we'll be here everyday. To be absolutely positive there is or isn't."

"Oh great. Pairs huh? Well...at least I guess I know I'm not crazy." Ann said that as she glanced to the ground to make sure nothing was underfoot.

"Now, my students and I methodically examined your house, looking for any kind of way that snake or other snakes could get in. It's secure. So don't worry or be afraid in your home. Okay?"

"I'll try. Thanks, Mark. I feel a lot safer knowing you're doing this for us."

"It's my job."

Barbara interrupted with, "I'd love to."

While Ann was confused, Mark wasn't. Pleased, he immediately said, "Good."

Soaking in this marvelous and welcomed expose' that he would have a beautiful, intelligent house guest, Mark focused back on the subject matter.

"Do you know anything else that could help us, Ann?"

"Only that Susan Hammer, who lived here for a while after her father died a couple years ago, talked a great deal to the town folk about the large snakes that lived out here."

"I didn't know that." Mark was staggered. He was usually called for these exact reasons.

"Charlotte, at The Diner, told me everyone thought she was crazy, because she raved about them being from outer space or something like that."

"Two years ago?" Barbara asked.

"Yeah, about two years ago." Ann nodded her head. Barbara and Mark gave each other a tentative glance.

Chapter twenty four

ANN WENT INSIDE, SO THE snake chasers could get to work tracking down the shocking bestial or to discover there wasn't one, whichever. She felt better that Mark believed her. He even walked her to the door and asked if she wanted him to come in and inspect the house. She refused, but thanked him and told him how nice he was.

Scrutinizing the kitchen walls, Ann felt a rush of fatigue come over her. She automatically decided to call her sister and visit instead, fill her in on the past two days. She picked up the inexpensive portable and sat down at the kitchen table. She could see Mark and Barbara through the undraped paned windows bearing towards the barn.

She relaxed with her feet up in another chair and dialed the number.

"Hey sis, how's school going?"

"What are you thinking?" Mark asked his lovely colleague, as they ambled along, assessing the picturesque geography. He had taken his jacket off, no reason to get it grimy, and rolled up his cuffed sleeves. They had grabbed a couple of flashlights out of his truck to help in their analysis of the oversized and decrepit structure, which stood about forty yards behind the Rock home. They agreed the dilapidated barn in the back would be a logical place to begin.

"I know snakes don't have ears like we do, but they do sense vibrations, Mark," Barbara began, sardonically; this probably sounded ridiculous. She explained her reasoning anyway, to the man she was going to spend the night with. Yeah, she liked him.

"After the examination of the large rat I took back to my lab, I do have a notion that loud noise must have something to do with why they hide or move away, disappear. It could be commotion of any type. The sensations they sense most likely alert them. I think it's possible they perceive the new and uncommon noises as danger. Of course, eventually they'll get used to the surface of the earth and to us."

"That sounds logical. Whenever I uncovered a suspected site, they seemed to vanish. I suppose coming from deep underground this world would be strange for them to adapt. The entire new ambiance they would feel and/or chemicals they would taste would certainly be diverse." Mark's thoughts went on to imagine how the outer planet would be different for the amphibians, compared to the inner topography.

"Yes, but they will adjust. You and I both know it. One of the things this Kingdom of snakes can do is acclimatize."

Mark agreed with her and at the same time pulled the faded red, heavy door to an open position, waiting to let the lady go first. This time she accepted his machismo. Stepping in directly after her, they took a rough glance throughout the building, while turning on their paltry equipment. There were many old chicken cages stacked in one corner and piles of hay opposite. The old hangar was spacey and there was typical farm junk in it strewn from one end clear to the large doors on the other end. It looked like a flea market sanctuary.

Looking around at all the stuff, "Let's check the loft first and work our way down," Mark said, remembering how fast the corpulent and expeditious ophite ascended the tree. He shined his light up above, carefully scanning the garret.

The twosome made their way over to the ramshackle ladder leading upwards, side stepping through shovels and tools on the floorboards, choreographing through the larger items; such as the lawn mower, a broken down tractor and a collection of tires. They whacked down cobwebs as they went.

"I'll go first," Mark gallantly told her. "Might be a loose plank." He nodded to her, being the male protagonist.

"My hero." Barbara made the comment in travesty, chidingly. Then deciding to be ornery and see what the man was really made of, she said casually, "At least I'll have a good view of your butt," just as Mark was taking his second step.

He waned and glanced down at her with amusement, then continued and countered with, "All women like my ass." She chuckled at him, the first time she actually let her hair down. Mark was grinning as he climbed.

As soon as Mark and Barbara entered the barn, the wily, obscured reptilian, without resonance, slid down the tree in a slow, purposeful method. Its long body arced and dropped with ease. The black luminous skin radiated a purplish tint that glistened in the sunshine. Using its prevailing strength, the head piloting the way, the fluid life force sneaked onto the top of the garage roof, never halting in shifting its silken hide.

It appeared to be watching Ann through the kitchen window with the unusual and aberrant eyes, as it kept traveling. The monstrosity regulated itself across and then down the side of the building and onto the ground, remaining soundless.

The creature snaked its way through the grass, clearly visible, if anyone were to be looking.

The head stayed higher then the rest of the body as it moved faster now, past and under the window on the side of the house, edging on its belly in a double S shape, continuously propelling forward. It slinked its way to the other end of the residence in a matter of nothing.

Thrusting its great and intimidating essence in the air, compelling its core up the side of the house in a tick, the snake glided quietly, giving off no clue of its presence. First its cranium, then the rest of its imposing existence crept through a hard to see opening between the roof and house, flattening its body with ease.

It only took a moment for it to completely vanish into the attic, because of its agility. The carnivore disappeared in entirety, undetected.

Ann was unsuspecting of the large creature entering her home as she talked enthusiastic and nonstop with Meg.

"I can't believe that actually happened to you!" an animated Meg exclaimed, on the other end of the phone.

"It wasn't anything I would prefer to go through again. Gees!" Ann was histrionic.

"I can only wonder. Boy, that's some story. Are you sure you're okay?"

"Don't worry, I'm fine. I'll just have to get used to these kinds of things, seeing as I'm a country girl now."

"Country girl," Meg repeated, then said, "Sounds nice, Ann. I hope you two are happy there, really, but I miss you not being here for me to pop in whenever I want. Selfish huh?"

"No Meg, I miss you, too. Hey I know, can you visit over Easter break instead of waiting until summer?"

"I can. I was hoping you'd ask. I didn't want to wait. "

"You don't ever need an invitation, sis. You know that." Ann was pleased she was coming. It would motivate her to get the house done in time for her sibling's arrival, give her something to look forward to.

"Well, I didn't want to intrude. I'm excited though, really. We'll have to stay up and have one of our all night gab sessions."

"Sounds wonderful!"

"Oh, I almost forgot, Ann. Your wedding pictures are in the mail."

"Did you get to see them? Are they good? Oh, I can't wait to get them! Thank you!"

No one suspected the cracks in the front and surrounding yard around the Rock's domicile to be of anything out of the ordinary. It looked like they were of consequence due to the dryness of the land. There hadn't been a great deal of rain lately, unusual for this time of year, but no one thought anything abnormal about the crevices.

Just as the other snake made its way out of sight, a new one came slithering out of one of the rifts in the lawn, sideways. It thinned its body to squeeze through and surface into the light of day. Once it was finally on ground, it was identical to the other two, having the vast dimensions and eerily funky eyes.

The snake coiled and sneaked its way to the house using the same motion; the head up and body S shaped, except this one was speedier than the last. It wasted no time climbing the house and slipping into the upper floor level, via another hard to spot gap under the roof.

Chapter twenty five

Mark and his corresponding partner in snake warfare continued to vigilantly search every square inch of the old barn's loft, while talking nonstop. They tiptoed through the rafters using their flashlights to consider each piece of hay, along with the breaches that let through small rays of light between the wood panels.

"I don't see any sign of infestation, Mark. Maybe we should be scouting out the land?" Barbara questioned, picking up a petrified bee hive.

"Look at this," she said, amused with her find.

"Cool." Mark shined his light at it to get a good look. "I'll take it back to my classroom. The kids will love it."

Barbara gawked at him. "You like teaching don't you?"

"Yes, I do. Very much," he answered her sincere, standing there watching her get a kick out of the fossilized colony.

"Why?" She watched him now.

"Well, I like to hear myself talk."

"Oh you're bad," she laughed. "Tell me the truth."

Mark only gazed at her maintaining his nonchalant expression. "No really. I was being straight with you."

"Stop it. I know better."

"That woman's intuition thing," he kidded her. Barbara tucked the discovery under her arm and started looking about again. He was funny. She did like his sense of humor. All the men at the university or the ones she'd met on business trips were all alike; old and boring, only talking about themselves. Mark was different and the more she was around him, the more she was interested in him.

"Yes, that." Stepping to her left as she answered him in a flirting manner, Barbara hit a weak spot in the edifice.

"Oh...oops...uh...well hell!" she mumbled first, then shouted, as her legs were going down into the flooring. The bee hive went flying and she dropped her flashlight when she tried to catch and save herself from the inevitable.

"Barbara!" Mark tried to reach for her, but he wasn't quick enough. He scampered over to the woman, his hands grasping wildly to grab her, before she went all the way through to the first floor. He lost his light during the tumult, too.

"Mark," she shrieked, at the same time the boards gave way to her weight.

Barbara fell the seven or eight feet and landed with a thud and groan as she creamed into the stall below full of weathered silage. She was unmoving at this point.

Mark couldn't get down that ladder fast enough. After watching her hit bottom, on his stomach, from making a last attempt at diving for her, he hurriedly pushed himself backwards towards the decent. He kept yelling, "Barbara, are you alright?"

Once down to the first level, racing to her aid, Mark stumbled over all the rubbish in the dimly lit building, practically breaking his neck, the incident replaying in his mind. Her expression was one of shock and fear, her eyes focused on him as she went down. He just couldn't get to her. They had been standing at least five feet apart. He felt absolutely horrible.

Knocking the gate open with velocity, Mark hurled to where the woman lay, unconscious. "Barbara! Barbara!" He felt panicky and responsible for her plight. Kneeling at her side he lifted her head into his hands.

Her forehead crinkled and she moaned softly coming back into his world. Then her eyelids fluttered and finally she opened her eyes.

"Barbara, can you hear me?

"Is anything broken?"

Realizing reality, she grumbled, "Mark...yes...I'm fine...oh brother... what an imbecile I am." She began to sit up.

"No, don't move. We need to be sure you haven't hurt yourself. Here, how many fingers am I holding up?" he insisted, concerned, shoving three fingers into her eye sight, leaving his other hand to cradle her.

"Oh please," she wisecracked, shoving away his intention and rolled over to get up anyway.

"Do you know how many falls I've taken in my line of work, Mark Gordon?" She acted tough sitting next to him and brushing herself off, trying to get over her embarrassment and brief oblivion. She should have known to pay attention to the job.

"The day I can't take a little tumble is the day I quit," she declared, flatly.

Mark was definitely in awe. She had grit, guts and genius. What more could a man ask for in a woman? He couldn't say a word. Mark could only stare at her with a twinkle in his eye. Love, lust and longing were in his heart.

As Barbara rubbed her neck and twisted her back, unaware Mr. Gordon was falling head over heels for her at that precise moment, her hand landed on a durable, rounded object buried in the moldy feed. She glanced down as she scooped through the muddle and pulled out an egg.

Quickly looking back at her new, special friend, she said, "Mark, I think I found something." Then noticing his pallid face and vacant look, she asked, "Are you okay? What's the matter? Did I scare you?" She was attentive to him, a bit worried.

"Yes, Barbara, you did. You scared the crap out of me."

She couldn't help but grin at the guy. "I'm sorry. I'm fine...really." Instinctively she touched his cheek. He was incredibly charming with his honesty. Barbara thought Mark was going to be hard to refuse. Not that she wanted to.

Coming out of his stupor, Mark saw what she had just picked up. "Is that a black rat egg?"

Getting over herself, "It appears to be," she said, dusting it off. "But..." Her gaze became absorbing as her word loitered in the air.

"But what? Here, let me see it," Mark virtually demanded.

"Sure." Barbara gave it to him and started to rummage around in the mulch to see if she could feel anything else. Right about the time she did find a nest, Mark realized what was so peculiar about the snake egg.

"There's more."
"It's empty."

They spied each other.

"The insides are sucked out, and look at the evidence of *who done it*." Mark showed her the imprints of fangs etched into the sides.

Barbara hurried to pick up the rest. "They're all barren Mark." Then she began to investigate their surroundings. Mark was already doing the same. Normally, when eggs are eaten by whatever, the casing is broken and the shells are scattered. But, this wasn't the strangest part about this unearthing.

The eggs had been hidden after having the life sucked out of them. Gordon and James were seeking traces of the culprit; however, they both had the same idea. According to the nicks left on the offspring, it was reasonable to think the newer family of Colubridae was responsible.

"Did I tell you the rat I caught a few months back ate my old blacksnake?" Mark asked, rather suspiciously.

"No." She looked at him funny, thinking the exact same conclusion.

"They're eating the normal blacks and their young."

"Mark, this implies that these unheard of animals are not only thinking, but working together as an intelligent race."

"Yep. And I think it's safe to assume other creatures are also being killed, probably at a pretty good rate, too."

"Right."

Chapter twenty six

"MEG, I HAVE TO GO, I'll call you back later." Ann hung up abruptly on her sister. She had an overwhelming need to vomit all of a sudden.

"Oh boy..."she sighed, getting up a bit too quickly, a big mistake. Her eyesight was blurred and fog filled her brain. Ann tried to blink the fuzziness away, but she was getting increasingly incompetent.

Three steps on her way to the bathroom, the weakness in her legs and the rest of her body took over. Feeling the faint consume her, she almost collapsed. Fortunately, she managed to lean on the kitchen cabinet, steadying herself.

This had never happened to Ann before. She was scared for her well-being, while trying to shake this spell. Her jaws were tingling from the need to heave, yet she couldn't go any further, because she couldn't see and she was too vulnerable to let go of the support.

Tears streamed down her face as she endured the bout. Ann raised her right hand feeling her forehead, checking to see if she had a fever or something, wobbling from the near fatal black out.

"What's...wrong...with me?" she whimpered, taking deep breaths, willing herself to stay conscious. As she held on, the lack of ability to function seemed never-ending, the nausea undying.

Ann remained parked in her kitchen, draped over the counter for about a minute, although it felt forever, before the hex began to pass.

113

Little by little, she gained her equanimity. Clinching her mouth tightly, not wanting to puke on her floor, alertness slowly made its way back, the stupor lifting. She moved her hand from her head to her belly and focused on the environment around her.

Even though she was still experiencing the feebleness, her vision finally returned. Ann decided she could make it to the toilet. Staggering through the doorway, holding on to anything that would help her maintain balance, she inched her way along, conjecturing reasons of why she was sick. The downstairs bath was right next to the kitchen, except it seemed miles away.

Ann practically fell to the floor in front of the porcelain god and boosted the lid with great speed. Her need to empty her stomach contents was the only thing of significance at the present.

In the split second before she closed her eyes to let lose, she glimpsed the golden, rhombus, slotted slits in the water, looking back at her.

As bad as she felt and as puny as her body was from the morning sickness, Ann was able to keep from hurling. She had that toilet lid shut in less than a glint and herself up off the floorboards in nothing flat. Yet Ann didn't scream or run. She couldn't. The shock of seeing the abhorrent snake in her latrine was too great.

Ann was backed up to the opposite wall, her eyes huge and hooked on the unbelievable. She looked like a statue with her hands and arms at her sides pressed against the support keeping her balanced, incapable of taking in air, frozen in time, so to speak.

But not for long.

Ann Rock gradually began to slide down the crutch she was propped against, her nails clawing the old and outdated remnants of wallpaper as she went. She continued to stare ahead at the reason for the immobility she suffered, waiting for the serpent to burst open the only thing standing between them. As her butt hit the ground, she involuntarily began to lose her vision again. Vertigo winning the moment.

In the next beat, Ann Rock lay lifeless on her bathroom floor, oblivious of her environs and of the need to give up her morning coffee. She was in la la land, caused by the immense jolt of horror she had just endured. Out like a light, she was ignorant of anything alien in her brand new home and brand new life.

The gigantic black snake jetted out of the water and the latrine with force, ramming the top closure open devoid a problem, at the very same time Ann lost her mental attentiveness. It seemed larger than life, considering the location. Its middle barely fit through the encircle of the ceramic as the perceived infinite escaped into the house.

The ophidian twisted its way out of the room, through the door using Ann as a stepping stone. The long, currently unassailable creature from the anonymous trekked over the sleeping beauty as if she wasn't there. Its head steered the body as it moved deliberately, with intention. The inconceivable knew where it was going.

The twenty foot splendor then made its way through the hall to the family room, twisting over the furniture to the fireplace. Never hesitating, the reptilian thrust itself aloft, scaling the bricks into the chimney, slithering on into the attic. There were cracks and separations inside the brick construction after all these years and the amphibian simply glided through.

A half hour later, Ann began to show signs of verve, sprawled out on her lavatory floor. Her eyes fluttered several times, before she was able to open them and she whined, feeling the surreal. The first thing she realized was that she was wet, almost soaked.

How did I get water all over me? Good Grief.

God...I feel miserable.

What am I doing on the floor?

Ann awkwardly rolled onto all fours. Exerting most of her strength, what little she had left, she pushed herself into an upright position. Clinging to the bathroom sink for assistance, Ann stood all the way up. Lifting her head, trying to remember how she came to be in this situation, she finally spied herself in the mirror.

Oh God, I look like shit.

I feel like shit.

What just happened?

Let me see, what's the last thing I remember?

I was talking to Meg. Yeah. She's coming for a visit next month.

That's right, okay.

Then I got sick. I had an irresistible need to earl.

Did I?

Ann studied her image in the reflection. She noted that she was ashen in color and her appearance was disheveled. Definitely not looking her best. She took hold of her orange shirt and glanced down at the dampness. Then at her sweats. Next, she noticed her Bear's ball cap on the ground. Confused, she bent over to pick it up. Ann couldn't comprehend what could have possibly come over her.

Did I just have a black out?

I don't remember anything like this ever happening before.

She moved deliberately to sit down on the toilet and rest a minute. Ann just couldn't quite determine what brought her to this point. She struggled to remember her morning events as she combed through her hair with her fingers, staring at the water on the floor. It never occurred to her she'd had to put the toilet lid down first.

I took Mitch to school and...

And Mark and that Barbara woman, from KU, were here when I got back.

That's right. I visited with them about the snake that chased me yesterday.

I remember thinking they were hot for one another. Yeah. They'd make a cute couple. Mark is so sweet to me. I hope him and Mitch become good friends.

Ouch, my hip hurts. I must have fallen on it.

Ann reached down and rubbed her injury through her sweats. Her mind was in absolute jumble. She concentrated for an inkling of anything that could have led her to being damp and passed out on the bathroom floor. This disruption had Ann shaken out of her fortitude. For the life of her she just couldn't remember.

Chapter twenty seven

"I THINK WE NEED TO WALK, what do you think?" A befuddled Barbara James asked Mark Gordon.

"You're going to wear my ass out today, aren't you?" Mark gawked at the woman he thought he wanted to marry. He'd never been this smitten with anyone. He amazed himself. He'd stay on his feet night and day just to get to be with her. But for the time being he would play the part of interested partner in discretion.

"Hope not. I'm looking forward to the dinner you're going to cook me." Barbara got a charge out of herself as she said that, getting up at the same time, smiling, not looking the guy in the eyes.

Mark's adorable and sexy grin emerged. He couldn't help it. She was the bomb. He shook his head at her assertiveness, surprised, but not surprised and got up, too.

"If you go to the store with me then I'll fix you whatever your little tummy desires."

Her heart skipped a little faster. Barbara tried to think of the last time she felt this way about a man. She looked him in his baby blacks now as she realized how long it had actually been.

"Okay, I'll go to the store with you." She shrugged her shoulders, hiding the desire she had for him.

"Well then, we have a date," Mark said, also keeping hidden his lust.

And that was that. The two strolled out of the barn, eggs in hand. They were evidence. Too bad they didn't have a camera with them to record the finding. Mark usually did, but his students were using it after school today to take pictures before and after they removed some of the crust sticks around town. He left it in his classroom this morning in case he didn't make it back.

His helpers knew what they were doing. Mark was a good teacher. And they were dependable and reliable. When or if he couldn't make it to the school early, all Mark had to do was call one of them to be there, take care of his critters.

"Let's go this way," Barbara said, deciding to be the leader of this expedition.

"From the angle of the barn verses the layout of the territory, gauging the rise and fall of the sun, I'd say any new life form would use standard radar to have a method of folly, wouldn't you?" She gave Mark a diffident glance as they trudged along into the wilderness to find – God only knows what. She had to do some philosophizing with a satirical edge about what they were doing since this wasn't a typical outing.

"You're the boss. Whatever you think is probably right." Mark didn't care about her guesswork. He enjoyed his circumstance, although what they were searching for could mean trouble. However, he was as determined as his cohort to be enlightened. He wouldn't let humankind go without a fight. Besides, she might essentially be on to something with her mordant supposition.

The brushwood splintered under their feet as they traipsed through the woods and out of sight of the Rock homestead. Mark and Barbara explored the ground as they walked and talked. Neither was ready to come to terms with the fact that they may have a new breed of intelligence to face. Or what it meant to mother earth, or to the human race, or to the animals it would prey.

Barbara rambled with her thoughts, "It seems logical anyone, I mean anything," she corrected herself, "novel to this planet would indeed blueprint the terrain using weather, light or darkness of course, and sound. Plausibly, the degree of revolve would factor in.

"And in an innovative milieu such as this, I would venture to suggest 'they' would conceal a safety zone." She used her fingers to make quotations again when she said *they*. "My reasoning is the longitude verses the latitude in the down under would certainly impact such an evaluation on the upper deck..."

"Enough already with the garbage. Let's talk about what we just found." Mark cut her off. She was interminable and he decided to call her on it. Furthermore, she might have blabbed that shit on and on all day if he let her. He thought they might as well lay the cards on the table and face the consequence, even though he loved listening to her talk.

"Why are you ignoring your true suspicions?"

Taking a deep breath, acting as if this decision was the last one she'd ever make, Barbara abruptly quit walking and looked to the sky for answers. Mark waited on her to get a grip, eyeing her flawless complexion. Was there anything wrong with this woman, he mulled over in his mind. This is crazy, he thought, to fall in love so rapidly. They had no chance of being together, living in separate towns and being miles apart in age.

"Okay, Mark," she interrupted his daydream. "This stays between you and me."

He smiled. "Sure it does. I won't tell if you don't tell, right?"

Reading between the lines, "Look, I'm sorry I'm worried about my reputation, Gordon. I worked hard to get where I am and I refuse to risk my job. I'm not young and idealistic anymore, I'm realistic, because I have to be," she told him, bluntly.

"You don't have to explain your fears to me, Barbara. But I want us to discuss what we **think** we know. That's all. You and me out here in no-man's-land. Let's go for the gusto."

She didn't answer for a while. They picked their hike back up and strolled in silence for a few.

So Mark went ahead and laid his reasoning on the line. "James..." he called her by her last name to lighten her mood since she called him by his, silently chuckling to himself.

"...I don't want to risk my reputation either. And I'm certainly green if we are discovering a new species of Elaphe Obsoleta Obsoleta, but I want us to go over everything we know. Can we please just do that?"

Finally, "Fine, Mark. Here's what's on my mind. Suddenly there is seismic activity on the rise and the private sectors are keeping quiet their research. More and more mammoth snake sightings are being reported, except when we get there they disappear. Ann being chased by one yesterday is bothering me and that we found zero evidence of the creature or where it hid, if it did. These black rat eggs empty and covered up, along with everything else is adding up to one thing.

"I think we have an intelligent race emerging from the unheard of and it scares me. I think they are big enough to kill a person without a problem. From seeing the babies they produce, in substantial sums I mind you, well, it could be a matter of days, before they *have* to start hunting larger dinners.

"You know, a couple years ago there was a report from a famous herpetologist, who by the way, has all the money he wants to do his exploration; you know who I'm talking about. Anyway, his conclusion on the Opheodrys Vernalis..." she used that term since Mark used the scientific description earlier. "...population was that they were swiftly decreasing in numbers. No one paid heed to the report at the time, but with what I know now, I believe this new breed may be the culprit and that they started eating them approximately five years ago. That these mysterious types of snakes began surfacing at that time, the reason for the green snake disappearance.

"Now, if you take what we already know to be true about the basic rats and theorize using these traits, well, it gets daunting." Mark paid attention. He had the same edge of logic and was ready to add to her assumptions.

"Right. The basic black is not only a good swimmer, it's ectothermic. It can live anywhere, really. And it has been speculated for years that the population of all rats is more than we ever suspected, because of their ability to blend in with the background of their environments. The female can produce a litter of eggs more than once a year, too.

"With their knack to protect themselves from predators, like hanging in trees..." They both looked upwards as he said that. "...I would say there are a healthy number of them. I don't think we give the snakes enough credit anyway, especially since they've been around longer than mankind.

"Of course, humans kill snakes out of fear, because of their size, but most rats would never attack without reason. May not be the case with this new variety, though. Is that what you're getting at?

"I've been wondering if they could or would and think we need to find out. Don't you?"

"I hadn't really thought about it as much as I was worried about the damage they're causing under my feet."

"I had one idea." Mark wandered with his thoughts about as much as his collaborator in science did.

"Since a normal male and female black rat can communicate using pheromones when they mate – and you said the snake you have is Asexual – why not think the new reptiles can communicate this way all the time?

"I've also been studying the one I have for the past six months. It has never shed the skin. We know the brille, the clear scale over the eyes, gets foggy and has to be shed, too. I think this new brood has enhanced eyesight, because it doesn't have this need."

"You're probably right."

Barbara had a sudden insight. "Mark, what if they eat **all** the other snakes? Then what?"

She suddenly stopped talking and moving forward. Mark also halted. The two were about a mile and a half from the barn when they spotted a populate area. The multiple holes in the ground in front of them were unexpected as well as frightening. And fresh. Mark could tell. He'd been around varmints his whole life.

While James kneeled down to get a better look, Gordon was gazing out into the open land looking for a conduit, of sorts. He didn't think these hovels were made from the snakes surfacing here. He thought they were made by the strange going inward, because of the way the dirt around the pits appeared. Meaning they were leading somewhere. A possible trail at last.

What Mark was looking for was any kind of earth raised by unnatural means. And he knew the general direction to look since he could tell which way they were traveling. Going into his thinking mode, he racked his brain trying to remember what laid ahead in the southeast direction he was staring.

"Mark, there's fourteen holes here," Barbara said, gazing up to him from her position. Seeing him stand motionless and with the very serious expression on his face, she stood and looked in the same direction, too.

"What is it Mark?" He didn't answer her. While he was speculating a course, he was also contemplating how the hell she could have been right in her supposition, concerning which way they headed to begin with. Which led them here. *What was it she said specifically?*

Chapter twenty eight

MITCH DECIDED TO CALL his wife on his lunch break today. If he had the car, he would have picked up some grub and gone home to surprise her. He knew she was probably working her ass off, stressed, wanting to get everything done. Ann was definitely a hard worker. He also felt bad about being such a dick to her yesterday.

The phone rang about ten times, before she picked it up. Mitch thought she was home, but had she not been, he wanted to leave her a message on the answering machine. He just sat there in the cafeteria waiting, piddling with his food.

"Hello?"

"Ann, hi, it's me. What took you so long to answer?"

"Mitch? What are you doing?"

"Talking to my favorite gal."

Silence.

"Ann? You there?"

"Yes, I'm here."

"What's wrong?"

"Nothing."

"Come on, I can tell when something's on your mind."

"I miss you when I'm away from you."

Again silence.

"Ann? What's up? Are you okay?" He heard her start sobbing on the other end.

"Sweetheart, what is it? Are you still upset with me?"

"No," she answered, in her mouse-like voice.

"Did you see another snake?" He was worried now.

"No...Mark's here...with that woman," she told him, between whimpers.

"I'm glad you're not alone, *sweetums*. Or did Mark upset you?" Mitch quickly remembered how detailed Mark's explanations were.

"No. But..."

"But what, Ann? Just tell me, please."

"I kind of...had a spell."

"A spell? I don't get what you mean."

Ann was afraid to tell him in reality. She thought it would make her sound crazy and she was already worried about him thinking that, although she was beginning to believe it. Her problems lately had sounded like the nervous breakdown she'd had years before. She wasn't sure what scared her the most. And that's the reason she got so upset with Mitch to begin with yesterday, when he said she'd imagined that beast.

"Ann? Are you there? I want to know what happened."

"Mitch, I blacked out. There I said it. I was talking on the phone to Meg and all of a sudden I had an urge to throw-up. And...that's the last thing I remember."

"That's the last thing you remember? Until when? Now?"

"No, I've been in the bathroom for a while trying to recollect what happened. I...woke up on the floor soaking wet..."

Alarmed, "What? Ann, do you mean you fainted?"

"I guess? I don't know."

"Are you hurt?"

"My hip. It's sore...bruised." Ann continued to cry softly.

"Oh honey, I wish I could be home with you." Mitch paused, then asked, "Can you drive?"

"I suppose, yes."

"Why don't you come and get me. I'll play hooky this afternoon."

"Mitch, I think I'm pregnant," she blurted that out of nowhere, and really started in with the blubbering.

There was silence once again. On Mitch's end this time.

"Mitch, I'm sorry...with everything going on I forgot to take my pills. Only I don't know which days. This is the third day off them since I made the discovery and I don't have any signs of starting my period...and now I'm scared since I blacked out...or fainted. What if something's wrong with me or...the baby, Mitch?

"Mitch, please...say something."

"I'll be right home, Ann. Don't move. Just wait on me." Click.

"But Mitch..." Ann was surprised by his knee jerk reaction. She simply sat there staring at the receiver in her hand after it went dead.

"Mrs. Weaver!" Mitch jumped up after hanging up on his wife, knocking his plate of macaroni and cheese off the luncheon table and then tripped over his chair.

"Mrs. Weaver, I need a favor!" He was speaking loud and animated, causing a scene as he stumbled across the lunchroom over to where she was seated with other teachers.

"Mitch, oh dear. What's wrong? Is everything okay at home?" She instantly became concerned, standing up, ready to help this fine young man in need.

Almost breathless he tried to explain, "My baby...I mean the baby... no my wife...Ann, my baby needs me. My wife needs me." He was a bit flustered, obviously. Mrs. Weaver took hold of his hands, her eyes large. By now, everyone in the cafeteria had his or her heads turned to see the commotion the new teacher was causing.

"Breathe slowly, Mitch. Like this." She imitated what she intended.

"I have to go home. Can you take me? I'm pregnant. I mean, I'm going to have a baby! Ann's pregnant. I have to go..." Relief showed on the older woman's face about the time the entire room erupted into applause.

"Mitch, congratulations! I'm so happy for you."

Approximately five minutes later, Mitch Rock was running through his back door, giddy. He immediately spotted his wife at the kitchen table still bawling, shamelessly. He was on his knees in a trice, in front of her, beaming from ear to ear.

"Ann, a baby? Really? You're pregnant? With our baby? Yours and mine? Now?" He was acting as if he'd never heard of the idea before; of two married people having a child together. Ann instantaneously stopped with the sobbing, completely bowled over by his retort and with the look on his face.

"Mitch? Are you...happy?"

"Am I happy? Hell yes I'm happy! I'm going to be a father! God, I love you, Ann." He laid one on the princess of weeping.

"When? How long? It doesn't matter. I'm so darn proud of you, sweetie." He wrapped her up in a big old bear hug.

Ann was way beyond stunned. *Mitch hates surprises. Didn't he just tell me he wasn't ready to be responsible for their new life? That he missed the old one?*

Mitch interrupted her bewilderment, "Ann, we're going to have a baby! Let's call everybody. Right now!" He stood up to reach for the phone.

Ann quickly got over the shock of him not being devastated by the news, now able to respond, "No, Mitch. I don't know for sure. I have to see a doctor first, before we can tell anyone."

"Right, okay got ya." He went straight for the telephone book Jeff had left them and looked up physicians. Ann could only sit there dumbfounded by the man she didn't know she married, wishing she could be as excited as her husband was about the possibility. *I would have never in a million years dreamed Mitch Rock wanted kids so badly. This is purely marvelous. But so out of character for the man.*

Ann subconsciously let the short period of unconsciousness slip to the unrevealed depths of her mind.

Mitch had an appointment set for Ann with an OBGYN next Tuesday. He had excitedly made the call. Then he went into town after putting Ann into a bath and picked up steaks to grill tonight. To have a celebration meal he added some potatoes, veggies and milk, along with a home pregnancy kit. He was walking on cloud nine and nothing could bring him out of his good mood.

The minute he got back to the house he made her do the test. It was positive. They both cried for about an hour and then sat discussing all the potentials that came with parenthood. They chattered until it was dinner time.

Mitch sat up the lawn chairs he bought at the grocers, while Ann summoned enough courage to sit outside with him. He whistled happily as he grilled.

Chapter twenty nine

MARK AND BARBARA HEEDLESSLY HIKED back to the Rock's house, deciding they needed an all-terrain vehicle to explore where the new earth race might possibly be in veil. They had spent the rest of their day walking, studying and discussing the budding and aloof reptiles; their theory on the apt living digs etc.

It was close to dinner time and the biologists were famished and near dehydration. Barbara felt stupid to have forgotten provisions. She was a professional and usually prepared for a long day in the field. Mark was feeling about as dumb. But the convo about everything helped them to ignore their blunder and inner rumblings.

Almost to the Rock home, the duo could see Mitch and Ann sitting on the patio, from a distance. They could also smell the aroma of food which instigated a quicker step to their pace.

"What do we tell them, Mark?"

"Nothing, for the time being. The reptiles are moving away from the residence and no one has actually been harmed by these snakes, so let's keep quiet.

"Let's leave these eggs here, so they won't ask any questions," Mark told her, pointing to a spot underneath one of the giant oak trees.

"Whatever you think is best," Barbara said, doing as he wanted.

Mitch and Ann watched Mark and Barbara walk to the house from about a mile out. The two looked to be on the weary side and Ann knew they had to be hungry. They'd been out there all day. She just got through telling Mitch, she wondered if they should go look for them.

As they approached, Ann hurried inside and grabbed two ice cold *brewskies* for her new friends, along with some cheese and crackers. Mitch unfolded the other two lawn chairs.

"Hey you two." Mark was extremely thankful when seeing Ann come out with the beers. "You have no idea how appreciative I am right now." He and Barbara slammed the alcohol.

"Thank you, Ann, Mitch. We were beating ourselves up pretty good on the trip back. Neither of us was prepared to be gone all day," Barbara told them, radically.

"Sit down, take a load off," Mitch offered, ushering them into the chairs. "Have some of our fancy hors d'oeuvres."

"You're saving our lives, guys," Mark informed the newlyweds, while chowing on the Swiss and Ritz.

"I don't know when anything has ever tasted better." Barbara threw in her two cents.

"Stay for dinner, we'd love to have you." Mitch was plain old happy and cheerful, making the invitation hard to refuse.

Seeing Ann grin from ear to ear, Mark thought, why not?

"Sounds great."
"I'm sorry, we can't."

At the exact same measure, he anxiously agreed, while Barbara politely declined. They slyly glimpsed one another a little uncomfortable.

Of course the woman's going to win in this situation. Barbara gave Mark a nudge. He promptly turned his attention back to the couple and also courteously begged off, however saying, "We'd love to stay, chat for a bit, though." He wasn't exactly going to let her get away with making the decision without asking him. Barbara shot the Rocks a large smile trying to cover her humiliation.

Ann knew Barbara turned them down, because – being a woman – she probably thought about the hassle of having last minute dinner guests. Whereas, men don't think about whether there is enough food or if it will cause a headache for the wife. She grinned at her, giving her a knowing wink.

"Let me get you another beer."

"Mind if I use the powder room, Ann?"

"No, please." She showed her into the house and pointed to where the bathroom was.

"You are a very gracious host, considering we literally walked into your evening."

"I don't mind a bit, Barbara. We both really like Mark and it will be nice to get to know you, too."

"Thanks, Ann," she said cordial, while practically racing to the relief.

Mitch turned the grill to low and covered the steaks as the four talked. The subject was the exhilarating news from today.

"You people don't waste any time, huh?" Mark chided them.

"I'm so happy for you!" Barbara was sincere.

"We couldn't be more excited," Mitch elucidated.

Ann simply acted shy about the whole concept, exhausted from her experience today. Then the women chatted, unintentionally disregarding the men.

"Did you two plan this?"

"No. We've always expected children would be a part of our future, but not quite this soon."

"How do you feel? Morning sickness or any other symptoms?"

This morning's incident came rushing back into Ann's head. "Yes, today, after we talked. I had a terrible bout of nausea and sort of passed out. It was weird. Do you think that's normal?" All day long, Ann had an alarm going off in the back of her mind concerning the episode, but she pushed it aside when Mitch became so keyed up, which still baffled her. Anyway, she was glad to have a chance to talk about it.

"I think it's completely normal. All women handle pregnancy differently and there can be a variety of symptoms. Some know right away, others don't. Some women get morning sickness slightly or not at all, then again there are women who are sick the entire pregnancy. I've heard of some expectant mothers gaining fifty or sixty pounds, while some gain hardly any. Try not to worry.

"Are you feeling better now?"

"Yes, tonight I'm fine. Except I'm afraid it might happen again."

"Eat. Eat, before you get out of bed and at least five times a day," Barbara instructed her.

"Really?"

"Yes. When do you see a doctor?"

"Tuesday."

"Good, be sure to tell her what happened."

"I will. I feel better just talking about it with you. Thanks. I have no idea what's in store for me. I've always thought about having kids; however, I know nothing about the pregnancy process. What goes on with a woman's body and how to know what's healthy and what's not. Everything really." Ann seemed her normal dramatic self as they visited.

"You'll do fine, Ann." Barbara was an exceptionally caring person. Her personal demure was completely dissimilar from her professional attitude. The two got along beautifully. It was nice.

Mark and Mitch just sat and listened. Mark was feeling lucky to be with such a stunning person, in looks and in brains, such as Barbara. Every so often she glanced over to him, making him feel special.

Mitch watched his wife with a goofy grin on his face the whole time. He felt lucky and special, too, having all his dreams come true. With a woman he'd loved his entire life.

After roughly thirty minutes of visiting, Mark finally announced they should go, "We'll let you guys get back to your dinner." Mark and Barbara had downed three beers and polished off the cheese and cracker tray, so it was certainly time to leave.

"We don't want to wear out our welcome."

"You think?" Barbara uttered, under her breath.

Chapter thirty

Once in the truck (Mark was driving) Barbara was concerned with what they were going to do for dinner. "I'm sorry, I'm starved, it's just that I didn't think we should intrude on the Rocks. Especially since they were only grilling two steaks."

Mark laughed at her. "I didn't think about that until after the fact. Good call."

"Thanks, but that doesn't answer my question." Barbara spied Mr.Gordon. He was younger than her, but it didn't really matter. They were a lot alike. All day long she had gandered his sexy looks and intelligent wit. This was bizarre for her. She never let herself get sucked in by a man's charm this fast, not that she'd ever met anyone like him before.

"Still want me to cook?"

"No, I can't wait. I have a fast metabolism and have to eat when the need arises. Or I get sick. Migraines. Can we pick something up on the way to your place?"

"Sure. I know where the best hamburgers in town are." He looked over at her and winked.

"Sounds wonderful. Thank you."

"You should have told me about your metabolism sooner. I wouldn't have made you sit there for thirty minutes."

"No, it was fine. I liked chatting with Ann. The beer and snacks held me over." Barbara glanced out the window in her thinking style. It did not go unnoticed by Mark.

"What?"

Miss James acted innocent. "I didn't say anything."

"As a man, I know something is on your mind. Let me in."

"Let you in? Why?"

"How about we make a pack and not play games, James."

Barbara was astonished with his bluntness. This man was more intuitive than anyone she'd ever been with. And aware and genuine and funny and caring and darling, handsome...

"Okay, no games." She went for broke. "I was feeling melancholy about never having my own children. Sometimes I regret not getting married and living as other women do." She cocked her head sideways, interested in his response to her honest disclosure.

As Mark was pulling into the Hamburger Inn, he said, "Does it make any difference if I tell you I don't want kids myself."

"Why would it make a difference, Mark?

"No wait, I take that back. No games, right? Yes it does make a difference. Tell me why, though."

"The whole *reproducing* thing turns me off." In the past that is, he thought to himself, but didn't say aloud.

"Every single woman I've ever met wants to get married and have babies, period. You're the first woman I've ever known that takes her career seriously. I like that," he told her, forthright, before ordering their meal through the drive-thru window.

"Hi Pete, we'll have two triple cheeseburgers with everything on them, two large fries and two large chocolate milkshakes. And make sure to put plenty of catsup packets in the sack. We want two large ice waters while we wait."

"Coming up, teach."

"One of your students I presume?"

"Why yes, Watson." Mark gazed at her then said, "Small town."

Barbara agreed, nodding her head, then asked jokingly, "So Sherlock, how was it you automatically knew what it was I wanted to eat?"

"Sixth sense. Besides, it wouldn't work out if we don't like the same food."

A man that takes charge without being pushy. *I like it*, Barbara kept to herself. She felt positive about this young Mr. Gordon.

Once they got the eats and finally made it to Mark's house, Barbara was suddenly full of questions.

"Do you own your home?"

"Yes."

"You decorate it by yourself?"

"Yes."

"It's nice. How long have you been a homeowner?"

"Six years. I was fortunate. I had a few dollars in the bank and this was a fixer-upper. I've been doing what I can, as I can afford it." They sat down at his kitchen table and began feasting.

In between bites, "What all have you done? What did it look like before?"

"I have pictures Want me to..."

"Yes I do." He got up and went into the other room to get the album, while Barbara observed every detail of the house. It was clean. There was absolutely no clutter anywhere. The furniture was arranged precise and the pictures hung accordingly.

Mark's home was a two bedroom bungalow with a screened-in porch and a fenced-in back yard, located behind the kitchen. Looking out the window, Barbara could see the perfectly manicured lawn. They had entered through the front door, directly into the family room. The bedroom doors were off to the right. They had walked through the main living area to get to the kitchen.

The carpet was new, Barbara could tell. It was a pretty reddish and indigo color, with the couch and two chairs matching impeccably. She was impressed. He had a big screen television and all the latest high tech gadgets in filming to go with it. His video camera sat on top the unscathed, beautifully stained pine coffee table.

134

Barbara gawked around the place as she ate, taking in the personality of this unexpected and surprisingly efficient romantic opportunity. The way he kept his home made him all the more attractive.

She was intrigued with the memorabilia that filled the crannies. In fact, when Mark came back, album in hand, she didn't notice him standing in the doorway staring at her. Sucking down the ice cream, she was busy inspecting the kitchen counter tops unaware of being watched. Mark cleared his throat loudly to let her know he was there.

Barbara flung her head around to where he stood, startled, eyes wide. "I didn't see you."

Grinning, "No, I guess not. You were too busy checking out my stuff."

"I can't help it. It's not just you, either. Wherever I go, I have this perpetual need to look at what other people do with their money. Sorry."

"It's fine with me," he told her, handing her the book.

"Cool." She immediately began going through the pictures, fascinated and awed by what he started with. Mark couldn't help but love her frankness. At least he knew what was important to her. She was funny, wanting to know everything about him. It made him feel that she was undoubtedly interested in him.

"Wow, how did you know where to begin? This is truly amazing, the about face of this house. How much have you put into it?" she asked, causally.

"I bought the place for eighteen-thousand-five and I've sunk about twenty into it as of now," he replied, frankly. If she wanted to know, well he might as well tell her. No one else had ever asked. Moreover, he was proud of his frugality and imagination.

Barbara studied the photos with great concentration, while Mark finished his burger. You could say this was her only other curiosity outside of work. "Did you hire out to do the roof?"

"Had to. It would have taken me a lifetime."

"Did you have to re-do the electrical and plumbing?"

"Yep. Everything. You name it, I've done it."

"Have you gotten an appraisal since you finished?"

"I'm not finished."

"What about insurance?" she asked, keeping her eyes on the book.

"I update every time I do a major project."

"Good, that's smart. What else are you planning on doing?"

Mark didn't answer her. When he didn't, she had to look at him. "What? Am I being too nosy?" She grimaced.

"No, I was thinking I'm ready for a shower and was wondering if you wanted to join me?" He looked straight into her vibrant brown eyes. She gazed back into his, unwavering. The mood in the place changing spectacularly.

"I've been waiting on you to ask me," she dared.

Without saying another word, Mark got up and held his hand out to her. She stood up, placing hers in his, unblinking, never letting her eyes leave his. He pulled her close. They kissed. A long and passionate kiss.

Mark took her shirt off as he guided her towards the bathroom. She loosened his belt, moving slow and deliberate, sexy, uninhibited. Mark kissed her neck and caressed her body. They leisurely made their way to the shower. Barbara enjoyed every second of his attention, letting him know by her movements. They quickly stripped out of the rest of their clothes and began exploring one another. She moaned with delight as he touched her. And she could feel he was every bit as turned on as she was.

The night ahead seemed equally promising to both.

Chapter thirty one

Ann Rock's eyes popped open from the dead sleep she was in, the feeling of *being watched* had summoned her consciousness. She became wide awake immediately upon realizing she had company. Ann didn't have to look and see if Mitch was in bed with her, she instinctively knew he wasn't. She was alone with the large, treacherous beast bearing down on her, assaulting her life.

The twenty some-foot beauty of a snake was intertwined around the end and on the right bed post, draping the spindle several times, engulfing the wood. The serpent dangled its head close to Ann's face, the tongue flicking continuously, the eyes focusing on hers. The snake's skin crawled sporadic and the neck slinked back and forth, but it was unmoving in the sense that it was going anywhere.

All Ann could do was lay there and stare back into the gripping slits of the giant metamorphous. Her fear ran so deep that she couldn't move. The shock of waking to something on this grandiose and fantastic scale was more than Ann's brain could handle, in the second or two, before complete awareness developed.

She had a feeling the large blacksnake wanted something from her, but it didn't behave threatening to her existence. Outside of it being an enormous, unfamiliar and unwanted bed partner, which was simply difficult to grapple no matter who you were.

Ann's thoughts shot to that of the baby as the unpleasant and unexpected, incredible in size, reptile studied her. Being this close to the obvious physically powerful surreal being was more than intimidating, it was humbling. All life seemed fragile at this particular blasphemous moment.

She couldn't help but notice the shining skin and smoothness to the monster's body, the way it curved and coiled with ease, for as big as it was. The snake's underbelly was ivory in color, sort of pretty. It seemed content to just spy her with its unnatural, yellow eyes, but Ann knew it could kill her without a problem at any time, if it desired.

Be calm.
Stay still.
Don't move.
Remember what you read.
Don't make it think it's in trouble.

Screw that shit. "Aaahhhhh!" Ann couldn't deal with bravery right now. At last, her own body was able to move, as well as her vocal cords. The thunderous cry she let out came from deep within her gut. Her arms and legs mechanically fought the covers to get out of the bed. She closed her eyes, while enduring to scream at the top of her lungs.

"Mitch!" she bellowed, just as she fell out of bed, the spread on top of her. Ann remained unrelenting in her desire to get out of that room. Her cries for help were non-stop and so was her bodily brawl with the bedding.

"Mitch, help me!
"Help!"

With the first utterance from Ann, the huge reptilian twisted away from her and in the flash of an eye, roved its way through the door. The faultless example of an amphibian used its great strength to move with speed, but without sound. It zipped its way to the attic, while Ann's loud and deafening, high pitched tone engulfed the house.

"Ann! I'm coming!" A frightened Mitch Rock shouted to his wife. The man hurriedly climbed the old staircase, two steps at a time. He had been up since the crack of dawn, on the internet researching human reproduction. She jolted him out of a nice quiet morning.

Upon reaching their bedroom, scared shitless, he found his frenzied wife on the floor, flinging the sheets here and there in an attempt to escape them. He guessed. Mitch couldn't see anything else menacing in the room.

About the time he made it to her side, moving with haste and bending down to reach her, she became free of the covers and was getting up at a rapid rate, clumsily. They collided with immense force sending both of them to the ground. The crack of their noggins thumping together was stomach-turning. They each grabbed their heads after the landing.

Ann stopped with the earsplitting blaring the very moment she was whacked, her eyes open big seeing her husband. Her head hurt, but she wasn't sure if it was from the intense roaring or the abrupt brute clash she just had with Mitch. She quickly and purposefully looked around the room searching for the uninvited.

Mitch was in a daze as he took the brunt of the accident. His eyes watered from the impact, only he wasn't crying. It was a normal physiological reaction. He blinked back the tears aiming to regain a center on his wife's pandemonium.

"Ann, are you alright?" he asked, vaguely. He couldn't actually get his bearings in order to get up just yet.

"I...I think so?" Ann was confused and sat unmoving, too, suddenly forgetting what she was looking around the room for.

"Why were you screaming, honey? Before?" Woo, this is going to be a nasty embarrassing bruise, Mitch thought as he rubbed his cheek.

"I don't know? I must have been dreaming, or something?" She acted as if nothing was predominantly wrong.

"You *think* you were dreaming? Jesus Christ, Ann, I thought the house was falling down." Mitch's expression illustrated his amazement.

"I'm sorry, I can't even remember what it was about. That's odd," she told him, in her mystified state.

"Mitch, are you sure you're okay?" she then asked, sympathetically. "You look as if you've seen a ghost."

The stress and trauma were wearing off for Mitch and he gradually got up to assist his wife. He curiously took a glance around the room, unknowing of anything to look for, except one of those creepy and oversized black rat snakes. He had a funny feeling and the hair on his neck began to rise. Mitch quickly remembered everything Mark had told him yesterday concerning the mysterious nature of the mutants.

"Ann, did you see anything...in here...that might have caused you to get upset?"

"I was sleeping, Mitch, why would I see something?" she questioned him, as he pulled her to a standing position, her face showing her puzzlement. The bump on her forehead was starting to swell. Mitch touched it tenderly.

"This needs attention." Mitch put his uncertainties on the back burner, for the time being. But as soon as he made sure Ann was okay, he was going to give Mark Gordon a call. He didn't like feeling vulnerable in his own home and he didn't want his wife hurt either. Something had to have caused her to panic, he felt it in his bones.

"Come on, we need to get some ice on our *bruisees*. Let's go down to the kitchen. And we need to get some food into you so you don't get sick again." Mitch took one last look around their bedroom as they ambled out the door arm in arm.

"*Bruisees* Mitch, what would that mean?"

"Okay, a *bruisee* is an accidental spousal knock-out. How about that?"

Chapter thirty two

Mark woke to an empty bed. Surprised to be alone after the romance last night, he dashed up, threw his clothes on from yesterday and darted out into the other room. He relaxed when he saw Barbara furiously writing notes in a small notebook of some sort. Then he spied the kitchen to see the coffee already made.

Nice.

"Morning, sexy," he said, walking over to her.

"Back at ya," Barbara replied, without interrupting her work.

"Okay..." Mark stopped. He could see she had a cup of brew, so he turned and headed into the other room to get himself one, thinking she didn't want to be bothered after that curt response.

"Quit sulking, I'll be done in a minute."

She must have eyes in the back of her head, he considered the notion. "Right..." Kind of creepy to Mark. His mom use to do the same thing. He quickly shook that idea.

Pouring his coffee into his favorite Chief's mug, Mark decided to sit on the porch for his morning routine, blowing off her mood. It was pleasant out. A cool and sunny spring day. What more could he ask for? The woman of all women was in his living room and he didn't have to make his own java. It was already a great day.

A few short minutes later, Barbara was standing in the doorway watching him enjoy his life. His innocent smile as he sat there gazing at birds in the backyard made her own existence worthwhile, in the present. He glanced over to her and winked, patting the couch with his free hand, wanting her to sit next to him.

No games, she remembered he said. *Guess I'll be straight with the man. If he's for real, he'll understand. If not, might as well find out now.*

"I lied to you," she said, without warning. Mark didn't flinch. He casually held his gaze. It wasn't exactly what he wanted to hear by any means, but whatever.

"Okay." She must have her reasons. He wasn't really worried about it. But then again he didn't ask either – because what if she said she was married, or something? Did he even want to know?

Mark didn't have a chance to speculate further. Barbara plopped down next to him and began her story starting with, "Here," and handed him her notes.

"They're written in code and I want you to know what it is." Mark opened the pocket sized book and took a spy. Looked illegible to him.

"Letters are backwards and I do not use M or N. Instead I use OO and PP. But it's the basic form of short hand. You understand short hand, don't you?"

"Yes."

"Good. Something ever happens to me, well then you have my notes," Barbara digressed.

"Why would something happen to you?" Mark was mystified here. He wasn't sure what to think about that remark. Or what to think about the lengths she took to cryptogram her notes.

"Don't worry, I mean if I have an accident or something. That's not even the point." Barbara got a little frustrated trying to come clean with him. It was harder than she thought it was going to be. She brushed her hair out of her eyes and tried again.

"Let me start over.

"I want to **share** my notes with you. I never have before." She rolled her eyes at herself. She sounded like an idiot and Mark was staring at her like she was one.

"I don't **share** these with the university or anyone in the field of discovery." She waited for a response.

It took Mark a second to figure out she wanted one. "I'm...honored?" He was completely in the dark here.

She smiled at him and calmed a little. He was charming.

"Okay, I know more than what I've told you...about the transformed surplus blacks. I've been watching them for years, Mark. And I wasn't **sharing** info, because I do want to be known in the herpetology world... for my unearthing of the new breed. I need the fame."

Barbara quit speaking, because as she said that the earth began to literally move underneath their feet. A slight tremor at first and then a full blown earth quaking started to shake their world. The two professionals reacted quickly, hitting the deck, covering their heads with their arms, an instinctual move. They were in basic survival mode.

It must have lasted thirty seconds, but seemed longer since lying on wavering ground in a state of panic wasn't the norm. Mark's coffee cup rattled during the quivering and fell off the whicker table and onto the cement flooring, shattering into pieces. The booming sound the earth made as it vibrated was fantastic. Neither had ever experienced such a circumstance. They hunkered down, unable to actually fathom the event.

When it was over they peered at one another barely moving, confounded by what had just happened. Moments later they could hear people shouting, bringing them into realism. Getting up carefully, taking a look around at the unbelievable, although there was nothing to see on the porch except the broken mug, they checked themselves to make sure they were okay. The two then hurried through the house, out the front door, to the street where the noise had seemed to come from. What they saw was more than unbelievable for Mark and Barbara. It was downright chilling.

There was a remarkable tear in the earth's surface that appeared to extend the length of the neighborhood. It was at least four feet in width and looked as if it could be a half of a mile deep. The biologists inched their way towards the phenomenal opening, the shock of the incident becoming real. They were both worried about the same thing. What if the atypical reptiles begin to surface, here and now?

Families were out of their homes gawking at the destruction that only took an instant in the making. Fortunately, it was located right down the center of the street and nobody's house had caved into the ground. Mark glanced at the one across the way, wondering if more structural damage had been done to the town or if this was it.

It didn't take long, before the residents began hollering at Mark.

"Gordon, what is it?"

"What just happened?"

"Are we going to die?" One overly affected woman wanted to know.

"Mark, are we in danger?"

"What should we do?"

"Stay back, all of you!" He commanded, thinking on his toes. Subsequently, sirens could be heard in the background, thankfully. This perforation in the ground needed to be roped and if something did emerge he wanted the sheriff here to kill it. He watched the earth closely as he instructed the town folk.

"I want all of you to calmly walk to the church. Don't go back in your houses to get anything. Just move, slowly and orderly, now."

Barbara stayed quiet, while hoping and praying there were no more bolts from the dark coming from the planet they lived on. She watched the people follow Mark's directions, but in her angst she also realized how much respect he ruled from this supposedly quaint town, making him all the more fascinating.

Chapter **thirty three**

Dᴇᴘᴜᴛʏ Dᴏᴜɢ Iʀᴠɪɴɢ ᴀʀʀɪᴠᴇᴅ within minutes of the disaster. An earthquake in one part of this town was heard throughout its whole. He was certainly aware of the trouble and the direction from which it came. Upon arrival, he wasn't actually able to drive Pine street where Mark lived, but blocked the end of the spanking tunnel with his county sheriff's car the very second he realized the cleavage. Surprised to say the least, he screeched to a stop and jumped out the vehicle. However, he was always ready for anything and everything and this disaster wasn't going to rock his world.

Running along the leg of damage, in control of his business, he radioed the sheriff inculcating the man to take Main to Walnut and come up Pine from the north. This way he could obstruct any traffic approaching from that end, in cars or on foot.

"It looks like the path of destruction is an entire block long, Sheriff. An extensive cavity in the ground in the middle of the thoroughfare. Doesn't look like anyone's hurt. Gordon's here, so I'll talk to him. Over."

Doug was stunned by the massive slit, along with the people who lived here. He'd never seen anything like this before and he'd been with the force for fifteen years, coming up in May. But he was a trained professional and he maintained his stature, wanting to prevail a dependable and reassuring attitude.

"Gordon!" He caught sight of the man stooped over, looking into the substantial fissure, which used to be a road. The neighbors were all leaving in a systematic and cooperative fashion as he approached.

"Doug, over here."

A breathless deputy made his way to the biology authority in their town. "This an earthquake, Mark?" Wide eyed, he also looked into the cavity.

"Yeah Doug, but it's a weird one. The earth only separated in what looks to be a half mile stretch. If I wasn't standing here witnessing it, I wouldn't believe it."

"You can say that again." It was an awesome sight.

Mark stood up and leaned close to the deputy in order to speak in a low and secretive voice. "Doug, I need you to keep this quiet, to yourself, okay?" Without a question Doug agreed, nodding his head, waiting for the scoop from his good buddy.

"You remember the snake from the other day?"

"Yes."

"I don't want the town folk to be alarmed, but I suspect there could be more. I want you to watch over this big hole here and look for large reptiles. If you see one I want you shoot it. Dead."

Doug's expression went from disturbed to disbelief "You mean to tell me that giant black rat wasn't uncommon, Gordon?"

He shook his head no. "I'm sorry I didn't tell you sooner. I couldn't be positive. I've been looking for them for some time now. I'm pretty sure they come from...well...inside the earth." Mark glanced back into the deep.

"Are you telling me giant snakes caused this rumble?" Doug was floored.

"Shhh. It's possible."

"Well I'll be a mon..."

"Doug, everyone that lives in the neighborhood is leaving. I instructed them to, because the last thing we need is a full blown panic. Understand? Don't let anyone close. If we do have some of those large snakes coming from within, well, you get the picture."

"Yeah I do, I can't believe this, but okay. Mark, I've got to tell the sheriff," Doug told him, just as he spotted the boss pulling up at the other end of the chaos as they spoke.

"Right. He needs to know. Just keep it on the low down.

"I have to go, Doug. I think I might know where a den is. If anything pops its nasty large head out of this place, just kill it. Got it?"

The deputy already had his side gun out and loaded. He was putting his walkie-talkie up to his mouth as Mark finished his sentence. "Sheriff, we got us a problem. Get those rifles out of the trunk, I'm on my way to meet you. Can't say what's going on over open frequency. Over." He never took his eyes off Mark Gordon, totally trusting the man he'd known forever.

Barbara approached the men. She'd walked a segment of the caved land and had been studying the unthinkable tremor, thinking.

"See anything?"

"No, this looks like the destruction was done months ago, possibly longer. The time was right for the collapse is all." She watched Mark's face, wondering if he understood the implication of the meaning. Barbara didn't want to be the bearer of bad news. Of course, she wasn't firm in her conclusion, although positive in the generality of it.

After examining the formation of the gully, Barbara's opinion on the geography beneath, was that the soil was undeniably weak below the entire town. Could be one quake after another or maybe there wouldn't be one for a year or two. She most definitely believed that more were to come, but no one can predict a certain timetable for quakes. Soon was her educated guess, though.

Mark let out a deep breath, staring at his love life. What a morning this turned out to be. He was having trouble coming to terms with being incredibly happy one minute and bamboozled into grief the next. He got her unspoken message.

"Should I call for the town to be evacuated?" he asked her, unsure of his capability to make decisions all of a sudden.

"That's your call, Mark. I don't know. This could be the worse one. Or not."

"Okay, that's a big help, James."

"I want you to come to Lawrence with me. I have an idea."

"Now?"

147

"Yes, now, Gordon." She gave him a funny look, then said, "Well..." he was unmoving.

"Doesn't look like I can get my truck out of here."

"No, but the school isn't far, we can walk to my car. Come on... what's up with you?"

"I'm in a little bit of a shock here. Want to give me a break?"

"But yeah...sure, we'll walk to your car. Let me get my shoes, my duffle and billfold." Mark forced himself to shake the gnawing feeling of guilt in his gut and get going. He knew standing here looking into the grand canyon would get him nowhere, but the possibility of his town sinking into the earth was very real to him now and he wondered if he could have prevented the destruction, had he been forthcoming.

"Doug..."

"Do what you need to, Mark. I can handle this town."

Barbara walked back to the house with him. She knew what was wrong with the man of her dreams. "Mark Gordon, this is not your fault," she told him, sternly.

"There's no way you could have envisaged this. You did the right thing keeping quiet. All we can do now is try to determine the extent of damage to Greenland and come up with a plan of action." He ignored her. Barbara took hold of his elbow and stopped him, stepping in front of him.

"Ouch, that's my sore arm." He winced in pain.

"Sorry." She quickly let go. *Oops.* "But, you're not going to disregard me. I'm telling you, don't beat yourself up. It won't do anyone any good." He looked into her big beautiful eyes. All he thought at that particular moment was that he was pretty damn lucky to have her care about him.

"I hear you. I know you're right. Just give me a few to deal, okay?"

It took about fifteen minutes for the two to get to Barbara's 1969 Mustang. Mark and Miss James walked at an intense pace, in silence. It was past seven when they arrived. There weren't any other cars in the parking lot, because the school was closed for a holiday. Normally, it would have been nice for Mark to have a three day weekend. He didn't feel *nice* right now, though.

Getting into the antique car, he looked around at what a mess it was inside. Papers strewn everywhere, old fast-food wrappers were lying about and there were various instruments taking up most of the room in the back. In fact, Barbara had to move books off the passenger seat in order for him to get in. She just threw them on the floor.

Once Mark buckled up, he did notice the fine condition of the leather. When she started the engine it purred like a lion. "Great car, wow. This is some ride." It took his mind off the other situation, however transitory. He loved cars, but didn't have the resources for a new one, since he made rational and logical choices concerning his finances. His truck got him around fine.

"I've had it since I was a sophomore in high school," she said, peeling out, showing off a bit.

Mark got a kick out of her. He grinned as they sped to the highway. "Can I drive later?"

"Sure. I got to drive your cool vehicle, so I suppose you can drive mine."

"Are you serious?"

"No. But I'll let you drive." She was being coy, glad he was unwinding some.

Barbara understood Mark was upset and she didn't blame him. She knew from experience how he felt. It's no fun to have a lapse in judgment on a professional level, but she also knew from experience to get over it, move on. Mistakes were made in this field of expertise all the time. It was the nature of the business. Mark was young and didn't have her working education, but he would soon. James was ready to tell the guy everything there was to know about her and her work.

Chapter thirty four

A FEW HOURS LATER MARK and Barbara were in Lawrence, Ks. They didn't talk much on the drive. Mark needed to absorb the calamity and Barbara was pondering scenarios. She was also thinking about why she wanted to tell Mark about her secret life. Was she in love with the man?

Maybe.

Yes.

But, it didn't matter.

It was time for it to come out, anyway.

Instead of heading to the university, she drove to her small apartment. It was located in the back of an old home, down an alley, above a garage and not in a very nice part of town. They parked and then climbed the outdoor steps up to the battered living quarters.

Mark was flummoxed by the poor conditions Barbara resided in. He spoke without hesitation about it, too. "Okay Barbara, let's talk about how you spend your money," he said, in complete astonishment of the small and what he thought miserable place to dwell. Shockingly, the inside was just as bad as the outside. He looked around at the nothingness she had. Not even a television or radio, he noticed first. All she did have was a dumpy old kitchen table and really torn up divan. This place was a disaster!

She didn't answer him. She slipped into her bedroom to change her outfit. He followed and watched her, remaining incredulous and asking more questions.

"I know you make a ton more money than me, so what do you spend it on? Why do you live this way?" She had a bed and plenty of clothes he could see as he snooped. At least this room was clean. That was something, but at the same time he wanted answers. And he didn't bother to hide his lack of understanding.

"Barbara?" He used a stern voice. "Want to tell me why you live here and in such squalor?"

She gave him a look and finally told him, in one word, "Gambling."

He was unwavering. "You have a gambling problem?"

"Yep.

"Come on, I'm ready," she said, in the next breath. She had a bag packed just as fast.

Mark trudged along with her, unspeaking, while considering her addiction. He felt sorry for her. She probably needed someone like him to straighten her out. Someone disciplined and informed in the world of finances. She deserved better than this. No wonder she was drawn in with his stuff last night. Wow, her first flaw. Didn't dampen his feelings for her, though.

Back in the mustang, "This isn't the way to the university...where are we going?"

"You'll see." Mark hadn't criticized her about her confession. The doctor appreciated that. He was a stand-up guy and she was now confident she wanted him involved in every aspect of her life, amazed by how fast the world turns.

Barbara drove to the industrial side of town and used a remote to open a large garage door, to what appeared to be in an unoccupied warehouse that stood yards apart from any other building. Getting out of the car once again, she led Mark to an old fashioned chained-link fence type elevator and slammed the door shut. Then she pulled the steel, hefty handle to control their fate.

Mark was perplexed by her surprises, but he let her lead him to wherever it was they were going. He noted the condition of the place and its whereabouts, but that's about it. He was interested in what was so important to this woman and also realized her secretiveness was just a part of her persona.

Once on the upper level, the squeaky door opened into an advanced, state-of-the-art laboratory. Mark was more than staggered. This place was boss. The first thing he observed was the spacious size of the room and the many different computers at hand. He gaped at the numerous microscopes, microtomes and the biological safety cabinets and was hypnotized by the modern incubators, as well as all the other scientific apparatus filling the ambiance.

He noticed that the two lab assistants working diligently were the same two men who had come to Greenland with Doctor James. They nodded to Barbara, yet kept busy with their operations.

The next thing that caught Mark's attention was the large mutant rat he'd turned over to her earlier this week and the numerous smaller ones in motion, caged adjacent to it. The considerable manmade habitat for the mother beast occupied an entire corner of the depot and was built with the snake's best interest, concerning its size and comfort. The glass enclosure contained an outdoor living area, basically. The snake lifted its head from the tree branch it was dangling, apparently recognizing new movement. Weird how they do that, Mark thought.

Trying to comprehend what this place meant exactly, Mark looked to Barbara for more answers. She was grinning at him.

"This is my gambling obsession." She took hold of his hand, obviously proud of her work.

"My own privately funded research center. Every dime I have is sunk into this place. And I spared no expense in the equipment. It's been years in the making and I intend on being recognized for **my** work one day."

Mark Gordon was in shock with all the latest technical advances in science surrounding him, although he didn't quite get her intention. "Please, feel free to continue to enlighten me," he said, while making himself at home sitting down in front of one of the many computers. He began typing at the keyboard. Mark wasn't shy. He assumed she wanted him to since she'd brought him here.

Barbara James stood behind him watching the screen. Mark was bringing up the main database of the Gender Neuro Ophiuroidea

Messenger RNA Envision she created, or the GNOME as she called it.

"Pret...ty...im...press...ive."

"I think so." Barbara wasn't bashful either.

"Mark, I stay at the university for the paycheck. I need investment money in order to take my ideas into the future and to be able to do that, I need to use this discovery, the fresh reptiles that surround Greenland and other territories.

"Enter the mapping section." Mark did as instructed, rapt by the technology unavailable to him before this very minute.

Barbara kept talking. "I exposed the misshapen race approximately five years ago. Here," she said, pointing to a position on the map outlined in red and green symbols.

"How could you know?"

"I've been placing cameras on normal rat snakes, rattlers, copperheads and kings, using small wide angled lenses placed over one eye, which last about four days if I'm lucky. I haven't figured out how to keep them from clouding over. The snake's normal brille stays in tact, because I found when removing it, well, the snake dies. Anytime you disrupt the normal functioning of the reptile, it can't survive.

"Anyway, I've been doing this for fifteen years. I put the snakes deep into caves to make their way out and record what I can via a receiver, retracting the signal. Doesn't work all the time, but as technology improves, I get more images. Five years ago, I got my first glimpse of one of these giant carnivores swallowing one of my experiments. I have a small collection of pictures of these novel creatures, but not in a group.

"Hit imaging." As soon as he did a black and white, hazy yet fairly good picture of one of the terrorist beneath his town, popped onto the screen. Mark then kept using the key to go to the next one and the next and the next, engrossed.

"A problem I am encountering now, is in the last couple of years it has been harder for me to find the ordinary reptiles. I think they're being gobbled up at an increasing and fast rate. It's my guess that the regular will be extinct by the end of the decade. But whenever I've gone to the spot of death, I can't seem to find the breed. They keep moving. And as you can see, they've passed through the northern end of Greenland. Expand the illustration. There, these ophidians are throughout all of Kansas.

"Unfortunately, my research stops here."

Mark concentrated on what she was saying, then asked, "Barbara, why not take this to the university? They would have the money to back you."

"Because they scoffed at my original theories all those years ago."

"Which were?"

"Which were; that we have alien life forms living inside the earth. I don't mean from outer space either," she said, in jest. Mark rolled his eyes, but thought she was quite entertaining.

Barbara went on, "We have the oceans, volcanoes and other planets getting more exploratory attention than the center of the earth. I could never understand why man didn't want to aggrandize erudition of what lies profound inside." She sat down next to Mark. He peeled his eyes away from the information highway in front of him, understanding he was only getting the tip of the iceberg concerning what she did. It was simply fascinating to him that she had such a brilliant mind and the fortitude to believe in herself, to this extent. He guessed he understood why she hadn't been forthcoming early on.

Mark also thought he grasped the risk she was undertaking regarding her professional career and why this place needed to be covert. At this point he'd help her any way he could, but he needed to know why she brought him here and what her plans were in the near future. He had to think about his town first.

"What's your idea, why are we here?"

"Mark, my team has already surgically placed the camera into the left eye of the mutant. What I propose we do is take it back to Greenland and let it go where we found the multiple hovels yesterday. We can hope it leads us directly to the den."

"Then what?"

"Then it's promising we'll be able to see the damage underneath your town. If it works, I'll also have a recording that proves the massive amount of these snakes, therefore proving a new race does indeed exist. I'll get the private backing I need to do future investigating. With that we can learn everything we need to know."

"Barbara, do you have any evidence that these snakes would harm a human being?" He had to ask. That question had been lingering after they had discussed the possibility yesterday.

She understood. "No. I don't. I swear to you if I did I would have gone public a long time ago. The safety of people is more important to me, Mark. I hope you know that. I also hope you know my interest in this research isn't specifically for fame either. I need the money, that's all. To continue."

Gazing into her eyes, Mark did believe her.

After a brief pause, he said, "Okay, let's do it."

Chapter thirty five

Meanwhile, back in Greenland, the Rocks were hanging with the rest of the town, all mesmerized at the unexpected damage, standing behind the law enforcement vehicles, gaping at the gap in Pine street. Everyone within a five mile radius could hear or feel some trembling of the ground this morning and all made their way to the site of annihilation. Mitch and Ann visited with Charlotte, while the sheriff and deputy patrolled the aperture from different ends and different sides, allowing no one to penetrate the disaster area.

"We were walking downstairs when we heard this loud, booming like noise in the distance and then we felt the house kind of shift slightly. It was bizarre," Ann was telling Charlotte, as Mitch looked around for Mark Gordon. The more he thought about how the typical blacksnake could blend in with its surroundings and why they lived so long (because there were no predators of the large adult) the more he had a hunch Ann did indeed see one this morning. It could have been outside the window. He knew from his own experience they could climb anything with great ease.

Actually, Mitch was worried about his wife. In the back of his mind he realized she had changed since she'd had that spell, or whatever it was, yesterday morning. And he was sure her attitude alteration had nothing to do with the pregnancy. He couldn't quite put his finger on it, but something was different about her demeanor.

He became aware of Ann's personality transformation last night, when they were grilling out. Not once did she look around for an unwanted pest or act nervous to be outside. Highly unlikely for her behavior this week. Wow, it's been a week today since we moved here, Mitch remembered all of a sudden. Seemed longer to him. Anyway, his jittery wife was calmer, insisting her episode this morning was just a nightmare. He didn't think so, because she'd never had those kinds of dreams before and he'd known her for how many years now?

"You seen Gordon around here?" he asked Charlotte.

"Yes, he left with that professor from KU. He told Doug he would be back tonight. He didn't tell anyone where he was going though, but Doug assumed Lawrence." She knew everyone's business in town.

"Thanks." Mitch was suspicious of the trip when this town just experienced something out of the ordinary. Something incredibly out of the ordinary. He became quiet, staring into the cavernous freak occurrence. Mitch Rock's mind delved into his own theories relating to the reasoning behind Mark Gordon's disappearance, on this anomalous morning.

Barbara James held a doctorate degree in the field of biology and was currently employed by the science department at the University of Kansas. She was the one Mark called when they captured the large and creepy blacksnake that had scared the holy shit out of his wife, and him, too, when it literally dropped on them from ostensibly nowhere. Miss James came and took the damn thing away.

So why would he be with her after an apparent earthquake?

Mitch quickly remembered the mutant rat in Gordon's classroom. In reality, he'd never forget either snake, but there was something peculiar with the recent events leading them to standing here, staring into a giant flaw in the ground. Larger than life reptiles, the earth splitting, Gordon gone with a snake expert as soon as it happens and the sheriff and deputy guarding the breach with rifles, was adding up in Mitch Rock's head.

Mark had said, "Where there's one there's two". He also mentioned underground springs when he asked them if he could study their land. And Ann was convinced the snake that chased her had probably hidden, possibly sliding into a hole they overlooked. If these giant reptilians existed in groups and lived in the ground that might be vulnerable to housing the reptiles, then did Mark think they caused this implausible incident? Were he and Ann in danger in their home? Was the whole town in danger?

"We better get going Mitch, we need to get started painting the kitchen," Ann said, bringing him out of his qualms.

"I know. Oh boy, let's get back to work." No way could he tell Ann his thoughts. He supposed he would have to keep this to himself for now.

Turning his attention, he asked, "Charlotte, will you call us if you hear anything about what may have caused this...trajectory?"

"Good one, Mitch Rock." She laughed at his joke. But, when the duo walked out of sight, Charlotte thought seriously about whether or not this large crack in the street could have been made by an alien object. Asteroids have hit the earth before. Maybe that's why the sheriff and deputy were armed and ready? She gazed upward to the sky as the Rocks left.

While it was for certain the folk of Greenland weren't going to get much done today, Ann had different notions. She wanted to utilize Mitch's day off and finish that kitchen, feeling positive about things again. "*Hey, Ya...*" she grooved to her favorite CD, Outkast, on the drive back to the farm. The video to this song is so funny, she remembered. It was a nice day out, she deemed. Life was good.

Of course, Ann was thankful no one had been hurt in the fright this morning; she just wanted to put her new home in order, before it got to the point where she couldn't lift anything. She'd heard from somewhere, if you lift heavy objects, while you're in the later stages of pregnancy, that you could strangle your baby. She didn't want that to happen. It was best to just get everything done as soon as possible.

The house looked so much better with having the grass cut, she thought as they drove into the drive. Ann wanted to hire a painter right away. The outside would at least be presentable with that huge job done. She glanced to the barn that stood yards behind the garage next, guessing it would also need an overhaul. *Wonder how much that's going to cost?* If she and Mitch did it themselves it would never be finished, she ascertained.

Getting out of the vehicle, Mitch hurriedly jogged around to the passenger side. He didn't want Ann susceptible. If there was a snake on the bend he wanted to see it, before she did. Protect her. He scouted every direction, including up, while making his way. Damn snakes were ruining their lives.

"I'm fine, Mitch," Ann told him, poking fun of his conduct. "You don't have to help me out of the car, for Pete's sake. I'm probably only a month along, if that. Wait until the end, before you baby me. I don't want you to waste all your caring for me now and when I'm nine months you're tired of the situation." She was in a great mood, for some odd reason, relaxed, kidding around with him.

"Oh no, I'm going to pamper you for the entire pregnancy," he told her, glad she wasn't aware of why he was really catering to her, but also taking note of her sudden lack of fear.

"Better take advantage of it. Second time around, I won't be so *romantadealized.*" Could he come up with words or what? This was one of his best.

As they walked to the door Ann said, "Okay, explain that one *Mr. Imaginalexis.*"

"That's it! That's what the title of our book should be. *Mr. Imaginalexis*! Good job, Ann." She was just as inventive, he had to admit that.

Mitch explained to Ann his new word meant he was romantic about the idea of having life be perfect. Then he began telling her about his research on pregnancy this morning, when he suddenly had that feeling again. That they weren't alone. He quickly scanned the house as they entered through the front door. Ann kept going, walking into the kitchen, but Mitch froze by the bottom of the stairs, staring upwards.

One of the house guests staying in the attic had been stretched across the banister, sneaking a look out the window as the two strolled up to the house, chatting. The long, hefty, oversized serpent spied the couple, until they reached the door and then used its mammoth strength to gracefully hoist itself to the second story, in a matter of nanoseconds.

Chapter thirty six

Mɪᴛᴄʜ ᴀɴᴅ Aɴɴ ᴡᴏʀᴋᴇᴅ like dogs painting the kitchen a dusty, organic white. They talked and listened to music, enjoying each other and the freedom to do what they wanted. The job was definitely a major improvement. It made a world of difference in the ratty old place, bringing great enthusiasm to the newlyweds at the prospect of truly being happy in the home they chose. It was going to look great when they were done.

Ann felt terrific and every time Mitch inquired about her physical health, that's how she answered him. Neither had a clue that the four foreign freaks from the inner orb were sunbathing on top of their shingled roof. And they hadn't looked outside, through the windows or the sliding glass door off the kitchen, to see several more of the beasts lurking in the trees on and around their immediate yard.

"It's a quiet day, don't you think?" Ann asked her husband. The kitchen window was open halfway to bring in the fresh air, allowing the Rocks to breathe without the fumes overwhelming them.

"Yeah, I like it. It's nice. Different from the constant traffic back home. Remember the police or ambulance sirens sounding day and night? I don't miss that a bit."

"You still miss your family?"

"Yes.

"Ann, I was thinking of us going home to visit next weekend, or soon anyhow."

"Mitch Rock, we just got here." She turned and gave him a look of madness; however, she was grinning at him. He was full of revelations lately. Being excited about her unplanned pregnancy, wanting to take care of her and oh so concerned with her health. But him, missing family and friends and wanting to visit after a lousy week, was a sweet contrast from the Mitch she thought she had married. He'd always acted macho all these years. It was nice to see the softer side.

"I know, but I want to show you off. Tell everyone about the baby." That wasn't the whole truth. Mitch had a desire to get her out of this house and if he could convince her, they would leave today. Maybe he was crazy, but he had a feeling of dread looming inside his stomach. He didn't want her to know that, though. He was using missing St. Louis as a way to sidestep the actual candor. He could tell it wasn't working.

Mitch Rock didn't normally rely on his inner rumblings to get him through life. He thought that was a woman's thing, intuition. Why he suddenly had a sixth sense, he didn't know or why he was listening to it. He supposed he had changed this week, too. After what he did to Ann, making her walk down the drive, he really felt horrible. Maybe that was one of the reasons she had changed? He had the intention of never hurting his wife again, sane or insane.

But, that was the thing. This hunch in his gut made him realize she wasn't loosing her sagacity, even though she wasn't acting nervous anymore. Actually, she was quite composed considering the morning events. Of course, with his suspicions about Mark Gordon not being straight forward about the wild, helped him go with his instinct. Mitch somehow understood his wife's reaction to the occurrences of recent, was not related to her neurosis several years ago. And that there could be a real threat out there prowling, hunting.

Mitch impulsively glanced out the window. His eyes searched the homestead slowly, carefully, until his wife interrupted his sentiment.

"I'm hungry. What about you?" She looked at her watch. "Its 2:30. Gees. Let's go into town and eat at The Diner, see if anyone has heard more news." Her beautiful eyes were glowing, the teal in them sparkling. She gazed at Mitch in anticipation of him saying yes.

"You're so cute. How can I refuse that look? You're like a child wanting a new toy or something." Mitch smiled at her in an adoring manner. He did love her more than anything else on earth. He was ready to get out of the house for a while, anyway. He needed a break from his peculiar notions.

The Rocks methodically cleaned up the mess, before heading to town. Ann washed the paint drippings from her face and hands; Mitch was extra cautious, he didn't have a drop anywhere on him. There was no reason to change clothes. They were only coming home to labor some more.

"Ready?"

"Yes, I want to drive."

"You got it." Ann had always liked being behind the wheel. This was normal.

Leaving through the side door this time, Ann walking out ahead of him, both Rocks stopped dead in their tracks just as Mitch shut the back door and they spied the Blazer. Coiled on top sat a copious, evil looking, incredibly intimidating and startling black rat snake or what they assumed was a black rat Genus. The head raised a good two feet spying them. The creepy appeared as if it could attack them in the beat of a drum.

Mitch flinched and leaned up against the locked door. The damned was only a couple of feet away. Ann stood still a small ways in front of her husband. Neither said anything. They simply watched the beast watch them, except Mitch was shocked and it showed on his face. Ann had a numinous, blank look in her eyes. She appeared to be in a daze.

A minute or so passed, before Mitch got his wits about him. Clandestinely, he grabbed Ann's arm, while he used his other hand to secretly unlock the door. His movements were minuet as he faced the serpent, pretending to be Houdini with the one arm twisted behind his back, trying to get them into the house, before anything bad could happen.

But the snake seemed to observe what he was doing, using those piercing, irregular eyes to stare at his actions. It was downright disturbing to Mitch; the thought of the remarkable being understanding of what he was doing.

In an unexpected, impulsive flash, the monstrous life form slung its body upwards, the head leading the way to the roof. In the literal identical movement, the tail of the twenty some-foot reptile struck Mitch on the left side of his head with great force. The unpredicted and very rapid, strenuous blow of the massive, preposterous creature hurled Mitch to the ground, causing him to drop the keys and knocked his glasses off, sending him into an unconscious state. He ended up on the dirt drive a few feet from his unmoving wife.

The rippling morph disappeared as quickly as it made the move, to the other side of the house. The speed and agility it demonstrated was genuinely amazing. And so was the powerful sting it purposefully and willfully dished out to the mathematics instructor.

A few moments later Mitch regained his consciousness, only to see his wife still standing motionless, gazing at the car. He held his face with one hand pushing himself up off the rough flooring with the other. It was the second time today he'd been knocked silly. Mitch wondered how many more poundings he could take as total alertness difficultly came back to him.

He was having trouble fathoming that he was just batted down by a large, sinister snake and his wife wasn't showing any signs of reaction. Is this even real, he questioned his memory, forcing himself with sheer will to get the hell up off the chat drive.

"Ann, are you hurt?" he managed to ask, limping the yard over to her. She didn't answer. Taking a hold of her hand he awkwardly pulled her to the house. His sight was blurry and he wasn't exactly in good shape here, but Mitch was coherent enough to find the keys and get them inside to safety.

"Ann, talk to me," he said, rather vexed, peering out the back door window once they were secure inside. The unreal was gone, but he had no idea of where to. He didn't actually see it climb onto the roof, because the incident had happened so fast and since he'd been blindsided. Which made it all the more daunting. A giant, let alone swift moving atrocity such as what he witnessed or thought he did, was sure to be dangerous, if not deadly. What he wasn't sure of is if the rat had intended to pummel him or if they scared it and the snake was only trying to get away from them.

Mitch began to feel faint. His perception was quickly fading. He stumbled over to the kitchen table and sat down. Ann was looking out the window above the sink and hadn't said a word. He was worried about her as well as his own physical condition in the present; however, he couldn't seem to function. Mitch felt nauseated and laid his head into his arms. This wasn't a good sign. Weakness began to take over. He couldn't utter another sound.

Mitch Rock slowly lost his consciousness, again.

Chapter thirty seven

Mɪᴛᴄʜ ᴡᴏᴋᴇ ᴛᴏ ᴀɴ ᴜɴꜰᴀᴍɪʟɪᴀʀ setting. His eyelids fluttered and he groaned, feeling his bandaged face with his right hand. He strained to get his eyes opened fully, then tried to comprehend the strange room and determine where he was, but it was problematical. His head bobbled and his eyesight was vague.

"Mitch! You're awake, finally," an exhausted and extremely upset Ann Rock said, rushing to his side from the chair she was sitting on next to his bed. She had been keeping vigil since yesterday afternoon when she'd had to call an ambulance after discovering her husband on the floor, insensible. Bad concussion is what the doctor told her.

"You scared me something fierce, it's been horrible waiting on you to wake up.

"Are you okay? Do you have a headache? Are you hungry?" She bombarded him with the questions.

"Can you see me, Mitch?" Ann suddenly realized he was squinting and rubbing his eyes. She hurried to hug him, enclosing her arms around him, still afraid for her man. Tears fell freely down her cheeks as she held on.

"No...I'm okay...Ann. Everything's just a little...fuzzy. I think. What happened? Where am I?"

Leaning back to a sitting position, on the side of the bed now, Ann looked at him seriously. She was trying to see if he could see, staring into his pools of blue.

"Oh shoot, Mitch, you don't have your glasses on. That's what's wrong. Where are they..." she asked more to herself then to him. Ann didn't remember them being in the kitchen anywhere. No, she was pretty sure they weren't. He always had his specs on, where could they be? This was odd.

Mitch concentrated as he focused what vision he did have onto his wife. He thought she was correct. It did seem as if his eyes were foggy from not having his glasses on. That was probably it. But his head hurt like a banshee.

"Mitch, you're in the hospital," Ann told him, collecting her thoughts. "The emergency room doctor said you took a nasty knock to your temple, that it was a serious injury. You have a really bad concussion. You've been out cold for almost twenty four hours. Do you remember anything?" She waited on an answer.

Mitch sat up a little bit nodding his head from side to side, very carefully, trying to shake the cobwebs loose and get his orientation. It was the wrong thing to do, though.

"Oh man, I need something for this pain. My head's killing me, Ann, get the doctor," he grunted. This was all he cared about at this very moment. It was throbbing and more than he could bear. Mitch laid back down, holding his head with both hands.

Ann immediately rushed from his side and ran into the hallway shouting for help. "My husband needs medical attention right away!" With that, two nurses scurried from behind their station and promptly came to his aid.

A couple hours later, a medicated Mitch Rock opened his eyes once more. Not as dramatically as before. He was in zero discomfort, the pain medicine working wonders, however loopy he was from it.

Rolling his head sideways, he could see an outline of his wife fast asleep in the chair next to him. "Ann?" He spoke in a soft, scratchy voice. His throat was awfully dry.

He reached for her and tried to stir her, "Ann...wake up." She didn't. She was out of it. Staying up all night and half the day, being a nervous wreck the whole time, had completely done her in.

Mitch decided to let her be and sat up a bit, making himself comfortable. He was dreaming of a Pepsi right about now. When he realized, which took a few minutes, that he was in the hospital, he looked around for a call button. The nurses would bring him something to drink, he bet.

One nice elderly woman did, with lots of caring.

"Here you go, how are you feeling?

"Do you need anything else?

"You're lucky you're not going to have permanent damage to your eyesight Mr. Rock.

"Let me help you sit up.

"Are you hungry?"

Must be a slow day Mitch decided, drinking that soda in record speed. He didn't hesitate to ask for another one. And yes he was hungry, what could he get?

"Thank you, you're very kind.

"I'm better.

"From the feel of this bandage, I guess I am lucky.

"I could eat a horse.

"A pizza would be great."

Ann came to just as Mitch finished his pepperoni pie and started on his third soft-drink.

"*Sweetums*, I'm so glad you're awake. I love you," he said, goofy.

"Well, I can tell you're feeling better," she told him, with a smile. It was obvious the drugs were working.

"Yeah, my head's all better." He grinned. Then in more of a reality mode he asked, "How are you doing?"

"I'm good, **now,** knowing that you're going to be alright." Ann straightened all the way up putting her arms into the air, stretching her back and cramped body. She had been in a crouched position in the chair, while sleeping. Then she grabbed Mitch's Pepsi and helped herself to a refreshing guzzle.

"That tastes good. We never have sodas. I miss pop."

"I know. I figured it would be okay considering the circumstance." He rolled his eyes at the room, then said, "I've been waiting on you to wake up. How did I get here? The last thing I remember..." his words trailed as he thought about what he did know.

"I went upstairs to get the paint off my face and when I came back down to the kitchen, you were passed out on the floor. I have no idea how or why you got there. You really scared me. I called 911 and..."

Mitch didn't hear what else she was saying about the incident as a tunnel vision suddenly walloped him upside the brain, about as hard as that snake did. The memory came flooding back to him in the tick of a clock, causing him to feel dizzy again. His color became pallid as he recounted the nightmare leading him to this bed, in this hospital. It took a minute or so, before he was able to comprehend his plight and realize the truth, the side effect of the painkiller wearing off some.

Digesting the recollection, Mitch waited until the malady passed, before speaking. "Ann." He interrupted her story. "I know how I got here. And you were there. Don't you remember going outside to get in the car and seeing one of those impious snakes on top of it? It hit me in the head when it fled, accidentally I think. I'm not sure." Mitch paused. *Could it have been intentional?*

Getting excited, "We probably scared it," Mitch continued his account. "Anyway, I managed to walk back into the kitchen and yeah, that's right, I got dizzy and sat down at the table. I must have passed out after that." Ann was staring at him as if he were a mental case. She did not remember such an event.

"Mitch, you must have really taken a jolt. We haven't seen another snake around our house for a while." That remark stunned Mitch Rock. *How could she not remember?* He was positive of his version.

He argued with her. "No, Ann. It's as clear as a bell. You were standing a couple inches in front of me staring at the black malevolence with me. It surprised us both. When we walked out the back door, it was there, right on top of our car in front of us. We both froze. It moved and I got smacked. Then it was gone." He repeated his account stubbornly.

"Mitch that's ludicrous as well as impossible. I'm not the one who was out like a light on the kitchen floor. You were. That's not how all this went down. I would know. It's your imagination or a dream or something like that. **You are** on drugs right now." Ann was feeling very uncomfortable.

"Where are my glasses, Ann?" he asked, emphatically.

"I don't know."

"I do. I'll bet we find them outside, a few feet from the kitchen door. Ten bucks, Ann."

"What would that prove?"

"It would prove where I was when I got sucker-punched. Go get the doctor. I want out of here." Mitch was becoming increasingly concerned about his wife. He began to think it was a possibility there was more than just this one incident she'd blocked from her awareness. That would make sense. Explain her behavior. This wasn't good. He needed to do something.

Chapter thirty eight

LAST NIGHT, BARBARA AND MARK made it back to Greenland around ten. They'd had a long day and went directly to his house, only to find out state troopers had the neighborhood blocked off, orders from the FBI. No one was allowed back in his or her homes on Pine street.

The duo were too tired to investigate why or from whom the commands were specifically given. They ended up renting one of those cabins in town, leaving Barbara's van and the funky reptile, in the parking drive out front. Mark figured he could get his phone messages at home in the morning, not really worried about it. He had no clue Mitch Rock was in Greenland Hospital. They went straight to bed.

What a trip it was for Mark and Barbara just to get the ornery black snake back into the portable cage. Once they made the decision to bring it here and let it lose with the ingenious eye-cam, the biologists tried in vein to persuade the large reptilian into the traveling unit. It was as if the damn thing knew what they were planning and was purposely incorrigible.

It should have been simple enough, too. The assistants had already sectioned off the baby snakes so they weren't a problem. The large habitat they had built, which could have been any snake's dream come true pertaining to a place to live, had a side panel. There was a round door in the center the snake could crawl through easily. All they should have had to do was open it, after already having the smaller pen in place with a couple mice in it to intrigue the reptile. But, the ophidian wouldn't budge, glaring at them through the glass with its head raised higher than the rest of the creeping body. It was not enticed by the meager meal.

The two assistants came to lend a hand, using the snake-poles to jab at the mighty being in an effort to coerce the black vertebrate. That's when it began to fiercely shake its tail, sounding as a rattler, however much louder. The noise and commotion it was able to make was deafening and shocked the foursome. They stopped at this point to watch the ferocious until it settled down.

Mark and Barbara were both unsettled, thinking the strange was dangerous, unless it simply felt threatened by them. It probably did, but the rate at which the thing moved its rear end was mind-blowing. The four stunned scientists watched in respect of the creature's dynamism. They had agreed it would be more than intimidating to run into and scare one of these giant snakes in the wild.

It was Mark's suggestion they try bigger food in the smaller enclosure to lure it in a more peaceful manner. He sent one of the other men out to buy a rabbit, or two. It took an hour, one of the reasons they were late getting back. Gordon and James had hoped to let the reptile lose and begin with the recording right away, but it didn't turn out that way. Meanwhile, while waiting, Mark looked through the photographs in the computer system Barbara already had.

Her camera worked like a video recorder, except the images came back in still photo. It made it possible to see every detail that came through, to be able to study the imaging thoroughly, yet then you could go through them at a faster pace and tag on the action.

Mark was impressed with Barbara's philosophy all those years ago; and her gumption; and her invention to produce.

Barbara stood the entire sixty minutes analyzing the unheard of. She stared at the epic snake. It stared back. She took note of the beat of the skins' constant movement. This wasn't a normal trait of a rat, one more thing making it stand apart from the Colubrid. And it wasn't flicking the tongue. Normally, this species uses the characteristic to sense everything around it. She pondered the way it used its optical sense and the enhanced reptile's intelligence level, how she could gain wisdom into the swine's intellect...

"Barbara," Mark said, startling her. She jumped, coming back into the day. He sniggered when he realized he scared her.

"What?" She turned to look at him.

"Our man's back."

Once the rabbits were in place, the giant amorphous became fidgety, but would not make a move towards the prey. It slithered around the habitat, in and out of the dirt, up and down the fake trees. It was at Mark's word they left it alone. He had an idea the nature of the beast's metabolism would be the answer to the problem. The energy it burned would eventually need replaced. Gordon had thought all along the snakes needed extra fuel, because of their growth tempo.

A couple hours later he was right and they were ready. All four were in motion as the snake abruptly snaked through the opening and coiled around both animals, squeezing them tighter with every inhale, not allowing the victims to exhale, causing the rabbits to slowly suffocate, before the snake swallowed them.

But, the rat was quick. When it had entered the mobile entrapment it was in the blink of an eye. Fortunately, they were expecting such a move and well, fortunately, it took a few minutes for critters to die. The snake was snared.

Barbara had the van backed up to the small, handy outdoor elevator. All they had to do next was push the enclose to the door and onto the rafters, using mechanical power to lower it. Once down and level with the backend, they heaved it into the vehicle. Mark and Barbara headed out as soon as the cage was secure.

Mark thought it ironic she wanted him to drive, now.

Chapter thirty nine

Mark Gordon and Barbara James woke at the same time, about six. They were both conditioned to get up early, probably one reason they were worn-out last night. Barbara suggested the minute they got out of bed that they go eat breakfast at The Diner. Mark agreed with her since he knew her need. He was hungry and thought it was a good idea, because he also figured they could find out the reason the government was issuing orders. He didn't understand why they would be involved or why they wouldn't let anyone back into their houses on his street, but he knew Charlotte would have the scoop.

Barbara didn't want to shower and get ready for her day, until she had some coffee and something in her belly. She was stubborn about it, too, insisting she was going now whether he was or not, putting her jeans and T from yesterday on, giving him the eye. Mark wasted no time doing the same since he didn't want her to go without him. He'd get used to how she was. He figured he would be the one to do the compromising anyway, cause she was pretty set in her ways. He had found that out in just the short amount of time they'd spent together.

Holding her hand as they crossed the street on foot – the cafe was only a short distance down the road – they walked instead of driving. They didn't want anyone at the place of business to spy what they had in the van.

Barbara enjoyed how energized she felt with him. "I'm glad I told you everything about me," she said, out of nowhere.

Mark squeezed her hand. "Me too. But you sure had me fooled when you told me you had a gambling problem."

"What would you have done if I meant that in the other way?"

"You want to know the first thing that came into my mind?" She nodded.

"Okay, my first instinct was that I could help you, that you needed me. What's your reaction to that?"

"I want to need you," slipped out of her mouth, before she had a chance to think about it. Mark laughed at her when she said, "Oops, I guess that was a little forward."

"No games, Barbara, remember? I want to know how you feel. And I'll be honest with you," he was matter-of-factly saying, while opening the door to The Diner. She didn't hate chauvinism coming from Mark Gordon and decided she would learn to appreciate this spirit of his. She knew she would probably have to do a lot of compromising since he was so young and set in his ways.

Charlotte spotted Mark the moment he walked in the door and was at their side in the next. "Mark, I'm so glad you're back. The FBI is in town and they're asking a lot of questions...about you Miss James." She gave the woman a cynical look when she told them that.

"What kind of questions?" Mark wanted to know.

"For one, like what's she doing here and with you for another? What's going on Mark? All the town folk are getting nervous."

"We came in for coffee and breakfast, Charlotte. Why don't you join us?"

She glanced at the two gentlemen sitting at the bar. They were regulars, so they were fine. It was early and the place was just opening. The rush hour wouldn't start for a bit and she had everything in order.

"Okay. What are ya having?"

"Allow me, Mark," Barbara said, with a smile. If he didn't like what she ordered, well then, it wouldn't work.

Looking at the waitress, "We'll have..."

"Never mind. I don't know why I asked. I know what Mark likes." She put Miss Barbara in her place and strutted off.

"I don't think that woman likes me very much."

"She just thinks you're the reason for the trouble in town. Come on, go sit over there. I'll grab us some brew." Barbara did as he wanted, walking over to where he pointed and sat down. She watched him converse with Charlotte as the waitress turned in the order and he poured the coffee up at the bar. Pretty soon, they ambled over to the booth and sat with her, Mark next to his love interest.

"Sometime after noon yesterday Paul and Doug came in for lunch. I had told them I would bring them some food after the usual crowd, but here they came walking through the door anyway. When I asked them who was guarding the pit the earthquake caused, they said they'd been relieved of duty and that the Federal Bureau of Investigation was taking over. Of what, they didn't know.

"So Paul made some calls to try and find out. He knew he had to report the incident to the USGS and did, but he has no clue as to why Greenland's small rumbling is of concern to any other part of the government, besides the Army's Chief of Engineers, he said.

"Anyway, they bring in state patrol and that's been it. No one is permitted into that area. Then, the men in suits start questioning whomever they see about your sidekick here, Mark.

"I'll be right back, foods up," Charlotte added, in a hurry seeing Pete signal her. She dashed up to bring breakfast. But not before she gave Barbara a dirty look.

Mark glanced at Barbara seriously and asked, "Do you know why they're asking questions about you?" She rolled her eyes and glanced away from him.

"Barbara?"

"Oh alright. Yes, I think so." That was all she said as she turned to stare him in the eye. She knew she couldn't lie to him.

"Well, are you going to tell me?"

"No." He stared back into her beautiful, now troubled big brown eyes without asking again.

"Foods here," Charlotte announced, interrupting them as she placed identical plates in front of them. Each had a large cheese omelet, wheat toast, jam, and a glass of OJ.

"Thank you."

"Thanks, Charlotte."

"Enjoy," the waitress said, sitting down once again with her own cup of coffee, but she wasn't sharing breakfast with them. She'd already eaten.

Without dithering, straight faced, Mark told her, "Well, you were right. Barbara is the reason the Feds are in town."

Doctor James choked on her first bite of eggs.

Chapter forty

Aɴɴ ᴜᴘ ᴀɴᴅ ʟᴇꜰᴛ Mɪᴛᴄʜ in bed, alone in the hospital, after the challenge. The doctor was coming in to see him anyway, as scheduled, but not for about an hour. She couldn't wait. She wanted to go home and find his glasses. It was really bugging her that he insisted on a different story, because she had a small inkling in the pit of her mind that she had blacked out again.

Feeling frustrated by the meaning, she drove fast. Truthfully, she was scared by the notion and tears were forming again. Ann had looked at the clock when she and Mitch decided to have a late lunch in town yesterday. And, she glanced at it again when he was out cold on the kitchen floor. The time difference was significant. Ann knew it was possible she lost a few minutes, maybe more.

This was very upsetting to her. She most likely thought she was nutty. What else could it be? The whole idea that there was another snake, only she didn't remember it, was utterly maddening if Mitch was right.

Almost to the farm, Ann was racking her brains trying to remember her nightmare the morning before. She never had problems sleeping or having dreams. Initially, she chalked it up to the pregnancy and her hormones changing, but now she couldn't be sure. Did she see anything? Mitch had asked her if she did. Why would he if there wasn't the possibility? *Maybe he saw something and just didn't want to tell me?*

Pulling into her driveway in a rushed method, chat flung everywhere. Ann didn't care if it was bad on the tires or not. She was on a mission to locate those darn glasses. She slammed on the brakes when she reached the house and left the door open and car running when she got out.

In a frenzy, Ann Rock searched the ground. She moved in circles, never looking up, along the outside of the house. She kept repeating, "Where are they, where are they?" Her concentration was solely on her immediate calling.

Then, surprisingly, she literally stumbled upon the eyewear almost breaking the frame. Ann bent down quickly and picked them up, focusing on the spot. She then turned to see the distance to the car. Realizing Mitch was telling the truth, Ann stood there in dread that she couldn't dredge up anything.

Was I out here when he was struck...by one of the large snakes? If it was on the car like he said, then how was I not whacked too? We would have both been right here, where I'm standing now. Where did the thing go?

With that thought, Ann spun around and looked up to the roof.

Gazing back at her was the mother of all snakes. The large, unbelievable creature was strewn across the roofline stretched out, the head was lowered and the neck was flowing boldly from side to side. The eyes seemed to penetrate her essence.

Soaking in her implausible fate, Ann made the decision to get over her fear. *I don't like losing time. I don't want to be crazy. I'm going to remember that I'm standing out here seeing this animal. And I'm going to fight for my home. It can't hurt me.* She gave way to anger. This snake wasn't going to ruin her life!

"I'm not afraid of you anymore!" she yelled at the preposterous, holding her ground.

It hissed at her. It was a long, deep, abrasive, aerated noise. Quite unlike anything Ann had ever heard before. It more than terrified her. The snake's hum immobilized her guts.

When she shied backwards a couple of steps, the snake lowered itself closer to her, eye level. The sun highlighted the shiny black and purplish skin as it moved towards her. Ann could literally see the strength of the reptile's muscles and at that moment figured she was a goner. She stayed still, fighting her urge to run.

Ann tried to summon her mind to face this taunt. She forced herself to evoke everything Mark Gordon had told her about the Squamata. But in her head the words were disoriented.

They're fascinating phenomenon of the cosmos, really.
It's not like we caught an anaconda.
It's okay to be afraid, Ann.
Farmers like them around here.
They strangle their prey..."

At the same time Ann remembered that sentence, the large creepy snake slid to within about an inch of her face. It studied her with those intent eyes. She could see the rest of the creature's body coming down from the house out of her side vision. Ann didn't have the tiniest hint as to what to do. Was this how fate was going to do her in?

Just as its face touched her cheek, underneath her left eye, she involuntarily screamed. One of those blood-curdling, gut-wrenching screams. Ann's instincts took over. She didn't move, she couldn't, but her vocal cords cut loose. Her screech came from deep within her soul. It reverberated across the land.

When she did hit the high pitch, the sneaky fauna backed off. Slowly. It did not react as before and move with speed out of sight. The unbelievable even hesitated as it reversed, still watching her. The body slithered backwards in constant motion and the slits kept vigil of her, while it inched away. Eventually it turned as Ann kept up with the dirge and finally slinked through the yard head first, into the tree studded terrain.

Ann continued her loud and annoying howling for almost two minutes. When she did stop, it was to catch her breath, before starting in again. She couldn't help it. It was all too frightening and too hard to comprehend. And she was isolated in her terror.

Chapter **forty one**

Mɪᴛᴄʜ ʟᴏᴏᴋᴇᴅ ᴜᴘ ᴛᴏ ꜱᴇᴇ Mark enter his hospital room.

"Hey Mitch, I just found out you were in here. What happened to you?" He acted concerned.

"How did you find out?"

"Charlotte, at The Diner. Everyone knows, Mitch. It's not a very big town and since we found that snake out there on your land, everyone knows who you are. Probably one of the nurses here told..."

"I get it." He waved him off. "Well, thanks for coming to see me."

"You going to tell me why you're here or do you just want me to hang out?" Mark made an attempt at humor.

"Yeah, I do, because when I'm done I want some freaking answers from you." Mitch gazed at him with meaning. Mark looked into his eyes, a seriousness coming into his.

"Go ahead," he said, sitting down.

"One of those Won't Hurt You If You Don't Bother Them Reptiles swatted me upside the head, Mark. It hurts, too. Knocked me unconscious for almost twenty four hours. Now, I want to know how dangerous they are, how many of them there are and whatever else you're not telling me.

"I saw the crater the earthquake left and the police guarding it with their Rambo artillery. I imagine you suspect these giant amphibians are the cause, am I right? Because if that's the case, I think I'm on a need to know basis."

Mark had walked Barbara to the motel so she could take a shower and then came directly here to see Mitch. When Charlotte mentioned he had an accident, but didn't know exactly what happened, Mark had the feeling the guy had run into one of the underground brood, and he was right. It was time to come clean with Mitch and tell him all he knew.

"Okay Mitch, yes that's what I think. I've been noticing movement below the earth's surface for about a year. I had no real evidence though, that these snakes were the cause. Only a suspicion. I just found out Doctor James has been clued into the unusual species, which by the way we suppose are a new breed of rats not mutants, for about five years.

"The reason I left with her was to retrieve the one we caught at your farm. She's placed a camera over one eye and we plan to let it loose on your land. We're hoping to find the den in order for us to accumulate data on the snakes. Find out if they are a threat to humans. We also hope to get some imaging back that might help us realize the damage underneath our feet.

"In all honesty, Mitch, we both believe that this is a bigger problem than just in or around Greenland. Barbara has some proof, but not enough to call worldwide attention to this, if we even want to. One of the reason's I've kept quiet is because I'm afraid of people getting panicky and possibly killing every snake they see, which would probably be the normal ones and we don't want that. The larger than life novel race hasn't shown their bad selves to many people.

"In reality, you and Ann are the first ones to actually experience a real problem. I'm sorry I couldn't say something before about how many there could be, but it really doesn't matter. Since we think this Class of snake is already plentiful in Kansas and possibly around the country, maybe the world, you see, it wouldn't make a difference where you live.

"Besides that, they're on the move continuously. I just can't be sure about anything."

Mitch didn't think whatever this guy said could shock him anymore, although this was shocking. "Should I get a gun, Mark?"

"I just don't know if they're dangerous or not, Mitch. Guess it wouldn't hurt. Yeah, get a gun. Better safe than sorry. But I project that they will behave as any other snake and would rather run from you..."

The emergency room doctor walked in about this time breaking off the conversation.

"I hear you're doing fairly good, Mr. Rock and that you want to go home." He picked up the chart and then said to Mark, "You here to get those stitches out?" Same doctor who treated him.
"Might as well."

The doctor released Mitch and also took the sutures out of Mark's elbow, giving both of them the thumbs up. It didn't take long and when Mark asked Mitch where Ann was and if he needed a ride, the man said he didn't know and yes he'd take him up on the offer.

Mitch had almost forgotten his wife ran out on him, after becoming upset with him, for arguing his story – the pain pills were messing with his mind. He decided he wouldn't take them anymore, unless he absolutely needed to. With everything that was going on, he didn't need to be out of his reason.

But, his head started throbbing horribly again when he was surprised by the fear-provoking monster in the back of the van. Mark hadn't warned him it was in there. He reacted as a girl, yelping as he climbed in.

"Sorry about that," Mark said, feeling kind of bad, yet trying not to laugh.

Mitch quickly popped another pill without thinking, since he had a prescription bottle in his pocket full of them. The hospital had filled it, before discharging him.

"Don't worry, it's a sturdy cage. It can't get loose. You sure you're okay, Mitch?" Mark wondered if the guy should have been let go. He didn't look good.

"Yeah, fine." He pouted, having been taken off guard like that. And he was embarrassed to boot.

Getting over hisself, "Mark, yesterday morning before this happened, Ann woke up screaming. Well, the day before, when you and Barbara visited, she blacked out in the bathroom. And then her demeanor changed. She's suddenly not afraid of these snakes." He wasn't making a lot of sense, but Mark was listening intently trying to piece together what he was saying.

"And she doesn't remember me getting knocked for a loop by the snake yesterday. I mean, it was on our car and we were both standing there staring at the crazy thing. I think something's wrong with her.

"Too, I keep having this feeling that we're not really alone in the house when we're there. I think Ann's seen more snakes and she's forgetting. Am I making any logic here or just being stupid?" he finally asked.

"Wow. I'm not sure, but it sounds like Ann's mind is in a protection means. You've probably heard before about people forgetting traumatic events. Like when a child sees something terrible happen to a parent, it's actually normal for them not to recollect the memory. Self preservation. I'll bet..." He stopped talking.

As they were pulling into the driveway, Mark noticed Ann standing by her running vehicle staring out into the yard, unmoving. It was weird. He couldn't imagine why she wasn't in the house.

Mitch saw her at the same time.

"What's she doing?"

"I don't know."

Mark parked behind the Blazer and got out of the van as quickly as he could, jogging to her side. Mitch couldn't move that fast.

"Ann? Ann?" Mark repeated. He could see she was in some kind of stupor and not responding to their presence.

"Look at me," he demanded, taking hold of both her arms, turning her around to face him. When he did, she came out of the trance-like state.

"Mark? Where did you come from?" Glancing at her husband who was now standing next to Mark, she said, "Mitch, you're home. What did the doctor say?"

Mitch and Mark looked at each other, worry covering their faces.

"What are you doing out here, Ann?" Mark questioned her carefully, letting go of her arms and acting normal, not wanting her to see his alarm.

"I'm just getting ready to go inside. Want some coffee?" She turned and walked casually as she spoke.

"You just going to leave the car running, Ann?" Mitch asked. When she didn't respond and went on into the house he turned the ignition off and pulled the keys out. Why the back door wasn't locked struck him funny. Then he noticed Mark was staring in the direction Ann had been.

"You see something?"

"No."

"Okay, well...are you coming in?"

"Not right now. Got to go get Barbara." Looking back to Mitch, he said, "I think you need to get her out of here," in a very serious tone.

Ann walked directly into the kitchen and straight to the cupboard where her cigarettes were. She robotically took one from the pack and lit it up, inhaling the smoke deeply. She stood and gazed out the window, while enjoying the soothing comfort her smokes brought. Mitch's eyeglasses dangled from her left hand.

Chapter forty two

"WHERE HAVE YOU BEEN?" a mystified Barbara James asked him, when Mark finally made it back to the cabin. He had been gone over an hour and she was ready in thirty minutes, cleaned up and sitting on the bed waiting on him in the rented room, watching the World Wide News.

"I got my stitches out, while I was at the hospital, visiting Mitch. Want to see?" He lifted his bandaged arm.

"No thanks." Mark shrugged his shoulders.

"Mitch was released, only he didn't have a ride home, so I took him." He sat down next to Barbara.

"What's Mitch's story?"

"One of those snakes side-swiped him. It was on their car when they walked outside. Mitch said it watched them for a minute or more and then in the bat of an eye it leaped and... POW!" Mark hit his fist into his other hand right in front of Barbara's face. She didn't blink. He chuckled when his joke didn't work. She just sat there giving him a look of annoyance.

"Anyway, Mitch thinks it could have been an accident that he was knocked over by it, that the snake might have been just trying to get away. He wasn't sure, though."

"Is that what you think?" Barbara asked him, a gravity to her voice.

"What I'm thinking is that I was wrong about them moving away from the Rock's residence. And check this out. When we got to the house, Ann was standing by their vehicle in the driveway, which she left running, glaring off into outer space. In a daze. It took a bit, before she came out of it."

"Is she okay?" Barbara's concern was genuine. She liked Ann.

"I don't know, she said she was, but Mitch confided in me that he thinks she's been seeing more and more of the reptiles and forgetting the sightings."

"You're kidding."

"Listen, I think it's probably true. It make's sense, since she was incredibly frightened of them to begin with. She could be experiencing behavioral amnesia. Chronic stress from this metamorphosis generation could have pushed her into psychodynamic chunking." Mark was affected. His gorgeous eyes radiated with his philosophy.

"Psychology degree?" Barbara got a kick out of him. But, she could do better.

"Poor thing. And she's pregnant. Justification for her etiology, I would presume." Mark knew at that moment he had a worthy adversary. He dared her with his rhetoric.

"Yeah, she sort of had a learned helplessness before. A selective conditional response in her cognition process to the stimuli would be based on her threshold of comfortableness. But false perception of safety could get her into trouble."

"Oh I didn't think about that. We have to do something. They can't stay at the house if she's coping with divergent thinking. Her perspective would inhibit her functionalism. The dynamic here is not good. Kind of a self fulfilling prophecy if you dissect it."

Wow.

"I see you're well versed in psychobabble."

"I majored in psychology, before switching to biology."

Mark was just as troubled as Barbara about Ann, even though they were trying to outdo each other in terminology. They sat on the bed for a time thinking about the situation. What they could do to help.

"I told Mitch to get her out of there when I left. He said he's already tried."

"Well, we could stay out there, with them. That way we'll be in the midst and we can gather data easier. I have to be back at work, at the university, Monday or Tuesday. I need everything I can get in the next two days. And we'll be there for Ann."

"Yeah, we could do that. I had better jump in the shower then. We're wasting time." Mark hurried to get ready for the rest of his day, pausing first to kiss the woman. She was fun to be with. He liked the idea of having challenging conversations with a partner he adored.

Barbara enjoyed Mark's antic with the fist, although he didn't fool her, as well as him being able to carry on an intelligent, yet twisted discussion. She thought she'd pretty much fallen head over heels for the man.

Dr. James toyed with the idea of confronting Ann's collective unconscious, while Mark was in the bathroom. The mental strategy of forcing Ann to face her delusional mind could possibly save the woman from making a bad mistake. Too, if they were all there together during the next sighting, then Ann's mental encoding might show her the threshold of what's been happening, the safety in numbers factor.

Barbara thought it was certainly best for them to stay at the farm under this circumstance. If Ann was left alone in her bogus perceptions for a long period of time, who knew what cornorbidity could develop. The id could take over her illusions and she could in turn lead a fictitious life, forever. The woman needed better coping skills. To dissociate herself from the real world was not the answer. Someone, herself probably, would have to do something.

Gordon and James headed back to the Rocks about thirty minutes later, snake in hand. It was time to free the organism and record whatever they could. Then, they were going to have to report the findings. Mark had decided in the shower, he couldn't keep his town folk in the dark any longer.

"How are we going to let that thing out? Without it getting spooked, possibly seeking revenge," Mark asked his cohort, casually.

"I guess we'll drive the van to the caurties and back it up. Open the rear doors and unlock the cage then..." she thought about this procedure. Where were they going to be?

"You brought your tranq gun didn't you?"

"No, it's in my truck. We wouldn't want to use it anyway." Mark turned to spy the size of the cage and the animal. The reptile was spying their every move. Its eerie eyes were as if they were giving him a death look. And the thing looked even bigger then when he originally captured it.

Shaking off the chills that just went down his spine, Mark told Barbara, "We'll move the entire cage to the ground and then I'll unlock it and jump back into the van. Think that'll work?"

"I guess we'll find out.

"Grab that small monitor, there..." she pointed. "...and turn the frequency until you get a picture." Mark did as she said.

"Wireless, cool. And it's so small."

"I told you I only buy the best equipment. The guys back at the lab will see the same images we do as it's recording."

"How much something like this cost?" he asked, playing with the gadget.

"Oh wow," he said next, not waiting on the answer, getting a charge out of seeing he and Barbara come into focus.

Chapter **forty three**

A<small>NN</small> R<small>OCK</small> <small>DID NOT REMEMBER</small> her latest encounter with one of the diurnal species. But, she was thrilled Mitch was okay and that the doctor had released him from the overnight hospital nightmare, for her.

He kept pestering her with questions, though.

"Mitch, I'm fine, just tired. I didn't get any sleep, because I was unbelievably worried about you, that's all. And I need to eat." Mitch was sitting at the kitchen table, woozy from his painkiller, while Ann was making herself some scrambled eggs. He watched her every little move, while fighting the effect of drowsiness.

The first thing Mitch noticed when he and Mark found Ann outside, with her glare glazed over, was that she was holding his glasses. When he asked her about them she said she'd forgotten where she spotted them. No matter, he pressed her anyway about the fact that she hadn't been inside since she'd gotten home, which had to have been an hour and a half he realized, so she had to have picked them up off the ground outside. But she wasn't exactly admitting to anything.

Ann kept answering him vaguely. "I can't remember. So what?" She tried to hide her own concern.

"Ann, do you understand that you left me more than an hour ago?"

"You already told me that, Mitch. Let it go, will ya?" she requested, a bit frustrated.

"Well, do you think you blacked out again?"

"I guess." She didn't want to think about it, let alone talk about it.

"Maybe we should take you to the emergency room, or the clinic or something. Find out why this keeps happening. You know, Ann, it could be something simple, hormone related, because of the pregnancy. I'm worried about you."

Turning to look at him, "Don't. I'm fine. I have an appointment Tuesday and I'll tell the doctor then. Okay?"

"I think we should stay in town until you do."

"No. I don't want to waste money. I didn't want to bring this up, Mitch Rock, but I'm not covered under your insurance policy. We need to be practical." Ann brought her plate over to the table and sat with him, her back facing the window above the sink, Mitch opposite.

"We have plenty of money, Ann, and you're healthy. I'm not concerned about covering the birthing cost. Now, you're going through something mentally and I want to get to the bottom of it..."

"Holy shit!" Mitch suddenly yelled, scooting backwards in his seat a few feet across the floor, the painkiller effects curbed. One of the heinous reptiles abruptly stuck its ugly head through the partially opened window. The yellow oblong eyes were fixed on him.

It appeared as if it materialized out of thin air, but had to be hanging from the roof, Mitch's rational mind assumed. The powerful neck slinked from one side to the other as the snake did what it wanted.

Mitch had been keeping a close guard on his surroundings, he thought anyway, knowing the large and uncommon were near. However, he hadn't expected something of this volume to approach through the cracked window. Although, he'd been chary that they could. This was incredibly spooky. He felt like he was in an alien world.

Ann sat there and ate, never looking at what her husband's eyes were hooked on, or even actually reacting to what had made him become so fearful out of the blue.

Mitch stayed unmoving after the initial shock. The carnivore didn't seem to want to come all the way in. It was only looking. And he wasn't sure what to do, anyway. He remembered how fast the animals can move. Then he grimaced when he thought about the word *they*, meaning there could be hundreds of them. Great.

191

The reptilian spied the man, its skin iridescent in the sunlight, creeping. The blackness of the body was amazing really with that ivory underbelly. The concentrated eyes with the black slits staring at him, as if with knowledge about man, were jarringly intimidating, yet interesting.

Mitch didn't know how long he could actually sit and watch the slithering beast, though. Horror was beginning to get its grip on him. He wanted to run, holler, attack or something. It wasn't easy to be a man and be still in the face of all evil. Even if the damned was normal in size, seven to ten feet or so, he knew he wouldn't be analyzing it in awe for the heck of it. This was mind-blowing.

As brusquely as the beast terrorized him, it disappeared. Out and upwards. Mitch reacted in tempo, considering his injury, sprinting over to the window and shutting it. He peered outside to see if he could determine where it was headed or if there were more. But he didn't see anything else out of the norm.

Nevertheless, Mitch was freaked out by the giant snakes, knowing they were somewhere. He glanced at his wife. She hadn't so much as flicked her wrist. It was strange. He temporarily wondered if the snakes had her brainwashed or something.

Mitch, old buddy, I think the painkillers are doin the talken. Get a grip, for the love of God. This isn't a sci-fi, you dope. It's only the dope messing with your head.

Jesus.

"Ann?"

She looked at him. "What?"

"What's the last thing you remember?" She gawked at him funny. He tried to explain.

"Did you see me get up and walk over here?"

"I don't know," she drawled her words, trying to think if she did or not.

"You didn't, did you?"

"Okay Mitch..." she let out a deep breath. "...you were telling me not to worry about money and the next thing I know you were at the window saying my name." Ann finished her last bite of food. She was getting upset. These blackouts were getting too frequent and the meaning of them devastating.

They both heard the van pull into the drive. Mitch was extremely relieved. He knew it was Mark and Barbara and he was happy they were here. Well, that was an understatement. He was ecstatic to not be alone anymore!

Maybe they could do something about this latest breed of Whatever Snakes? He could only hope. He walked over to the back door and waited on them. While doing so, he looked over the land, up and down, obsessed with the haunting. He thought he was beginning to know exactly how Ann had felt, before...

When the biologists reached him he flung open the door and started in, "One of those damn black snakes just stuck its revolting head in my kitchen window, Mark! There has to be something we can do! I'm going to get that gun, I swear, and kill all of them!" He had moved to one side, so the people could enter the house, while yelling at them and then he slammed the door shut.

"Calm down, Mitch," was the first thing Mark said.

"I understand and we're here to help. And we're not leaving you two alone. We'll be staying with you. Now, let's sit and talk for a few minutes. Did the snake try to hurt you this time?" Mark and Barbara both had their hands full of widgets and proceeded to set everything down on the table. Mark nodded to Ann. He eyed her carefully trying to get an idea on how she was.

"Hi, Ann," Barbara whispered, staying out of Mitch's tantrum. Ann artificially smiled at both of them.

Weird.

"No, and it didn't act like it wanted to. It just stared at me. But, that doesn't mean I want the unnatural living on my roof! Or in my yard!"

"I'm going to take a look outside. I'll be right back," Barbara told everyone. Then she scurried out the door to examine the milieu.

"And those beasts have done something to my wife! She can't remember..." Mitch suddenly became lightheaded and almost fell over. Mark grabbed his arm and helped him to sit down.

"Mitch, try to stay relaxed. You have a nasty bruise and getting upset isn't helping." He looked at Ann and said, "Why don't the two of you stay in town for a while."

"I don't want to," she flatly refused.

"Okay, well, Ann, how do you feel?" Mark was getting Mitch a glass of water as he asked. He quickly checked to make sure the window was latched.

"Fine I guess. Tired, but I'm good, thanks."

Barbara came back into the house. "I didn't see anything out there. They must have a hiding place." Scanning the three, "Mitch, are you alright?" He looked white as a ghost.

"Yeah...sure." He drank the water.

"Ann, tell me about your blackout spells." Mark decided to come right out and ask her. Barbara froze, waiting on a reaction, a bit stunned by Mark's bluntness and decision to come out with the information.

"Great. I guess Mitch told you?" Surprised, she let out a sigh. *Might as well spill my guts.*

With her head cast down she began, "I'm not exactly sure how to explain, but you see, when Mitch said there was a snake on the Blazer, I just, I don't remember, but, well, he was probably right. I mean, the first day I saw the giant snake, it was on the car. I was really scared, too. And the one that chased me, boy I remember that one, but I haven't really seen anything since. I know I'm not remembering some time frames. I can't be certain if it's because I *might have* seen another gross and huge snake or not. And I simply didn't see what Mitch did a little while ago. Mitch was sitting across from me one minute and...the next he was at the window. I don't know how to tell you what's going on." She hated this. It was obvious by the way she nervously rambled.

"Will it make you feel any better if I could?" Mark asked her. "Or if I tell you you're having a normal reaction to something that terrifies you?"

"Really?" There was hope in Ann's eyes. She looked at Mark now waiting for his reasoning, ready, relieved he understood and didn't think she was loony.

Mitch quickly regained his alertness. "You know what's wrong? It's normal? Say again?"

"Yep." Mark didn't want Ann or Mitch to think her reaction was anything abnormal, thinking it would help Ann to overcome her own minds capabilities.

Chapter forty four

GORDON AND JAMES PUT INTO plain words their theories to the Rocks. The married couple listened closely and then Ann began to cry. Tears of relief that she wasn't crazy came pouring down her face this time. Mitch was also incredibly thankful to hear the account. And it made sense to him. He had been so worried, he was beside himself.

The newlyweds asked a ton of questions, before Barbara told them her idea; of confronting Ann with the unthinkable. That she might remember if she was forced to and suggested they all go out to the van and look at the ophioid they had caged. Maybe for Ann to examine the creature at length would be enough to trigger her subconscious.

Ann wasn't positive why she had to. "I mean, if it was a really scary incident then why would I want to remember it?" She was totally innocent.

Barbara was direct, in her professional mode. "Because if you keep blocking the memories, it will keep happening every time you see one of the large snakes. Ann, if they pose any kind of threat, you won't have the *mind* to protect yourself."

"Oh." She thought about that for a minute.

"But they haven't hurt me, so why would they in the future? I like not knowing they exist. I want to live here. I...we..." she corrected herself "...want to raise our baby in our home. And not be afraid to do so."

"Ann, listen to me," Mark gave it a try.

"Selective memory can be unhealthy to you and your baby. Uh...it can be habit forming. You can't let your brain trick your slant anymore. Look, since it has only been a few days, you have an excellent chance of reversing this without a problem. I know you're scared, but sometimes it's better to just be scared. Feel it. Run away or whatever. It's a natural reflex to have. It keeps us out of dangers way. If you let this continue, it could start to pertain to anything that alarms you. Understand? Anything. Say there is a poisonous spider in the house one day and you ignore it. What about the baby?"

Mitch piped in, "He's right, Ann. You have to fight this. You have to be tough. I'll be right there with you." His eyes were as wide as they could get. He didn't want anything to happen to her and the baby.

"Me too, Ann," Barbara encouraged her. "All of us."

"Oh, alright. I'll try. I don't want the baby to get hurt, because I'm afraid of snakes and unconsciously decided to pretend there aren't any. Gees."

"Good girl," Mark told her.

"I'm proud of you, *sweetums*."

"It'll be okay, Ann."

The foursome slowly walked outside to where the van was parked and on around to the back. Mark asked Ann if she was ready, before sliding the rear end door open. She nodded her head that she was. Ann had her arms crossed in front of her with an uneasy expression on her face. Mitch had his arms enfolded around her shoulders and Barbara was standing right next to them. It was time.

But when Mark shoved the door open and they all four peered inside, the enclose was broken and the snake was gone. Mark and Barbara's mouth dropped to the ground. Mitch and Ann stood there confused. No one noticed the van window was open.

"What the...

"Get the equipment, hurry," Mark yelled at Barbara, while he slammed the door back in place and headed for the driver's seat.

"You two, go back inside or head to town. We have to get this recorded." Mitch and Ann followed Barbara into the house immediately, as ordered. Mark stopped the van next to the back door and hopped out, helping his partner in crime. She tossed the flashlights and two-way radios into the back and scooted into the passenger side, via the driver's seat. Once they were both buckled up, he peeled out.

Barbara had the portable high-tech television turned to *on*, playing with the knobs to get reception.

Mitch and Ann watched the pair bounce their way out of sight across the rough terrain. They were both a little frazzled by the ordeal. Mitch went around to every single window and made sure they were all locked tight. Ann followed behind him, gabbing about the development.

"I am so relieved I'm having a 'normal reaction' to fear, even if I do have to work through it and remember everything. I was getting really freaked out about losing chunks of time. I thought I wouldn't be able to be a good mother if it kept happening. How could I raise a baby like that?

"I'm ready to face it too, Mitch, now that I've had a chance to think about it. I guess by not admitting I had a problem before, made me, well, not have a problem. You know what I mean? I was afraid of being a mental case."

"Actually, I think I do know how you feel. I was so upset when Mark and Barbara got here that I felt...I didn't only feel crazy, I acted crazy. Boy, seeing that snake look through the window and after being pummeled by one, I was scared shitless to be honest. Still am. I want them gone. I don't blame you one bit for using a memory lapse to cope. You poor thing. Out here by yourself when I was working."

"Mitch, lets try to jog my memory ourselves. Because you're right, we have to get rid of the stupid things. Maybe I can remember something useful, given that they didn't hurt me." Mitch thought about this for a second. He wasn't feeling that great and really needed to lie down.

"Sorry, Ann, why don't we take a nap? We're both exhausted and we've got the Snake Busters out here, so we should feel fairly comfortable. Maybe after that we can think of something."

"I am beat. I know you must be hurting. Are you feeling any better?"

Mitch took hold of her arm and walked her upstairs and into the bedroom. "I'll be fine. I think maybe the painkillers are making me sick. I just need to rest a bit.

"Hey, have we ever done this? Take a nap in the middle of a Saturday afternoon?"

"I don't think so. We're living the high life now, aren't we?"

"Yeah, we are," he replied mordant, teasingly. "I suppose it's the last chance we'll have, anyway. When the baby gets here I doubt we're taking siestas."

Ann smiled at him as they laid down. "I'm getting excited. I've been thinking about the horrific so much of the time, that I haven't had a chance to really focus..." she quit talking.

"What is it?"

"I don't know. Something about the baby has something to do with the snakes. I don't know what, though. Umm. Weird I would suddenly know that.

"Oh never-mind. I'm just being silly now." She fluffed her pillow, laid her head down and yawned. When she glanced over at her husband he was already out like a light. Ann caressed his face, then closed her eyes, finally able to breathe a little easier.

Chapter forty five

"I'M GETTING SOMETHING!

"I've got dirt, dirt and more dirt. This snake is gliding through the earth with effortlessness. Outstanding. At a very rapid rate, too. I wish I had all my tools so I could know the exact speed and scope, but my men should be getting this footage and will have some readings for me when I call in." Barbara was in her element as they sped across the land.

"Any clue to its whereabouts?" Mark Gordon asked the lovely doctor of biology.

"No. Not without letting it go ourselves. Damn. How in the name of God did that thing get out of my thermoplastic invention? I put that cage through the Dog-Bone test myself!" Barbara was tense, something Mark hadn't been privy to witness before. He listened to her rant, while he drove the vehicle through the uneven countryside, dodging the trees, stumps, potholes and thick brush.

"The tensile strength of that structure couldn't be any better. I considered the temperature and duration. I knew what I was doing. The strength reduces as the temp increases and the strength reduces as the dura is extended. It was child's play. There's just no way that amphibian was strong enough to put a tear in the side of it. With what? Its head? Damn...damn, damn."

"I think maybe it did. Uh...it's right there in the back if you want to take another gander."

"Yeah, funny. I guess I underestimated the power behind the muscle." *Or this is one heck of a phenomenal beast.* "I should have known. Oh, I'm so mad. I could ruin everything." She never took her eyes off the monitor on her lap.

"James, chill. We're probably going to find out a whole lot of things we think we should have known. Hell, maybe even the answer to the age old question; what is the nature of the forces propelling the plate tectonics?" He thought he was witty. Especially in such a serious situation. Mark liked the fact that he could keep a sense of mirth.

Barbara didn't pay him any heed. She was busy trying to determine the precise position of the subject, pissed she'd been so stupid, if she was. She couldn't afford to mess up this opportunity. One, she'd been waiting on it for a very long time, and two, it was very important to her research that she know the exact location if and when they found a den.

"Damn it! Earth, nothing but earth. Where in the hell is this guy going? Why do you suppose he's in such a hurry? Is the monstrous scared? Or does it have a purpose in the tribe? I have to know those answers, Mark." She was becoming fussy.

Finally, Mark spotted the hovels and halted the swift, bumpy ride. He shut off the ignition and began searching the area with his eyes.

Nothing.

Shit.

Barbara grunted as she took a quick glance to see if there was a new opening or anything.

There wasn't.

Crap.

The duo sat in silence as they waited. On what, they didn't know. And all Barbara's monitor showed was that the snake was on the move. They couldn't even tell if it was going up or down.

"Now what?" Barbara was impatient, making Mark wonder how she'd lasted this long on the job.

"Want to tell me why the FBI is looking for you?" He had a hunch and went with it.

Waiting a minute, before answering, Barbara gave it up. "Gordon, do you really think that after all these years a new breed of an undiscovered Kingdom would rear its feo head, suddenly, to mankind?"

He took his eyes off the land and gave her a stupefied look. "Yes?"

"I'm beginning to wonder.

"You see, about six months ago one of my lab assistants saw a suspicious car parked outside the warehouse. He wrote down the license number. I had a 'friend'..." she did the hand thing again, "...run it through DMV. It was a phony.

"That particular car was never spotted again, but all three of us began paying close attention whenever we were coming or going. There have been numerous dubious vehicles driving around the area or parked along the street since. It seems when we did start noticing, they would disappear.

"Then one day, a couple of weeks ago, I found a small listening device in my car. No one can get into my warehouse or my lab with the security measures I take, so I guess they thought I might say something, while driving. Oh brother. I don't know. But, it has the FBI written all over it.

"Now, the reason I think that is because I did some checking. No one else would have access to my purchases, home address, real estate contract, orders, bills etc. to have a chance to discover what I'm up to. Plus, the many different cars used to survey us and the type of electronic bug used were palpable clues.

"Anyway, we've all heard rumors that our government decided to explore genocide warfare years ago by using reptiles. What if they actually did? What if the defense department created a perfect killing machine, with a degree of intelligence?

"I became even more wary of this concept when I heard they were in Greenland, watching the crater and asking questions about my labor. Of course, my biggest fear has always been that another herpetologist would or could steal my work, the reason for the guarded positions I take. But if the government is interested in it, there's no guarantee about my fate.

"If these are their experimental creatures, they wouldn't want them to be discovered. I have felt like I'm being followed for weeks now.

"Nevertheless, the breed is new to the surface of the planet, whoever created them, God or man. And they are growing and multiplying at a rapid pace." She finally took a breath.

"Jesus, Barbara. No wonder you want proof and location. If some form of the government did cause this horrific life form, wouldn't they want it controlled?"

"Right, that's what I mean. In control and hush-hush. I could be a problem, Mark."

Mark didn't have to think about that suggestion. "Let's go public with what we have then. We have enough proof." He jumped the gun.

"What about causing panic and alarm among the population?

"That's why I was trying to get money for this undertaking. To study them and find out if they pose any harm or risk to the environment. Before educating the people. And now, I'm worried about what the FBI is willing to do, if my guess work has any validity to it at all. Which I think it does."

"I think I do remember hearing about that covert operation."

"Mark! Oh my goodness! Look!" Barbara had been periodically glancing to and from Mark and the screen. This time when she looked down she saw what she wanted. The pet with the camera in place just slid into a cavern. She was getting her first glimpse of open space, filled with a grouping of the overgrown species.

"There...must be...hundreds of them," Mark barely got out. He was shocked. Just shocked. So was Doctor James. The revelation they were staring at came with an unanticipated variable; the massive amount of reptilian's theory being real. Their snake stayed on the move, intertwining with the others.

"I can hardly believe this."

"Christ, this is a huge find. This, right here, is the corroboration you've been working for."

"Oh good Lord, Mark, I know. This is incredible. I guess. The implication, the unearthing of the clutch, the toil on the world," she breathed her words. James was way beyond excitement. Her mind was working in express trying to understand the jolt on society this would have.

"Unreal...you did it Barbara." Mark grasped the concept, even though it was intimidating.

She looked at him briefly, too wound up to concentrate beyond the fantastic. "I can't screw this up, Mark. Promise me you won't let me."

Mark knew he was definitely in love with the vulnerability she was showing right now. He scooted closer to her, wrapping his arm around her and did promise that he was going to be there for her. After that, they were both entranced with the pictures in front of them, each thinking of different potential developments.

Mark Gordon thought about the impact on all living creatures when this brood finally emerged. What would happen to the eco system and what would happen to the earth physically? Barbara concentrated on the potential race in itself, how it survived and developed the acumen level and whether or not it was natural.

Although, neither could get over the numbers of the unheard of living lurid.

"Look at that rock formation..." Mark said hurriedly, because the snake was still in motion and the images they were getting were moving quickly, he barely got a glimpse of it. They would be able to analyze the videoing once back at her lab, but for now they didn't have a replay button.

"It had to have been tunneling downward the whole time, according to what I just saw. Barbara, I'll bet money this location is directly under the Rock's house. And we can figure the distance when we get an accurate rate of speed that it traveled, but my ballpark is two miles according to the loam, what I can make out that is"

Chapter **forty six**

As dusk settled in Greenland, the biologists sat hunkered down, mesmerized with the television portable, unaware of their surroundings or what time it was. Mark kept trying to pick out the approximate region the new breed were hovering, while Barbara was interested in the statistics, praying nothing would interfere with her expensive and hard earned revelation.

While the monitor only showed black and white, Gordon and James were positive the eyes were all the same weird color of yellow. It's what stood out the most. The lucent pairs against the backdrop of dark, elongated bodies.

Mark explained it this way. "Have you ever gone outside at night with a two-million-candle-watt flashlight and shined it on the ground? What looks like dew are really spider eyes."

"Would you believe I have?"

"Yes. Strange we're so much alike. Anyhow, that's how these eyes appear." And there were many sets of the oblong ghostlike pearls flashing across the screen in front of them.

"Have I told you about the time I went frogging with my brother?" she asked, watching the snakes creep below the surface.

"No. Actually, James, I don't know very much about you. Please, enlighten me."

She instantly looked into his gorgeous black beauties and beamed. Only for a second. They were on a mission here. Except, she figured there was nothing wrong with passing the time telling stories as they explored. The initial shock was wearing off and Barbara was feeling pretty damn good. Pay dirt had been a long time coming. She was almost giddy.

"I think I was about eighteen and he was sixteen. My brother's name is Robert and he lives in Alaska. In fact, he's also a biology major. Runs in the family."

"What's he do?"

"Marine. Works with the whales."

"Cool."

"Anywho, he takes me down to the neighbor's pond around midnight one summer night, we had to sneak out. And of course, we had snuck some alcohol and taken it with us. We're shining the flashlights around, talking and giggling, when suddenly we spot this snake, and it had..."

Mark cut her off. "It's a stupid joke, Barbara. I can't believe you would even try to pull it on me. It's as old as the hills and twice as dusty."

She laughed. "You're bad."

"That's right. I am." He winked at her.

A short time later, "I can't believe I'm getting all of this imaging. I'm so relieved and excited, Mark. Do you know what this means to me?"

"Yes, I think I do and I'm excited too, darling, but we need to think of how we're going to go about bringing the attention to this that you need. I hate to be a damper, but the FBI is in town and you do have suspicions. Remember? We need a plan of action."

"Oh, shit, you're right." She sat up, uncurling from her position of lying on Mark's shoulder. She had been comfortable sharing the best day of her professional life with precisely whom she wanted. Barbara didn't really want to think about the mess she...they...could be in.

"And it's getting late. We should get back to the Rocks and check on them. Your guys are getting this right?"

"Yes, and I need to make some calls. I have the numbers encoded in my book of the *right* people to contact with this info. It's important for me to get connected, now, tonight, as soon as possible. We probably should go."

Just as she said that, the ground beneath them began to rumble. A low murmur enveloped the atmosphere. It quickly became full fledged vibrating quaking, like before. They looked to one another with dread in their eyes realizing it was happening directly below them.

"Ah-o. Hold on." Barbara put the monitor on the floor and grabbed on to Mark. He steadied himself clutching the steering wheel, starting up the vehicle. The van soon began to rock with vehemence on the unsteady ground.

"Get us out of here!"

Gordon stepped on the gas. The wheels spun. "Shit!" He put it in reverse and again stomped on the pedal. They moved about an inch. He repeated the process, putting the gear into drive and then reverse, each time hitting the gas. The ground beneath them was beginning to crack trapping the tires in the groves, the sound was unmistakable.

"Come on, come on," Mark kept saying, but he kept his wits about him. He wasn't the type to panic or be foolish in a tricky situation, even though if they didn't get out of there now, they would most likely be swallowed up by the trembling planet.

Eventually the tread took hold and they shot backwards ramming into a tree. The two were jolted forward. Barbara hit her head on the windshield.

"I'm fine!" she hollered, before he asked and sat back, placing her feet on the dash, still holding on to Gordon.

Mark threw the van into drive and steadily began to outrun the splitting soil. Barbara turned sideways cranking her neck as much as she could, keeping vigil behind them, blood trickling down the side of her face. It was getting fairly dark, but she could see the outline.

The van was extremely difficult to drive, Mark avoiding the tree studded land, while it shook brutally. Both humans were taking a beating and were afraid for their lives, but the professionals remained in their cognizant minds. Barbara did the best she could to determine the abrupt change in the planet and steer them to safety.

"Mark, turn it south! The earth's opening to the north," she yelled, recognizing the bearing the rip was taking. Mark was desperately trying to control the jerky vehicle. He pulled the steering hard to the right as

she said, barely missing one of the giant oaks. Then, suddenly one of
the trees came pummeling down right in front of the van, crashing
loudly.

"Look out!" he yelled, yanking the wheel back to the left, just
missing a collision.

"Faster Mark, go faster!"

"I'm trying, Jesus Christ," he shouted, right before they crossed
in the path of the oncoming fracture. The wheels hit a loop in the
uneven ground causing them to bounce upwards with immeasurable
force as the van continued to pitch side to side. They both let out a
wail knocking their heads on the ceiling. The tossing was taking a toll
on them. The van tipped to the left as this happened and almost went
completely over.

Mark stayed with it though, and managed to keep his hands
gripped to the wheel and his foot on the pedal. Just when the tires met
the earth once more they were off and running, dirt and rocks flying
into the air, burning rubber. Mark was disoriented as to the course they
were heading, only paying attention to the immediate pathway he was
taking, that's all he could see. It took quite a bit of concentration just
to manage this task.

Being jumbled about in the darkness of the night, steering around
obstacles while only able to see a foot or so in front of him, trying to
out maneuver a cracking earth in God's country, yet maintaining a
calm nerve through all of it, showed Mark's tenacity, boldness and
courage. He was impressive in an unexpected and hairy situation.

As suddenly as the quaking started, it ceased, like the first time. It
took a second, before they realized they were out of danger, Mark still
driving as fast as possible evading the foliage.

"Mark stop the van, I think we're safe," Barbara barked, her fear
ruling her voice, but not her. He hit the breaks. They catapulted forward
coming to an abrupt halt. The duo sat still, while they tried to regain
their sagacity, wanting to be positive the unanticipated was for sure
finished, staring at one another.

Barbara's eyes were wide with disbelief, although she was in control
of her reactions. She breathed a sigh of relief, a tear streamed down her
face mixing with the blood from the cut on her forehead.

Mark was in a state of astonishment gazing at the woman he wanted to be with, forever. "Are you alright?"

"I think so, you?"

"Yeah, boy, man that was close."

Smoke suddenly began pouring from the engine and the van started making strange noises. After a couple clanking, out of the ordinary clamors, it completely died.

"Great," she said, with a guffaw; however, a calm was setting in. Barbara spontaneously threw her arms around Mark and kissed him. He grabbed hold of her tightly and responded with great affection. They were both shaking. Neither could help it after the immense adrenaline rush. Biology.

Hugging each other for a time, Gordon and James knew they were lucky.

"Looks like we're walking the rest of the way, you up to it?" he finally asked.

"Yes, let's see if we can find the flashlights in this mess." They rummaged through the strewn about devices and did find them. One worked, the other didn't. It was fine. At least they had some illumination.

Getting out carefully and slowly, Mark directed the light source to the novel fissure. They walked a couple paces to the sight, glancing into the amazing. They couldn't really see that much. Just blackness looming from the hole. The light didn't have enough beaming power.

"Let's go, Mark. I have a weird feeling we're not alone out here."

"Me too." He hurriedly shined the light all around the immediate night and into the trees, but they couldn't see anything, like a snake. That was good, but still it was creepy outside in the dark, a mile or so away from civilization, especially after what just happened and knowing the new breed were somewhere.

"Okay, well I'm spooked," Mark told her. "Come on let's move."

Chapter forty seven

When the bed began wavering, due to another minor earthquake, Ann Rock was jerked out of a peaceful sleep, alone. She sat upright, her eyes large, immediately panicked by what was happening. The earth sounded as if she was next to train tracks bearing a locomotive and the room was as rickety as the bed. It was hard to focus. Things were falling off the dresser.

She held on to her mattress for dear life as she bounced helplessly. Where was Mitch? Ann wasn't even sure what day it was, having been forced to consciousness like this. Using her fortitude, she managed to look outside to see that it was dark. Strange. The whole ambiance was unreal.

No way could she scream. Waking up to the house doing the mamba wasn't unerringly a standard for Ann. She was alarmed, really. Was the fantastic never going to end in Greenland, Kansas? My God, ever since they moved here it was one thing after the other. Now, suddenly she was praying she wouldn't fall out of a joggling bed. And her husband wasn't anywhere near. This wasn't easy to grasp.

Ann was hoping that she could possibly be dreaming when abruptly, the rumbling ultimately stopped. In a state of shock, she glanced about the room trying to come to grips with where she was and what just happened. She had to force herself to think of the last time she was aware. Again.

Okay, Mark and Barbara were here. They left because...oh yeah, because that snake wasn't in the van. Let's see, Mitch locked all the windows and that's right it's Saturday. We laid down to take a nap and talked about how we never do that. Where is he?

There was a knock at the front door, startling Ann out of her remembrance. *Shit, who could that be?* Ann looked at the clock next to the bed realizing it was seven at night, not seven in the morning. That still didn't answer her question, though.

Getting up, shook over her peculiar awakening, Ann staggered out of the room and down the stairs. "Who is it?" she hollered on the way.

"Sheriff Stone, Ma'am. You alright in there?" The deep voice on the other side of the door wanted to know.

Thank God, Ann thought as she quickly let him in, answering before she could see him. "Yes...yes, thank you." She was ready to greet the man and not be alone right now, although she was haggard looking from sleeping in her clothes, her curly hair a mess.

"Please come in." The sheriff stood on the other side in uniform with his hat in his hands, a gentleman. He was a burly looking fellow with trenchant dark eyes. His build was at least six foot, Ann derived staring up at him. Sheriff Stone's hair was perfectly slicked back and he was very handsome in looks, yet his manner came off intimidating without him having to move. He was probably in his late fifties, early sixties. Been around, she could tell that. He had that hard look to him.

"Thank you, Mrs. Rock. I was patrolling the area when I heard the commotion out here and I came to see if you and your husband are okay." He walked into the home surveying the place, as if he had the right, which she guessed he did, but whatever. Ann took a glimpse outside, before shutting the door and escorting him into her kitchen.

"I'm fine, thank you very much. It's a pleasure to meet you, Sir. Can I make you some coffee? It's no bother," Ann replied, using her best manners. She felt secure with him here.

"If it's not a problem, that would be great. It's been a long, tiring day." He was just as polite. "And you can call me, Paul. Everyone else does." When he smiled, Ann knew right away they would be friends. He was a good man, she felt it.

"You can call me Ann, Paul. Come this way and please, make yourself at home."

"I appreciate that.

"Ann, I would have sooner rather than later I hope, been out here to meet you and your husband properly. It's just that's it's been a hectic week.

"Where is your husband by the way?" he asked, setting his Stetson down on the table, taking a seat.

While Ann scurried around, she said, "I'm not sure. I was napping and he must have gone into town for something. I woke up when the earth decided to quiver again. I guess you felt it, too?"

"Yes, and I could tell the quaking came from this area. I also knew Mark Gordon was out here with the woman from Lawrence, so I figured this was the place to start investigating."

"Oh, yeah right. They are here, out on the land somewhere, doing... uh...some science stuff." At that moment she heard Mitch screeching into the driveway. She smiled sweetly at the sheriff, hoping he didn't hear the recklessness.

"Sounds like your husband's home."

"He doesn't always drive that way. I'm sorry. He's probably worried about me," Ann confessed right away and acted innocent.

The sheriff grinned. "It's okay tonight. I'm glad he's here."

"Thanks," she said sheepishly, then went about finishing her task.

Mitch, the worried husband, came barreling through the door in the next instant, yelling, "Ann! Where are you?" He had been in town getting something for them to make for dinner when the reverberating occurred. It was all he could do to pay for the groceries after the event sounded. And he knew it came from this direction. Then seeing the patrol car out front really demoralized him. *I should know better by now not to leave Ann out here alone. I am such an ass!*

He saw the sheriff first and then his wife. "Ann, you're okay?" Mitch was reassured.

"**Now**, but I was pretty scared when the ground started shaking." She gave him a look.

"Mitch, this is Sheriff Stone. Sheriff, this is my husband, Mitch."

"Please, call me Paul. The only one around here that calls me *sheriff* usually is the deputy." He stood to meet the man, smiling and held out his hand.

Mitch shook it with his right, while holding the groceries with his left saying, "It's a pleasure, Paul. Please sit down." Mitch moved over towards Ann after the introduction, sat the sack on the counter, kissed his wife and got out some coffee cups.

"I'm sorry I wasn't here, Ann. You were sound asleep and I thought I could get to the store and back before you woke up."

"I'm glad you're back."

"Me too." Mitch gave her an endearing look, and then brought the cups over to the table and sat down with the sheriff.

"Any word on why Greenland is having these quakes?"

"To be honest, I was hoping Mark Gordon would have the answers."

There was a short knock at the door, before it opened. Mark and Barbara entered without waiting on anyone to answer. They both appeared a bit ragged and edgy.

"Paul, I'm glad you're here," was the first thing out of Mark's mouth. "Ann, Mitch, everything safe in here?"

"So far," Mitch told him, while getting up to get more mugs. "Sit down, I'll get you some coffee. Looks like you could use some."

"Thanks, that sounds wonderful," Barbara exaggerated her words. "Hi, I'm Barbara James," she introduced herself in the next second, walking over to the sheriff.

"Ma'am, pleased. Uh...you okay?" he asked, seeing the cut on her head.

"Oh...yes, thank you, I'm fine." Actually she'd forgotten about it.

"Barbara, let me see." Ann was concerned. "Here, I have a first aid kit, let's get you fixed up." She guided Barbara over to the sink and pulled out her box of bandages and some Neosporin.

"Mark, where were you two?"

Gordon took a load off as Mitch suggested and then answered with, "Scouting the land. We ended up right on top of where that damn earth started cracking. Wrecked Barbara's van trying to outrun the dividing. It was delicate there for a while. Not something I hope to do again."

"I'm glad the two of you made it back in one piece." The sheriff was trying to comprehend such a situation. "Where about was this, Mark?"

"Couple miles due southeast."

"Was it as big a quaking as the one this morning?"

"No, I don't think so."

"Mark, can you explain to me exactly what's happening around here? You probably know the FBI and state troopers are snooping around, but they won't talk to me. I know they were ordered by the Army's Green unit, but that's all I could find out."

"The Green's, of course," Barbara said, her words lingering. Ann had her head cleaned up and bandaged and was pouring everyone a cup of the freshly brewed coffee. Barbara abruptly excused herself, asking Ann and Mitch, "Do you guys mind if I use your phone for business purposes? It would be long distance. I'll pay you back."

"Please, do whatever it is you need to do."

"Yeah, really don't worry about it."

"Thanks, this won't take long. I'll be right back." She got up and went into the other room taking the portable with her.

Mark sipped the java as if he'd never tasted coffee before this very minute, thoroughly enjoying it, then he focused on the sheriff speaking slow and deliberate. "Greenland has been experiencing very minor earthquakes, even though it seems to us they are bad. Barbara doesn't think the quaking will get any worse than the one in town, it's just that we can't predict where they could take place next or if there will even be another one. There have been smaller ones that we couldn't actually *feel* before these.

"Now, the reason this is happening here is because we've had some extremely large snakes tunneling underneath our town. Exactly like the one we caught. Doctor James and I have just recorded the first evidence that there are many." The sheriff's facial expression never changed as he absorbed what Gordon was telling him.

Mark went on. "We can't be sure if the reptiles are a breed never explored before; either because they are being unleashed from deep within our earth for reasons of an isotonic rebound or if pesticide use is affecting or if the Army has experimented with snake genetics, wanting to invent a new form of weaponry. That's the theories we're looking at right now." He didn't want to use the term *genocide warfare* and scare everyone. As if this news wasn't scary enough.

"We have no idea if these snakes are a menace to mankind. Barbara is on the phone now to get a go ahead to begin an in-depth study on the Phylum in order to find out. The Rocks here have had a couple hanging around their house, but so far, other then the scare they cause when seeing one, they haven't hurt them. Well, I was bit by the one we captured, but that was the reason, it was threatened. Mitch was snagged by one when it got spooked yesterday.

"Anyway, I think they're like the black rat snakes. If you don't bother them, they won't hurt you." He paused to take another drink of the delicious coffee.

"Sheriff, I would venture to say the government wants to keep these unusual reptilian a secret from the average public. Barbara wants to educate the people. We might have a bit of a fight here between the two." He shrugged and waited on a response.

The sheriff was staring at Mark, stoic.

The Rocks and Gordon waited silently on what the man would have to say.

After a good long minute, thinking carefully he made a decision. He trusted Mark just like everyone else in town and thought he knew what to do. "I think I should hold a press conference right away. Inform the town of the snakes, while letting them know what you said, to leave them alone. That they are being interpreted by a professional in this area of expertise.

"Mark, I also think the citizens of this town have a right to know about the government skinks intention. Nab them in the bud if that's what you want. They won't be able to keep anything quiet in my county."

"Barbara and I have agreed we need to make people aware of the snakes. Thanks."

Paul stood, grabbing his hat. He wasn't the type to waste time when something as important as this was taking place. "Mark, I'll tell everyone to report any sightings to me. Then I'll be in contact with you.

"Thanks for the mighty fine coffee, Ann. I hope we get to visit some more soon, get to know one another. You too, Mitch. I'm sorry you've had some trouble out here. Whatever I can do I will. Feel free to call the department any time. Meantime, I think I'll be sending the deputy out here periodically to keep check of any problems."

"Thank you, sheriff. I'll see you out," Mitch said, as he also got up.

"He didn't act shocked at all," Ann whispered to Mark, amazed.

"That's why everybody in town likes the sheriff. He never gets rattled."

Chapter forty eight

"ANN, SORRY WE RAN OUT on you. It's just that we had to try to get a recording of the underground and luckily, we did. It's very exciting for people in our field."

"Don't apologize, Mark. Mitch and I slept all day, anyway. But will you tell me what you did discover. Maybe I'll remember something?"

"Let's wait on Mitch and Barbara." Mark wasn't sure if he should go into detailed graphics about the snakes until Mitch was around or even if he should at all. He had some psychology courses, sure, but he wasn't a practicing psychologist and didn't want to make Ann's problems worse. Barbara was the one confident in her decision to force Ann's memory, by making her look at one of the wild Chordates. Which didn't work out.

"Alright, I suppose I could start dinner then. Mitch went to the store and I'm going to make lasagna. Sound good?"

"To tell you the truth, Ann, anything sounds good right about now. I'm starving."

"Oh, well, Mark, why didn't you say something? I have a ton of cheese and crackers. Mitch and I lived on stuff like that in college. I always keep plenty." Ann hurried to get him a tray filled with saltines this time and sharp cheddar.

"Ann, you're a sweetheart. Whenever I can get back into my house, I'll fix you and Mitch a meal fit for a King." Mark stuffed a mini sandwich into his mouth. He nodded his head yes at her, while moaning how good it tasted, without actually saying the words, giving her the thumbs up at the same time. Ann laughed at him.

"We'd love to." *Our first real friend here in Greenland. Cool!*

"Mitch, I had no idea you two were having problems out here with large snakes. I saw the one Mark captured and I was stunned, but I thought it was a freak of nature. I couldn't have imagined in a million years there being more. And you two kids out here in the country, new to the area, dealing with the unusual reptiles by yourselves. I feel mighty bad.

"Now I was serious when I said call me for anything. That's my job, I'll be here." Mitch and the sheriff chatted as they strolled to the patrol car.

"Thank you, sheriff."

"Paul."

"Right. Well, it was really nice to meet you, Paul. Thanks for coming out and checking in on us."

"My pleasure. I would stay if I didn't have important business to attend to. But, the deputy will be here later." Paul got into his seat and shut the car door. Rolling down his window he'd had an afterthought.

"Say Mitch, how many of those darn things have you seen, anyhow?"

Leaning down to the window, "I've seen two for sure, possibly three."

"Lord Almighty. And one of 'em knocked you unconscious, huh?"

"Yep. And I had one stick its head in my kitchen window earlier today. I'm telling you Sher...Paul, they're down right menacing when you're this close to them." He made a distance with his hands.

"I'll bet that ain't no fun."

Ain't? Did he just say ain't no? Oh man. If Ann heard him say that... "No it isn't. I can't tell you how glad I am that Mark and Barbara James are spending the night." He began backing up towards the house. He knew the guy needed to go.

"I'll be around. You take care.

"Oh and Mitch, slow that driving down."

"Uh, yeah...Yes Sir," Mitch mumbled, feeling like a kid in trouble, waving stupidly as the sheriff backed down the drive.

Barbara was in what was going to be a dining room, which was empty at the present, standing-up holding the phone to her ear, gazing out the window at Mitch and the sheriff. Actually, this was the third number she'd tried to call and couldn't get an answer, so she was basically listening to the phone on the other end ring.

The numbers James had listed in her pocket-size notebook were hotline numbers. Someone should have picked up each one she dialed. These were to the richest investors in the world. Hard to get attention from, but she'd made the list of callers a couple years ago. There wasn't reason for no one to be answering. She was beginning to wonder what was wrong.

Hanging up, she figured she should call her lab assistants. Maybe they'd heard of something concerning the contacts she had. A change in numerals possibly. That was highly unlikely, though. Dialing the laboratory, Barbara watched Mitch walk back up to the house and the sheriff pull out of the drive, thinking there was surely something rotten in Denmark. Maybe with the FBI on her tail, it was scaring off some would-be backers.

"Steve, Barbara. Tell me you got everything."

"That's a roger. Congratulations, Doctor James."

"Congratulations back at ya. We all did this. Isn't it amazing? Can you believe the perfect imaging we got this time? Our foot is halfway in the door, except for one thing. None of my numbers will work. You know something I don't?"

He didn't answer.

"Steve? You there?"

"Yeah, just a sec. I'm getting something different on the screen. Are you seeing this?"

"No, my monitor broke. There was a slight earthquake and we had to... never mind, just tell me what you're seeing."

"Barbara, where are you?"

"I'm at the Rocks. Why?"

Silence.

"Steve? Steve? Hello? Can you hear me?" Barbara took the phone away from her ear and stared at it. It simply went dead. When she tried to turn it back on it wouldn't work. *Umm. Must have something to do with the quaking.*

"Barbara, we can see the van. If you're anywhere near it, you need to get out of there now. Barbara? Can you hear me? Barbara?" Steve slammed the phone down when he realized they'd been cut off. He looked at Jim worried, shaking his head.

What the two men could see was their modified-snake-eye-lens filming the giant reptilians moving up through a split in the earth where the doctor had been, they deduced since she mentioned a small quake. They were sure of it, when once the snake was on the surface the first thing their videoing showed was the wrecked van. Barely. The amphibian was moving at a pretty good rate of speed.

"What should we do, Steve? If Barbara's in the proximity to where these things are headed, then she could be in some trouble." Steve watched one of the computer screens very carefully. They had different still photos on most and one running the event as it was happening in the now. Jim worked the controls and froze the van's image on his computer.

"What's the GNOME count so far?"

"As far as individuals that this snake has passed, three-hundred-forty-two."

"What about how many surfaced before our friend?"

Jim punched a couple keys. "Nine surfaced ahead of our camera. Can't detect what's following."

"Wait, what's that? Freeze the slide!" Steve saw something he didn't like.

"Son of a bitch...call the FBI. We have no choice." The snakes were aiming to a homestead. He could see part of a foundation. They just didn't know whose, but it didn't matter. They had been instructed by James to react if they suspected trouble.

Chapter forty nine

Mɪᴛᴄʜ ᴄᴀᴍᴇ ʙᴀᴄᴋ ɪɴᴛᴏ the house via the front door, double checking the outside, from the inside, before locking up for the night. He spied Barbara on the phone in the dining room right next to him, acknowledging her on his way by. She signaled she would be just a minute. He gestured okay bringing his thumb and forefinger together in a circle.

Upon entering the kitchen, he said, "Want some help, sweet pea?"

"No thanks, I have it. Sit and relax, Mitch. You've had a trying day. How's your head?"

"I think I'm better. Haven't taken a pain pill for how long now?" He snatched a piece of cheese and stuck it in his mouth as he sat down next to Mark.

Looking at their guest, he said, "I guess you and Barbara will have to share the couch, Mark." Mitch smiled large in a knowing way. Mark grinned, looking sheepishly at him.

The two male humans detected an alien presence just as the mathematician finished teasing the biologist. Mark was facing the doorway, so he saw it when it showed its nostrils. His grin quickly became a frown. He was shocked speechless, his eyes as big as silver dollars.

Mitch had his back to the significant, sinister swine, but he could feel its aura. The all powerful eminence. Gazing at Mark's facial change confirmed his instinct. He slowly turned to see the beast lingering into the kitchen.

Mitch froze when he realized he was the closest to the menacing monstrosity, half twisted in his chair with his neck cranked all the way to the right. The ominous ophidian was coiled at the bottom and the head was stretched to eye level. The snake stared directly into his. All he could think about was how quietly it had snuck up on them, when it was so gigantic. Pretty freaky.

Mark was in complete awe of the surprising company. Not only of the size and the unrealistic nature of the animal, but of the stance it was holding and the curious characteristics it was demonstrating. For a normal black rat snake it would be in an attack mode, but this novel breed seemed to be looking for something. It wasn't a typical snake and even different in behavior from the one they let lose earlier. This wasn't a good sign.

Ann Rock continued scurrying around the kitchen as if nothing was intruding on her life. She was busy making four hungry people a meal to satisfy. Although, she could have noticed the devious vertebrate at any time since it was governing the karma, she subconsciously chose to ignore it.

Barbara was just giving up on making phone calls tonight, strolling back to the kitchen, when she glimpsed something extremely unusual in front of her. A monstrous, black, devilish serpent spooking its way through the kitchen door, twenty feet or more in length, she knew by looking at it. The giant thing more than startled her. Walking up behind it, without ever hearing any kind of noise from the being and certainly not expecting one of the latest reptiles to be in the home, she let out a loud gasp as she stopped dead in her tracks.

The sneaky snake moved with the greatest of speed and used its massive and powerful body to reverse. The corkscrew, overgrown ophiomorphous flipped its tail with force and took Barbara James out in the glint of a falling star. It hit her on the right side of her head sending her flailing to her left, over the family room furniture and up against the wall like a rag doll. She landed with a thud, unconsciousness ruling. Doctor James never had a chance.

Mitch and Mark flew up out of their chairs reacting to the sudden terror. All Mitch could think to do was grab a couple of steak knifes that were next to him on the counter, handing Mark one as they made their way to the doorway. What they saw was unsettling to say the least. The giant, unnatural life form had rapidly slithered on top of Barbara and had her skull to her chest wrapped in several loops with its influential body. The black and purplish skin crept continuously. The head was up as high as their height, watching the two humans as they were gaping, disbelieving the action on the other side of the room, unknowing of what to do. Except they had to try to save the woman.

"Barbara!" Mark yelled, faintly. It was hard to speak right now. Time seemed to stand still. His thinking was idle. The love of his life was about to be strangled or crushed. He had to do something, although he was iced in fear. First time in his life.

He knew the horrific was ominous, looming, but at the same time he abruptly realized it was an exceptionally intelligent creature. The slits grew bigger he noticed in his fiery dread, meaning to him it was hesitating in its decision to kill. He kept his focus on the part of the body covering Barbara's face, while looking into the eyes of the slick, quick, grandiose trouble. It wasn't squeezing her to death yet. It was waiting. But, he wasn't sure if she could breathe and whether or not the surreal would know that.

Okay, Mark. This thing can think. Get over it. Try to communicate. Or do something you dork. Why does its skin crawl and what does that mean? Could it be a clue to a weakness? Damn it.

The snakes have never hurt Ann.

Ann. She has to be the answer.

"Ann!" He took his eyes off the atrocity and glanced to her. She was still cooking. *Man, that's weird.*

"Mitch, get your wife in here, now!" he demanded, while stepping a few feet into the room, knife held up in a threatening manner. He guessed he would try to use it if he could. But when he made his move, hoping him and Mitch could kill it, the snake followed him with those creepy yellow eyes and the body curled tighter around Barbara.

"Shit, Mitch! Drag her in here, damn it! It's killing Barbara!" He took a swipe at the monster, willing his courage and his own strength to win the day. The slippery dominant slinked its neck and he missed.

The snake quickly curled forward after the dodge and butted Mark with its vast head, in the stomach. He tried to move faster than the reptilian, but it was impossible. He went down to his knees just a foot or so in front of the ungodly.

Mitch's eyes were about to bulge out of his face seeing how fast the astonishing organism could strike. He was in complete and utter horror; however, he was able to react. "Ann, get over here now!" His voice was commanding. It startled Ann out of her project and she turned to look at her husband with a baffled look covering her face.

"We're in trouble! Get over here!" Ann slowly put the hot-pad down and ambled over to him, even though she was in one of her trances. It was the fear and emergency tone in her husband's voice that forced her to move, endearing her subconscious desire to disregard what was happening to let her conscious mind react. She wasn't completely aware of her environment. Only of Mitch's cry for help.

The minute she was in reach, which Christ Almighty Mitch thought took an eternity for her to get that close, he grabbed her with force and pulled her into view of the snake.

"Ann! Look at it!" She was staring at him, her eyes glassy. Mitch was insistent. He knew it was Barbara's only chance, to have Ann remember why the snakes from hell didn't hurt her.

Mark was catching his breath and carefully backing away from the snake, trying to stand back up. He could see Barbara begin to show signs of life. Her legs were moving slightly and her hands reached for the hideous body wrapped around her being.

He shouted, "Ann! You have to help her! She's going to die!" In that instant Mitch took hold of his wife's head and jerked her to face the carnivore that was in murdering mode. Ann's eyes gradually became connected with those of the beast. But her attentiveness of the situation remained secret from her cognizant mind. She simply looked at it, unmoving.

"Ann, you have to remember! It's her only chance. The snakes never hurt you, Ann. Why? Please remember!" Mark was desperate.

"Ann, the baby's in trouble!" Mitch was playing the only cards he knew. "Do something. You have to save our child's life! Oh God Ann, please!"

Barbara began to struggle intensely with the slick, smooth body of the outrageous. Her feet were kicking and she was twisting at the hips, the rest of her engulfed by the massive. Mark made another effort, jumping at the impious slug with the knife in forward motion.

When Mitch realized Mark was making another attempt, he also reacted. He lunged toward the ophidia, his blade also ready. The huge, ugly head went down in a flicker and in one solid shift, slid suddenly across the room striking each man at the knees, knocking them down. Both let out a whimper. Mitch rolled as he hit the floor. Mark stayed where he landed growing more and more upset. James was dying and he couldn't save her. Her struggle was becoming violent. She was suffocating and he knew it.

"Ann! You have to help Barbara. I can't do it! Please, Ann!" This was hard on Mark. He was losing his composure, starting to cry.

Ann watched the action taking place, completely thrown. She could see Barbara's fight, but not the oversized snake. And she saw her husband rolling in her peripheral vision. She could hear Mark's grunt and pleas for help. But she remained mystified as to why.

The baby's not born yet. How could he or she be in trouble? I don't understand what Mitch wants me to do.

What's wrong with Barbara? Why is Mark yelling at me? Why is Mitch on the ground and what caused him to fall?

I'm fixing dinner.

The entire time these thoughts were going through her mind her eyeballs were gripped on the huge orphiormorphs. It now focused on her. Still pinching the life out of Barbara, the gigantic snake raised once more and made eye contact with Ann. The pupils again became bigger.

I want to remember. I don't want the baby to be hurt. I don't want to be crazy.

Tears began to roll down her cheeks as she stood there trying to summon her nerve and fortitude. *Be tough, Ann. You have to get used to varmints if you're going to live in the country. I can't let a dumb snake scare me away from my home.*

It was the word *snake* that brought Ann back into realization. Very slowly she remembered the eyes staring at her from within the water of the toilet. She was sick and needed to puke. But there were large black slits surrounded by yellow, gazing at her.

Ann remained motionless, while she watched from her side view, Barbara's struggle with the giant reptile stop. As her hands drifted to her sides and her legs became still, Ann gradually began to recollect the mother of all snakes on the roof, coming down and touching her face in the driveway. She could picture the nasty thing slowing sneaking away from her.

Ann was alert to the fact that Mitch was groaning. His head was already bad and now he could barely withstand the pain throbbing from temple to temple. She could tell. They were married and had been together a long time. Ann wanted to rush to his aid, but couldn't. She didn't know why.

When Mark begged again desperately for her help, sobbing freely now and seemingly in agony, her mind remembered the reptile that peeked in their window. And she also unexpectedly remembered the scary snake in the bedroom. She could see her husband getting walloped upside the head.

Fear began returning deep down into the depths of her being.

The scream that came from Ann in that very instant, overwhelmed the chilling evil taking place in her home. She stood still gutting out the misery in her heart and fright that grasped her clear through to her bones. The past images filled her mind. And the snake that was now terrorizing her beloved husband and best friends came into focus. Ann never took her eyes off the giant creature that choked the life from Barbara James. The snake in the present, she now realized that had just hurt her man.

Ann could finally see what was happening in front of her. She instantly understood Mark and Mitch's pleas for her help. She knew the amphibian wouldn't hurt her if she just kept blaring in high pitch. One thing she had no problem doing since she was incredibly afraid at this very moment. But she would face it. She would never be so pathetic again in her life if it meant her child could get hurt one day. Ann held onto the courage she beckoned from God. She now understood she needed her fear.

The huge and strong reptile responded to her in a heartbeat. The unreal let loose of Barbara and in a flash was directly in front of Ann. Coiled at the bottom, its body S shaped, the head and eyes eyelevel glaring straight into hers. It was almost touching her face as before.

Mark and Mitch watched, unmoving and in wonder of the spectacle.

Barbara gasped for air and rolled onto her side trying to regain reality. She tried to see what was happening and comprehend her environment, except she was dazed from her near death experience and was having a problem focusing her own eyesight, let alone breathe.

The snake began hissing at Ann. Different from before. It was louder and sounded with substance, like a scratchy whistling noise. As if it was trying to imitate her. The two beings were at a stand off of sorts. It was purely astounding.

In the very next time frame, Deputy Doug crashed open the front door, his gun drawn. He moved with haste. He had been making a drive by, shining his light around the land when he heard Ann's ferocious, thunderous ear-splitting screaming. But he became ineffective due to the bombshell he faced and stood immobile in the doorway, taken by such a revolting surprise, yet pointing the weapon at the implausible, unsure of how to precede. Unusual for him; however, this was an extremely unusual circumstance.

The inconceivable beast turned its head and spied the man with those weird eyes. The animal flicked its tongue and shook its tail making a booming noise, shaking the house like the earthquake, scaring everyone even more. But before Doug could pull the trigger or do anything, it hoisted its colossal and powerful body past Ann and into the kitchen, using its head to break the window and escape. The profane was gone as fast as that. The real life nightmare over.

For the time being that is.

Chapter fifty

"WHAT...IN THE NAME of God...is going on?" Doug maintained his stance, now pointing his gun at Ann since she was behind the snake to begin with from his position, unintentionally. In fact, they were all staring at her. She had stopped with the acute screaming and was breathing heavily, tears flowing freely. She couldn't move either. No one could until the initial stun wore off.

Mark was immensely relieved when the snake let loose of Barbara. He knew she was grasping for air, alive, but couldn't comfort her, because he was subsequently engrossed in the impossible bizarre taking place in front of his eyes. It all happened unbelievably fast, yet he was affirmative the snake was trying to communicate with Ann. *Wow.*

Catching his rationale, before anyone else, he looked over to the woman he was positive he would marry. He never once dreamed he could care for someone so much that he would be capable of losing control of his poise. Water ran down her face as freely as Ann's did. She quit with the coughing and gasping and began breathing at a fairly regular pace. She would be fine, he instinctively knew it.

Barbara glanced at Mark. She'd never actually experienced a close call like this. She'd been hurt in the field before and had been through some harrowing times, but she was embarking on a white light a minute ago and it certainly had a profound impact on her wits. She realized she loved the man staring back at her right now with all her heart. Barbara couldn't imagine being without him. From the hint in his eyes, she knew he felt the same way.

"I'm okay," she whispered. Her voice was a bit raw.

Mark smiled. "I know. You wouldn't be in the game if you couldn't take a few falls, right?" Barbara couldn't help her grin. He did keep his sense of humor in traumatic situations. She cherished that about him.

Mitch wanted very much to get up and hold his wife, he just couldn't. The pounding he was taking in his head was too much to bear. It hurt to even keep his eyes open. She was crying, but he couldn't be a man. And when she needed him the most.

This was the worst feeling in the world to Mitch Rock. He was powerless.

Ann's mind was going nuts. *I did it* – was her biggest revelation. She remembered everything and stopped the large, ugly slithering creature from killing Barbara. Everyone was okay, thanks to her. She faced her deepest most inner fears and saved the day. Ann was so damn proud of herself. Aside the issue that her heart was racing awfully quickly, from the enormous amount of fright she'd experienced.

Ann let herself cry. She deserved to.

While Ann stood there collecting her mind, she suddenly remembered Mitch wasn't okay. She needed to call upon more mental toughness and use her inherited grit to help him. She knew she could. At that precise moment, Ann was glad she was a strong person. And this recent test of her resolve had proved to her, without a doubt, she could handle any situation she was confronted with. It was a good feeling. Especially since she was having a baby.

Finally, her breathing seemed back to normal. The first thing she said was, "Deputy, please put your gun down."

He did. Doug was staggered when he comprehended what he was doing. Standing there in a very unprofessional manner, shocked stupid by a gruesome reptile. Her request jolted him out of his coma. He practically ran over to Ann.

"Are you alright?"

Mark was clued in to Mitch's problem and was crawling on his hands and knees to where he lay in pain. Barbara was shaking off her physical and emotional trip and was stumbling over to the man, too.

"Doug, call an ambulance."

Ann was at Mitch's side in the next beat, down on her knees hovering over him. "Sweetie, it's going to be okay. We're going to get you help. Hold on." She grabbed his hand and squeezed it. He tried to squeeze it back, but he was rapidly losing his bearings.

Mark put his hand on her shoulder. "You did it, Ann. You hear that Mitch, your wife's a hero." Ann gave him a worried look. Her thoughts about saving the day were gone. The only thing important to her now was her husband.

Barbara checked Mitch's pulse and then placed her hand on his forehead, to see if he had a fever. She didn't know why. She was just trying to help. The bump on her face was beginning to swell and it was possible she didn't have all of her reason about her.

The giant amphibians from down under were secretly surrounding the Rock homestead, hidden in the dark of night. There must have been fifty or more of the Phylum lurking about, closing in on the unsuspecting people inside. The audacious were roaming as close as the front door, which was left open.

Several climbed the house, while others hung in the trees. The black snakes all looked the same. The head propelled their motion, all of them slithering in that twisting type of way. And they made no noise as they crept closer and closer.

"They're on the way." Doug announced, now bending over the other four. "He gonna be okay?"

"I think it's a migraine," Barbara announced. She looked to Ann trying to comfort her.

"He's never had one before."

"Could be from the blow he took yesterday and then again..." She didn't really know.

Doug's radio went off. "Sheriff?"

231

One of the creepy slinked in behind the humans. It glided effortlessly through the entryway and then raised its head to spy the people. Its body was upside the corner of the wall, almost unseen even if someone was looking. The eyes slits widened as it watched.

A second Squamata came down from the attic and hung on the staircase, curved around the banister several times; however, the neck held its S shape higher than the rest of the squirming physical substance. It, too, scouted the five foreigners in its view. The remarkably black skin with the touch of purple was in constant motion.

"How long will it take the ambulance to get here?" Ann asked, extremely worried about Mitch's condition. His eyes were closed and he moaned softly.

"Should be here in nothing flat," Doug reported.

Mark said, "Hang on buddy," as he started to get up. He needed to get off the floor at some point he decided, a little hurt from the powerful snake's forceful blows.

A siren blazed in the distance.

Barbara stood up with Mark, both of them a bit shaky. "We should probably wait outside." Noticing his slow and premeditated movements, she then asked, "You hurt?"

Hating to confess, "A little. That damn thing packs a punch. What about you? You took a pretty good rap. It knocked you out." Mark was favoring his left side.

"I can't feel anything right now. The adrenaline I guess."

"You need to have your face looked at, get some ice on it or something."

"I think we all need to see a doctor."

Suddenly, Mark had that funny tickle go down the back of his spine. He quickly turned to spy the room. A little too quickly. He hurt his neck and he groaned, grabbing a hold of the back of it. But he didn't see anything unusual. He'd had a weird feeling that he was being watched, though.

The sirens were blaring next to the front door about this time.

Which had scared off Mother Nature's newest inhabitants.

Chapter fifty one

SHERIFF PAUL STONE HAD a strange inkling on his way into town. He decided to take the other road on a whim. The old dirt path that would bring him around the back way. He would end up a block behind the main street, close to his office.

He was glad he did, too, when he saw the FBI over-running his sheriff station. He parked the vehicle out of sight and got out, niggling his way to a window. He wanted to see what was going on, what they were doing without being detected. Stealing a look, raising his head up just enough after removing his hat, he spied three agents.

One of them was on the phone, while the other two stood chatting. Paul eaves' dropped on the conversations taking place. Because as luck would have it, the window was cracked. He could hear the guy on the phone ordering the Army reserves to report to Greenland immediately. He said something about combat duty.

The other two coats were discussing the evacuation of the township. They conversed about the large reptiles and the reasoning behind their decision to block all roads leading into town. That they didn't want this to get out. If no one was here to see what they were about to do, then they could contain the problem from the rest of the world.

Paul listened intently trying to understand the gist of the meaning. It sounded to him like they were bringing in troops to take out the large snakes Mark was talking about earlier. He thought this was very odd. How many could there be? To call the Army?

When they mentioned Doctor Barbara James being a problem, the sheriff made the assessment to warn Gordon, right away. He did an about take and hurriedly proceeded to his car, carefully and slyly. Paul also felt that this was a serious enough situation to enlist the neighboring counties. But, he knew he shouldn't use his radio. It was most likely being monitored.

Climbing into his car, he heard the unmistakable roar of helicopters in the distance. That was certainly fast and suspicious. This must have been planned for a longer period of time than just a second ago. The Army was probably waiting in the wings, waiting for the go ahead. Why? Paul was beginning to get apprehensive about the situation.

The sheriff determined he'd better be smarter than these fellows were. He needed to get out of town without being spotted, so he could go live with the information. Good thing he'd lived here all of his life. He would indeed make that broadcast. Paul Stone was a man of his word. Only now, it would be to a larger audience. He knew exactly who to go to.

At the same time he took off, without his headlights on, he heard the deputy call for help over the two-way, from out at the Rock's home. He thought for a moment. The FBI would probably expect him to contact his deputy to find out what was going on. He quickly picked up his radio and appealed to Doug.

"Deputy, what seems to be the problem? Over."

"Sheriff, we had a run-in with one of the...uh...large black snakes. Mitch Rock is down. Over."

"Is it serious? Over."

"I don't think so. Can't really tell. Uh...everyone out here is shook-up, though. I'm making all of them go to the hospital to be checked. Over."

"Good, I'll meet you there. Over."

The sheriff hoped to possibly buy himself some time. He didn't really have the intention to go. Couldn't take the chance now. He had to make the fast decision of whether to warn Gordon or get this news out to the public. He knew he wouldn't have the time to do both.

Paul didn't like the bureau taking over his town and he automatically assumed it meant him as well. He went for the neighboring county in his haste and would just have to wish it was the right thing to do. Stepping on the gas, he headed toward the cornfields.

Sheriff Paul was taking all the old roads zig zagging through the farmland, in and out of the crops when need be. He could see the major highway all the while. And there were numerous trucks storming into his municipality. He had no idea what they were for. It was crazy. However so, he kept his mind focused on his job as he made his way out of Greenland.

Chapter fifty two

THE AMBULANCE CREW RACED into the Rock home arriving in record time. The man and woman paramedics were effective and efficient. They had Mitch strapped on the stretcher in nothing flat, IV in place, then talked with Ann, Barbara and Mark about their injuries as they were loading him into the vehicle. It was decided they would all go the hospital in the ambulance and/or in the deputy's car.

Ann rode with Mitch. Mark and Barbara went with Doug. The trip was short and uneventful. The hospital wasn't busy and the same emergency room doctor that took care of Mitch previously, examined all of them, dishing out a few painkillers to Gordon and James and treating Mitch for his migraine like pain in his head. The doctor wanted him to spend the night so he could keep an eye on him.

Next he did a blood test on Ann to verify her pregnancy and told her firmly, she needed rest. He would put Mitch in a double bedded room where she could get some shut eye, too. Mitch would probably be spent for the night, he explained and if she couldn't go to sleep he would give her a mild sedative.

"Don't worry about your husband. He'll be good as new in no time."

Mark, Ann, Doug and Barbara all followed Mitch down the hall, who was being wheeled to his room on a hospital bed by the doctor, who was ordering the nurses to bring food and drinks. The two were more than happy to be of service. It was a boring night.

Once Mitch was set, the emergency doctor wanted to know everything there was to know about the snakes. He sat with the five and had a sandwich with them, asking questions and listening, disturbed by Mark and Barbara's tale. Ann lay on her bed, weary from her remembrances a while ago, also interested in everything they had to say. And Mitch was sleeping peacefully just as the doc had said he would.

Barbara and Mark were excited, despite the fact that she was almost strangled to death and he was a little banged up. The two were positive the snakes had a higher than expected intelligence level and that they were undeniably trying to connect with Ann Rock. Mark projected that the pregnancy and her hormones, based on his early assumption that the snakes communicated with pheromones all the time, not just when mating, was the reason they were interested in her. And the reason they did not hurt her.

The biologists were thrilled with the idea of studying this new race. Maybe learning a way to actually live among them without fear, interrelate with the strange, somehow. Barbara wanted to figure out a way to use Ann's scent or whatever, in order to be around them.

They dissected the fantastic event that took place. How the one overgrown reptile didn't kill Barbara right away and instead watched and reacted to Mark's actions. The difference in the slits or pupils' size meaning. The way it amazingly listened to Ann's scream and then tried to imitate it. How the thing recognized it was in danger when the deputy pointed a gun at it and then the amazing escape. The incredible sight before that, when it shook its tail, and how domineering it seemed.

They talked about the numbers of the gigantic brood they spotted with the eye-cam on the rogue and how fast they travel. The achievable depth of the earth they could have originally came from and speculated on why now the unfamiliar decided to surface. Mark and Barbara didn't bother to delve into the other theory – about the government's potential experiment causing the new Class. And whether or not they were worldwide. Because it didn't matter any longer. Whatever the reason on the how and the why was a moot point. The race existed, period.

Doug questioned if they should warn the town, now, not later. Mark and Barbara agreed they should immediately, but said the sheriff was supposed to make an emergency announcement. About that time they began to wonder what happened to that idea and where the man was.

An hour into the hype there was a knock at the door. Before anyone could ask who it was, four men entered. Two suits and two fatigued. They were not friendly looking or acting. They wanted Barbara James and Mark Gordon to come with them.

Doug was already apprehensive, before they entered, because the sheriff never showed and he didn't radio with alternate plans. It was unusual for him not to be where he said he was going to be. So when Doug got a load of the muscle these orangutans were trying to pull, he was suddenly positive the sheriff must be on to something. He had a notion using the two-way wouldn't be wise.

The deputy interceded on Mark and Barbara's plight. He figured he couldn't really do anything, except maybe he could find out a hint as to what these butt's were doing. He stood up immediately and walked over to them, shoulders back, chest out, with a serious attitude.

"I'd like to see your identification, all four of you." His posture was sturdy. Gordon and James were still sitting, dumbfounded. At least he thought they were. They'd been pretty informative the last thirty minutes. Doug believed he knew all that they did.

The men obliged. Doug took his time studying the ID's. "What do you want with them?"

"Miss James," one of the suits talked around the deputy. "Your partners called us to intervene on your behalf." Barbara's eyes became wild with worry. She'd completely forgotten her and Steve had been cut off earlier. He must have thought she was in trouble.

Why would he think I was in trouble? What did he say before he hung up?

"Please come with us, now. We've already seized your laboratory. If you want to avoid any..."

Barbara was off her chair in a split second, livid. She was at the man's throat who just spoke to her, in his face, yelling. "You have no right! You egotistical obtuse asshole!" Gordon jumped up and grabbed her shoulders.

"Come on, Barbara, calm down. Let's just go with them and find out what's going on." He knew they needed to cooperate as the men wanted, if they were to learn anything about their involvement in the creation of a new Kingdom. Barbara needed to be in control of her emotions in this very critical time.

She unwillingly reigned in her anger and did what Mark wanted.

"Ann, I'll be back to check on you two." Mark winked at her. She had sat up pretty darn fast when the men entered. However, she kept quiet.

"Try to get some rest."

That was it. They left with the men, however strange.

The doctor and the deputy eyed one another. Things were not right in their town. But, that was the argument; it was *their* town. They needed to discover whatever they could and take immediate action. Protect the citizens.

The doctor told Ann he'd be back to look in on her later, meantime she could ring for the nurses if she needed anything. Then he stepped outside the door with Doug, shutting it behind him. Ann glanced over to her husband, before she laid back down, closing her eyes and drifting into la la land, instantaneously. She was too tired to understand the importance.

"I'm going to follow them," Doug said.

"Okay, I'll call the mayor and see what I can find out. Where do you suppose Paul is?"

"That's a good question, but if he hasn't contacted me, then there is a reason, so I won't try to get a hold of him, say if he's undercover. The sheriff said over open frequency earlier he would be here and I suspect since he never showed, he's having trouble with his mission of informing the public and had to go to an ulterior plan." Doug was matter-of-fact. The sheriff was a smart man. He was doing what was right for the people and Doug knew it, whatever it was.

The two good guys shook hands before Doug left, promising to keep one another advised.

Chapter fifty three

As Mark and Barbara were escorted outside and into a black suburban, they noticed the men in green guarding the streets. And while they drove to wherever they were going – no one was saying a word – they saw the citizens being forced to leave, out of the south side of town, ropes and tanks blocking off certain streets. All being made to take a certain exit in their cars.

It was bizarre. It looked like the community was in a war zone. These people weren't here an hour ago. How in the hell does the government do things like this, Mark wondered. In all veracity, it was creepy. The clout and supremacy this commanded along with the domination principle was hard to take in stride, to say the least. For his town to be taken over in one hour was certainly humbling, as well as maddening. And apparently there wasn't anything he could do, but cooperate with the thugs. *Unbelievable.*

A little ways outside of town, Mark and Barbara could see their destination. A couple of extraordinary yellow tents were set up in the middle of a farmer's crop of what used to be corn. Looked like the field was harvested early. Typical stuff you see in the movies, Barbara thought to herself. She and Mark hadn't as much as whispered a word to one another, but she knew he was thinking the same thing she was. That the government definitely created this newest earth family. They were probably carting them off to convince them to keep their mouths shut. She rolled her eyes at her own ideas, still dealing with her frustrations over the current matter.

Mark was staring absorbedly at the same thing Barbara was. He was more worried about her than he was himself. The agents had said they'd taken her lab under federal security. Why? He felt like he knew. It was because she discovered their experiment and they didn't want the news to get out. How in the world would they keep these large, fast growing and in need of food, rapid offspring producing, cunning, thinking and communicating creatures a secret from the rest of civilization? He had suspected all along the reptiles could be worldwide anyway, so this didn't make sense. *Do the thick even know how intelligent these reptiles are?*

The duo was led out of the vehicle and into one of the modern, portable canvas shelters. Doctor James figured they'd have a giant hole dug in the ground with futuristic ladders leading downwards and men in gray sealed jumpsuits looking for the beast, just like in that one movie. *What was the name of it?* But as she walked further into the place, she didn't see anything like that.

The temporary building held some long cafeteria style tables and a lot of metal chairs. There were men working telephone cells and busy doing paperwork. Or something. It wasn't interesting or impressive at all. Mostly military personnel. Some computers.

"Boring," Barbara said, under her breath. She was only getting more and more irate at these rude and obnoxious people.

"You okay?" Mark whispered. He noticed her fuming beneath the skull. Once more he marveled how she kept her cool all these years and got to where she did. Then again, he wasn't the one who just lost his life's work. He had a notion she wasn't going to agree to remain quiet. Could mean trouble. Of course, he'd be there for her no matter what happened next.

The two were ushered into a plastic enclosure and the make-shift door was shut behind them. They were alone, imprisoned so to speak.

"No, I am not okay! These imbeciles took away my lab. They can't do that." She was pissed.

"Barbara, remain calm so you can think of the bigger picture. Understand?" Mark figured they were being overheard.

"Fine. I'll be calm." She exaggerated her words. "But this is still my discovery!" Barbara was stubborn. And not really calm.

"I'm sorry, darling," Mark said, moving over to her. "I'm behind you one hundred percent. It's just that we obviously can't do anything right now. Let's not **say** something we might regret." Mark wished she'd get the drift without him having to come out and tell her that they were being listened to or shut-up already. He reached to put his arms around her. He'd never had the chance to hug her after her ordeal. Just thinking about the serpent strangling her made his heart hurt.

She batted him away. "I'm too angry and upset, I'm sorry. This sucks!" Barbara stomped around the tiny area glancing out the windowed enclosure. Her arms were crossed. A sure fire sign of her growing aggravation.

Mark understood. "Will you marry me?"

It just popped out. He didn't know why now, but it didn't matter. Their lives may never be normal again. Why not ask?

Barbara flung around to look at him, her brown eyes wide with shock. She uncrossed her arms and stood there with them hanging at her sides, her mouth opened. "What?"

"You heard me."

"I...but...uh I...well...umm...shit....Mark?

"Now? What about...ug...Jesus...I...don't...know...uh..." She stared at him grinning at her, completely bowled over. Common sense was trying to rule, but in her heart she wanted to say yes immediately. It just wasn't coming out. Barbara was struck dumb and it showed. This was certainly a surprise. She was fuming mad a second ago and now she couldn't even think of why. Mark Gordon had completely diffused the situation and she was more than a little dazed.

The two locked gazes. Neither approached the other. Barbara maintained her stupefied expression, while Mark held his crazy smile. They were a perfect match.

About this time they heard explosions sounding in the near distance.

Doug crudely pursued the suburban. He wasn't going to hide the cold stone element that he was following. Or that he wanted to know what was going down. This was his homestead after all and he wouldn't be ragged. Of course, the feds hadn't told him a thing so far or the sheriff either, for that matter. But that didn't mean he couldn't stumble upon their enigma, or at least be a thorn in their sides.

When he saw the Jefferson's farming land, he was mad as a bucking bronco. The brass destroyed their produce and these unsightly, bright yellows tents were covering their once beautiful income. *That's not right.*

"Who do they think they are?" he said to himself, pulling up to the gates behind the other vehicle. A pair in gear strolled over to him, proper.

"Deputy, mind parking your car on the left, over there..." the man pointed. "...so we can keep order?"

"Oh sure, anything I can do to cooperate with you gentlemen." He was being sarcastic.

"Thank you." They nodded as he drove in. He rolled his eyes.

Doug kept an eye out scoping anything he could espy. He walked on in the first tent as if he owned the joint. Then he watched daring when they took Gordon and the woman to another place, but sat down where they asked him to. He waited, while one of them brought some coffee and then listened when the suits began explaining.

The deputy didn't like what he was hearing. He sure in the hell wished the sheriff was around right about now. They weren't asking him to make a decision or anything. Just to understand this was top secret information his government was sharing and they expected him to keep it that way. He got their gist. Doug had a feeling he'd wind up dead if he did talk.

And they needed his allegiance, because he would have to explain something different to the town folk when they were allowed back into the limits. When that would be they didn't say. Doug never agreed or disagreed. He only said, "Yes" when they asked if he understood or not.

Doug became suspicious of the reasoning behind killing the surprising, practicably inconceivable snakes. That is not how they did things here in Kansas. It wasn't that he wanted the unexplained novel animals in his backyard, but around these parts they would in the very least, study the darn things first. Maybe capture them and move them, if they were extremely dangerous, to another place where they could survive. They weren't in the habit of killing a species of whatever, just because they didn't like them. Hell, mountain lions, bears, you name it, could all be extinct if man were animals in that way.

He began thinking about everything Mark and Barbara had said. They were both elated at the prospect of a new breed of amphibians. They thought if people left the snakes alone, they wouldn't hurt anyone. If it's true, they weren't sure after what happened, but that's the point. Shouldn't they find out first? Before destroying an entire populace? He also had a notion the government was responsible for this mysterious company of late.

Doug flinched when he heard the first boom.

Chapter fifty four

Aɴɴ Rᴏᴄᴋ ᴡᴀs ᴊᴀʀʀᴇᴅ ᴏᴜᴛ of her safe and peaceful slumber with the sound of mortar shells dropping from the sky. She dashed out of that hospital bed and over to the window, instantly wide awake.

"Oh my God!" The blasts were coming from the direction of her house. She could see the helicopters flying overhead. When she furiously looked down to the street, she saw several of the tanks roaming, engulfing, this once nice town. And there were no people in sight other than the GI Joes' marching in sync with the armor.

"Mitch! Mitch, wake up!" She turned and went to his side and started shaking him. He didn't budge. Mitch was in a deep, deep sleep. She hurriedly checked though, using her hand to feel for his breath. He was alive. Probably fine, she decided, thinking she was being silly. The nurses did come in and look in on him periodically.

Making a rash decision to find out what was going on near her residence, Ann yanked her shoulder bag off the floor, running out of the room and down the hall. She spotted the militia guarding the elevators right away and came to an abrupt halt, ducking to one side, so they wouldn't see her. *Shit*. Ann's instinct told her to avoid these guys. She bet they were also watching the steps.

Quietly, hunching down, Ann sneaked back into the small room. She shut the door softly, so as to avoid noise. She looked at Mitch sleeping soundly, while tiptoeing to the window. Ann forced it open. It hadn't been open for a long time she knew, because it was hard to do and it took all her might. But she did it.

Spying the casing, she saw the emergency staircase directly under her. Except it wasn't as close as she would have liked. Taking in an encouraging breath and telling herself not to be afraid, Ann began to crawl through the window. It was tricky to maneuver out and down, feet first, while trying to get a footing on the steel shaft. However, she maintained her endurance.

The explosions yonder were even louder now. Ann tried to get a good look at the overall bearing of the tumult. She hesitated in her James Bond fashion, while she twisted her neck. To her, it looked as if it was specifically her house that was being bombed. It wasn't like the neighbors were close together out there.

Feeling the panic and craze within, Ann forced her movements. When she did hit the first step of the fire escape with both feet, it made a sudden deafening noise. The entire set of stairs fell to ground level causing an enormous racket. Ann held on to the window seal for dear life, her heart racing from the fright.

The steel was still under her, it was only that the ladders of steps had been secured together and they let loose with her weight. She guessed they were supposed to do that.

Gees, that scared me.

Waiting a moment to see if any of the armed bodies heard the sound, possibly busting through the door any time, before she let go of her support, Ann took one last look at Mitch. Poor thing really took a hammering the last two days, she thought to herself. I hope he'll be all right.

"Love you, sweetie. Be safe," she whispered.

Sighing with relief that she didn't appear to alarm anyone, she slowly let go and now holding her breath, she cautiously bent downwards. Her hands reached to find the bar to hang on to and steady herself with, for the three flight trek back to the planet. Ann had always hated heights. In fact, Mitch always wanted to go to Six Flags and she wouldn't. It would have been a waste of money since she knew there was no way he'd get her on one of the rides. She remembered how he used to rib her about that.

This memory relaxed her some. Ann kept her eyes focused on the window, until she could grasp the railing, very carefully. Then she gazed down and placed her foot on the next step. Slowly, she did the same with the right one, then again the left and so on, until she hit pavement. Her hands and legs were shaking incredibly bad from being tense, when she was finally able to let go.

Whew.

Once she was done with that task, Ann took a furious look around. She wasn't sure how she was going to get to her house. Did she chance the walk? Not seeing any means of transportation and taking a second look at the patrol, she thought that yes, she would have to walk or run, duh. No other cars were even on the road. Thank God she had put her tennis shoes on tonight.

Hidden in the shadow of the building, Ann crept to a parked car and hid behind it, continuously gazing about, before heading down an empty street. She kept up a pretty good pace as she ran, glad she kept up with her workouts over the years. And she was thinking and planning at the same time. Once she made the end of this street, she could cut through the backs of the houses and end up on the dirt road that led to her home. But Ann wasn't exactly sure how she was going to remain unseen. She worried about it; however, never hesitated in her undertaking. Her orange bag flopped on her back as she went.

Ann made it through town and to the street leading to her house without a problem. But once she got to the four corners, she realized it was being heavily scrutinized. Sneaking a look from behind a trash dumpster close by, she watched the array of trucks, tanks and vehicles, heading down her road.

Just as the idea entered her creative mind, one of what looked to be a camouflaged dump truck, came roaring past her. She went with her impulse and sprinted towards it, grabbing hold of the tail end and jumping up on the tailgate. It was easy. She could only hope she wouldn't be seen.

As the truck rolled passed the guys in uniform, Ann made herself as small as she could, crunching into a ball, except for her arms gripping the tailgate above her. It was kind of hard to hang on this way, but if it worked she didn't have to run the rest of the five miles.

It did. The two soldiers never even turned around to check the back of the vehicle.

Chapter fifty five

THE SHERIFF'S CAR WAS POUNDING down stalks one minute and soaring onto the highway the next, no headlights. The Monte Carlo SS converted, came barreling out of the cornfield at a rate of about fifty miles per hour. Which was fast considering the driving conditions. It hit the asphalt road with a bump and a thud, the tires squealing, burning rubber as they grabbed hold.

Paul Stone punched the gas pedal to the floor, while he held tightly to the wheel, keeping control of the steering. The car tilted from side to side momentarily, but was soon speeding smoothly down Interstate 60. Nice car.

The sheriff missed the road block by about a mile, now on his way to Mission County. His best friend and hunting buddy, Sheriff Arnold, was who he expected help from. They'd known each other for years.

Paul went ahead and flipped on his lights, thinking he was most definitely out of sight of anyone who cared. He was getting more and more angry as he drove. This sheriff didn't like having to tiptoe out of his town. As he drove and thought about the situation the car hit a hundred miles per hour.

Sheriff Stone couldn't understand why the government would swing into his place unannounced, uninvited and unwanted and then try to keep him in the dark. All over a bunch of snakes to boot. He could have handled the problem. Probably knew more about the critters than any of these officials, anyhow.

Once he finally drove into the limits of the next county, just minutes from Hayden at that speed, the sheriff let up on the gas. Checking the time, he decided to go straight to the house of his colleague, figuring the guy was home for the evening. Paul absolutely did not want to use his radio unless he had to.

It wasn't long before he was parked and out of his SS, walking up the steps to the two-story home. He rang the bell, then waited. The sheriff's face was grim under his hat. He glanced around the yard and neighborhood as he stood there.

When the door opened, Bob Arnold greeted him soberly, instead of enthusiastically as usual. "Paul, I've been expecting you. Come on in."

Paul was a bit perplexed by his behavior. Suspecting he knew something, he said, "Maybe we should talk out here, Bob?"

"That'll work." Bob strolled out of the house and onto his large wood porch. His manner was cautious and deliberate. He held eye contact with Paul when he began to explain why it was he knew the sheriff would be visiting.

"FBI has already been in contact with me." No reason to sugar coat anything, he felt. Paul's eyes narrowed.

"Now let me tell you what they told me, before you get all out of sorts," he quickly added. "And I know you're probably steaming mad, Paul, but just hear me out. Because good buddy, you don't have a choice."

Paul's jaws clinched. "I'm listening."

"Alright, here's what I know. First the feds figured you'd come to me. They know everything there is to know about us. I don't like it any more than you do. The way I see it, is we might as well do what they want. We'd be fighting a losing battle." Bob paused for a minute, while the two sat down on the outdoor wicker furniture, Paul sighing heavily, clearly unhappy with what he was hearing.

"The government created the snakes. They're going to dispose of them. They want it kept quiet and your job is in jeopardy if you don't cooperate. As far as the town kin, whenever they're permitted back into their homes our story is this; chemical spill on the main highway. We'll tell them that's why the good citizens were evacuated out of Greenland via the old bypass. All the people forced to leave are set up in a temporary shelter over in Junction City." Bob Arnold was direct all the time.

Sheriff Stone eyed his pal, before saying anything. He respected Bob as much as he liked him as a friend and law enforcer. Except it wasn't his town getting taken over.

"What if it was..." he didn't get a chance to finish.

"Already thought about it. Your hands are tied. Mine are tied, period. Plus, we cooperate now, it could help us in the future. It's not wise to piss off the government. You know that."

"Yeah...right." He shook his head, while absorbing this information, disliking and not approving, but understanding what was said.

"What else do you know, Bob?"

"The snakes surrounding Greenland are not fully grown. They are dangerous, were generated to be, and in about another six months its speculated they will start killing larger animals, such as deer. Something about how fast the normal ecosystem will change, thus life as we know it could come to a devastating end if the animals live.

"Look Paul, the officials admit they are the cause of this mess. Greenland will be rebuilt with their funds. Any damage done will be taken care of and any hardships compensated.

"You have to look at the big picture. This is the best thing to do, for your entire community." Paul thought about this for a moment, gazing out at the peaceful surroundings.

"Apparently there's no alternative. And it sounds like a serious problem. But I'll tell ya, Bob, I do not like any of this. The big wigs could have come to me in the beginning instead of shutting me out."

"Yep, the two men that came to see me said it was a mistake. They thought they could contain the problem without alerting anyone, initially. Said something about a Doctor James they were originally after. That's about all I know."

"Okay, well, I guess thanks for being straight with me."

"What are you going to do?"

"I'm going to head back and see if this James woman is okay." He stood up to leave, then hesitated, before heading down the steps when Bob spoke.

"You remember what I said, Paul. Think about the town and the folk. The money infused will be good for your economy. You oblige by what the feds ask of you, whether you want to or not."

Paul turned to look at him. He took a deep breath to steady his anger, then answered with, "I hear you." He wasn't mad at Bob, just the state of affairs.

"Good.

"By the way, you see any of 'em?"

"Just one. Mark Gordon captured it. To be truthful we all thought it was a fluke. A regular black rat snake that had grown unusually big. It was certainly a remarkable sight.

"You know, Bob. It's not like I want an infestation of giant reptiles to deal with. I just don't like being run out of my office. Being kept out of the loop. I don't like dealing with the FBI, anyway."

"No one does."

"I suppose. But now I have to suck up their ignorance and play ball. Why in the world would they create something like giant snakes, anyway? And how did it get out of control to this extent? They tell you that?"

"No. You're going to have to ask them yourself. But I'll be honest with you, I was shocked by what they were saying. All I did was keep my mouth shut and agree to convey the message. I've never heard of such a thing before. I think my veins were bulging to the brink the whole time."

"I'll bet you were a bit shocked. Candidly Bob, I am, too."

"You going to be okay?"

"Sure, ego's a bit bruised is all."

"Say Paul, how did you get past their barriers? They said you'd show up here, but how was it they lost you or how did you lose them?"

"I'll save that story for one of our fishing trips, old buddy."

"I'm ready whenever you are."

"Thanks, I'll be in contact." Sheriff Paul Stone walked to his car hurriedly. He was worried about the safety of his people now. He knew the entire population of Greenland couldn't have been evacuated. And he was anxious to know exactly how the feds were going to remove these large snakes, wondering how dangerous they really were.

Chapter fifty six

THE DOOR TO THE PLASTIC enclosure Mark Gordon and Barbara James were waiting opened. An Army official decorated with medals came in and introduced himself.

"I'm General Sprigs, in charge of the Green Unit. I'm sure you've both heard of our branch and what we do."

"Are you killing the new breed?" Doctor James asked, heatedly the second she finished, uninterested in the prologue.

"Yes," he stated, flatly.

"If you'd like to follow me I'll be glad to fill you in on all the sordid details."

The general turned and walked back out. They went along with him having no other option. Mark noticed Barbara wipe her eyes as she filed through the door in front of him. He knew this news was devastating for her, on top of the other. Wasn't anything he could say or do to make her feel better, though. Just be there for her, he supposed. Mark felt really bad for this woman.

In another secured area within the large tented headquarters, the biologists took a seat where shown at one of the sizeable tables. They were offered food and coffee, whatever they wanted. Both declined. The man in uniform sat across from them.

"We **have to** destroy the snakes, Doctor James. We've looked into all other alternatives and there aren't any." Barbara sat motionless, glaring at the man. They had her lab, her life's work and she wondered what would be next. There had to be a reason for why they were suddenly willing to talk to her.

Sprigs continued to inform them, "Twenty years ago a group of our scientists had this crazy idea to genetically alter black rat snakes. I'll be honest in the logic. It was for warfare. They wanted to produce the perfect killing machines.

"They mutated several genes in the strands of DNA for several purposes. One, size, so they could kill a man. Intelligence was enhanced thinking we could some how teach them to obey. I'm not going to get into all the technicalities here, but basically the skin was changed for durability and the eyesight was improved.

"The first generation of this brood was not exactly what was planned. The fruition of the theories was not acquired. The idea was scraped. The snakes were supposed to be destroyed back then, but there was a mix-up and they were let lose instead." Barbara made a face and shook her head; however, she kept quiet.

"In the beginning, no one considered it a big problem since the snakes that were created were neither large nor aggressive. The skin was tougher and smoother and they could see more vividly. That was the only real results. They didn't show any signs of intelligence as anticipated. So, as time passed, the snakes were forgotten. On to bigger and better things.

"Then, close to six years ago we began hearing complaints now and again, about abnormally large reptiles with strange eyes and started investigating. We've managed to snag a few over the years. What our people have been able to determine is that with each fresh batch of snakes, they get bigger, stronger and more intelligent. The genetic disruption done all those years ago is what caused the latest threat to earth and mankind. We now have a completely new variety of Elaphe that are growing rapidly, reproducing rapidly, of high acumen capacity and dangerous to man, since they were projected to be. Apparently, it took years for the genetic structure to actualize the changes.

"I wasn't involved in the making all those years ago, but I head the damage and control unit. When we find a den we raze it.

"Doctor James, Mr. Gordon, I'm sure you both know by now we're not quick enough. And this past six years we've discovered that these novel snakes have split into many different lairs. They're on the move constantly and we suspect that natural genetic changes are taking place for survival purposes as well. As with any other species. Anyway, I've had to call in additional coffers and personnel every year since I took over. The problem is getting out of hand.

"That's where you come in...may I call you Barbara?" She nodded slightly, still not uttering a word.

"We need what you know; the reason we seized your lab. When your assistants called us, it gave us the legal means to do it. Your work is impressive and very crucial, beneficial to us, especially now. We're losing the battle with these things.

"I have as many as fifty helicopters cruising the skies day and night, all over the states using our infra-heat technology to find a suspected grouping. Then we have to use dirty bombs to penetrate twenty feet or more of soil and troops to finish off the ones that survived. This private war is costing the government some big bucks." He finally took a break in the unearthing and asked the two again if they wanted something to eat or drink. This time both took him up on the offer, a bit humbled by his honesty.

Mark was sober trying to comprehend the dangers this type of enemy could impose. He still wasn't convinced that they would be an actual threat to a person as far as fulfilling its hunger need. Nevertheless, he wasn't stupid and he could envision what a massive amount of these reptilian could do to the planet.

He knew the general was telling the truth when he said they reproduce fast and grow at an incredible rate. And of course, he'd dealt with two of them now and he saw how many were shown by the pet-cam, so he was fairly positive the carnivores could take over a specific area easily enough. But what he was most concerned about was the food they would need when there will probably be tripled as many as now in about five more years. That thought alone was demoralizing.

Mark Gordon had a problem with killing off a complete race, though. Then again if the mutation process keeps improving each brood, then what would happen?

Barbara hadn't thought about these implications since she didn't know about most of this. It was depressing. Her entire life changing right before her eyes, in a matter of minutes. She uncovered nothing. What a fool she thought she was. Barbara could have kicked herself, mainly because she should have suspected the snakes weren't *natural* to begin with.

As much as she didn't want to say it, she could see why the Army was trying to keep this a secret. The pandemonium that would surely wreck havoc with the world would be extreme. Oh and the political backlash on the United States would be horrific. What a mess. All because a bunch of idiots years ago thought about taking out North Korea without effort and without blame. (Could have been any country, but that's what came to mind.)

She wondered how they were going to continue to keep this on the lam when there were certainly more people like her on the earth already delving into the idea of creatures living below.

"The sooner we contain the species the better. You're both biologists, so I'm sure you appreciate the meaning of why these measures are necessary. Also, the reason why killing the snakes needs to stay a covert mission.

"Just so you do understand I want you to know I'm not an egotistical, power happy bastard. If and when the need arises to inform the public, I'll make the call. When it's undoubtedly at the point of no return, I'll concede." He took a sip of his coffee. Another man had brought all three of them some.

Barbara decided to ignore the loss of her life, when the entire world seemed to be in peril. Kind of silly to be upset when this problem is on a much grander scale. She was still let down, but not immature.

"Doctor James, I'd like to ask you to come on board with us. Help us," he said, startling the woman.

"Beg your pardon?"

"I want you working with us. It's that easy."

"Because I'm a security leak if I don't?"

"Not exactly. Let me be frank. We need your expertise. Your approach and educational history in the field. I think you'd be a great asset to us in finding the defunct snakes.

"Think about it." The general abruptly got up. He had been signaled to take a telephone call. He immediately left the room, leaving Mark and Barbara alone.

Chapter fifty seven

THE VERY SECOND THE DUMPSTER that Ann was hitching a ride on slowed down to turn, she jumped off and sprinted into the ditch, directly across from her house. The rumination that she was in large snake terrain suddenly impeded into her mind, but she didn't know what to do about it now. Taking a quick spy around her immediate ground proved nothing, thankfully. All she wanted to do was get into her house and make sure everything was okay.

Squinting to see further in front of her, Ann could see trucks in the distance, men on foot, but mostly lots and lots of smoke bellowing in the air. There seemed to be a cease fire at present. No more bombs going off that is. Ann could scarcely make out a foggy outline of her dwelling fifty or so feet away. It was a relief to see it still standing. What kind of shape it was in, she couldn't tell. She thought the men on each side were guarding it, she guessed.

Slowly, she got up off her knees and hands. Stooped down, Ann quickly darted across the street and yard, fanning the smoky air as she went. Her eyes were blurry and it was hard to breath, but she was making progress. Inch by inch she slinked to her domicile. There were shouts in the background and the rumbling noise of those dump trucks...

"Hold it right there!"

Ann let out a whimper. She was taken by surprise thinking no one spotted her.

"Turn around!" She did. And fast.

"Who are you?" It was one of the army men holding a gun pointed at her mid section.

This was the second time today someone aimed a gun at her. Ann was thinking she was an English teacher or wanted to be, for God's sake. A simple girl. Wanting to lead a simple life. What happened to that idea? How on earth had their dreams come to this? And why would she be a threat to this asshole?

"I'm Ann Rock. I live here and get that damn gun out of my face, mister," she demanded, forcefully. She was going to have to get control of her life somehow, wasn't she?

"What are you doing here?" He lowered his weapon.

"I want to check **my home.** I have a right. I pay taxes."

He took a walkie-talkie off his belt and radioed someone else with the information that he had a young woman wanting to gain access to her house. Then he asked Ann to please wait one minute.

Finally, "Okay miss, we can go in. There was no fighting in or close to your house. It all took place a ways from here."

Fighting?

"I suppose I'm to say thank you?" Ann looked at him with disgust, before whirling back around and marching on into her home. The soldier went with her. They entered together, him scanning every inch of the area. The house was a little smoky and filled with dust, but everything was in order. Ann was a little disheartened realizing the cleaning that would need to be done when they had already spent so much time on the place. She sat her purse down on the kitchen table and herself in one of the chairs. What a disaster this was turning out to be. The guard followed her and stood in the doorway.

"Someone is on their way in to talk to you."

"Why? I don't even know what's going on. Why don't you tell me?"

When he didn't answer, all Ann knew at that moment was the young man in uniform had suddenly became a solid, thick, black moving spiral in a freaking instant. The speed and agility one of the titanic ophidian displayed was beyond description. One second he was standing there in his army duds, gun in hand talking to her and the next he was enveloped by the unheard of. The snake had him completely bounded from the head to the toes. He had no chance and hadn't so much as made a sound, let alone a struggle. No one could have fought against that quick of an attack. Especially by something you couldn't hear coming for you.

Ann didn't move a muscle. Couldn't. All she could do was watch the man die. The snake's unnatural eyes were focused on her as it used its dominant and mighty body to squeeze the life out of the human. And it didn't take long. The atrocious wasn't suffocating him. Ann heard the sound of bones breaking instead of the man's actual breath being forced from him slowly. It was a horrifying scene, gross to hear and an unreal situation to be in, but happening so fast there was no time to react or feel the fear. Or comprehend in all pragmatism. Ann and the scary locked gazes.

When the snake uncoiled instantaneously after that wicked splintering and crunching, it was in Ann's face in the next tick. The mysterious hissed that whistling murmur. The massive body curled to an almost standing position leaning forward with its neck skulking. The purplish skin jerked as usual, she suddenly remembered.

This time she saw the great white fangs as its mouth was opened. But Ann still couldn't move and she couldn't scream either. Out of the corner of her eye she could see the body of the person that was just murdered in front of her, crumple to the floor. That's how quick this snake was. When it let go of its prey, he was still in a standing position. His eyes were wide open, death covering his face. It was sickening. There was a thud when he hit the floor.

The slick, silent beast turned and disappeared abruptly just as Ann blinked. Which was her only body part to budge. She barely caught sight of the tail slipping through the doorway over the dead guy.

Ann stayed in her somber state. She wasn't going to forget this, ever. The realization of how dangerous the reptiles could be struck her in the gut. She also knew in that moment they hadn't hurt her when they could of so many times. Why? Was the baby saving her life, she wondered. Mark mentioned her hormones could be what they identified with.

The unbelievable breezed in here and slaughtered that soldier, but only hissed at her. Was it because she had never been a threat to any of them? And the man was? It dawned on her the Army was here blowing up the place around her house. They must be trying to kill these snakes!

Maybe the snakes are fighting back?

Just as that thought entered her head, she was able to gain control over her body. She awkwardly and hurriedly shoved herself away from the table and onto her feet. Ann stumbled to the door in her trauma. She had a need to see what was going on in her patch of the world. And get away from that dead soldier.

Forcing her will, she ran through the kitchen door and outside. Without faltering, Ann Rock broke into a jog, then found the energy and strength to run through the hazy nightfall, choking back tears. Tears for the loss of life she just witnessed and tears for the strange life form from down below. It was bewildering. Ann had no idea where the emotions for the hideous snakes were coming from. Maybe it was because they showed signs of intelligence?

Ann was breathing hard, but had made it about a mile into the country. She could see more trucks and men in large bombarded holes working furiously. Blood was everywhere. The smell was horrific. Indescribable really.

As she glanced around, she instantly became aware there was blown up snakes scattering the once beautiful land. The lights from the vehicles made it possible to see the ugly mess in front of her. She'd never seen anything like this and prayed to God she never would again. Ann's mind was racing, trying to come to terms with what lay not far from her own immediate backyard.

She stopped to catch her air and watch the unfathomable taking place before her very eyes. They had demolished the new breed of reptiles Mark and Barbara had discovered. There was no way she could guess at how many had been destroyed, but it looked to her there were scores. It was a gruesome spectacle. One that would be ingrained in her mind forever. And it was extremely hard to understand.

Ann had been afraid of the terrorizing monsters, yet she was learning about them whether she wanted to or not. For some odd reason they sought her out, to communicate with. That's what Barbara had thought. And now all she could think of was that if she hadn't been so afraid of the different, then maybe they wouldn't have had to be massacred. She felt responsible. That young man back at the house wouldn't have had to die. And just because she was frightened of something didn't mean it had to die either.

Guilt and sorrow filled her soul. What she was seeing wasn't right. She could feel in her bones this wasn't necessary. And it was totally her fault. If she could have just tried to listen to them...

Ann fell to her knees. Liquid spilled from her eyes, but she kept them open. She watched as the pieces of snakes, the blackness of their once living bodies were being loaded into the dump trucks. When one was full it drove away and another took its place. The men out here were all picking up what was left of the once living and getting rid of the novel race. And there was nothing she could do. Not now, it was simply too late.

Chapter fifty eight

Ann Rock didn't know how long she was kneeling in the God forsaken, what used to be, picturesque landscape, watching the unimaginable take place before her. Or why she was even torturing herself by staying here. But she couldn't seem to find the motivation to get out of this hell. All she could think about were the events leading her to where she was presently.

Her perfect wedding entered her head. The daffodils and the lily's were so beautiful. It hadn't been that long ago since she was naive, happy and idealistic, starting a brand new life, here, in Greenland. Never in a million years would she have thought this was how things would end up. She had no idea if she would ever get over the strange and heart-breaking experience. Let alone all the fear her body endured during the recent tribulations. And now it was angst she was dealing with.

She hoped Mitch was okay. And she had a dire need to see her sister. She guessed being amongst this repulsive catastrophe was making her miss her own family. These dead snakes were probably related, she thought. How sad it all was. For all of them to be killed, in such a violent manner.

Watching snake after snake body parts being hauled off and all the men out here dutifully carrying out these orders, without a word, was as if being in another world. No one even noticed her, or so it seemed.

They were getting rid of evidence as quickly as they could, traipsing all around her.

Ann noticed the air clearing some and a sparkle of daylight beginning to shine through the tree tops. She had no idea what time it was.

A voice catapulted her to quickly turn around and see who was behind her. It was Sheriff Stone she saw. He surprised her. She hadn't heard him walk up.

"Ann, you okay?" She gave him a slight smile. It was one of grief and sorrow. Seemed like that's all anyone ever said anymore – *you okay?*

She simply nodded. She didn't really feel like talking right now. He reached his hand out to her to help her off the ground. She took it and slowly got up, glad he was here. As they began to walk to his car, Ann couldn't bring herself to look back. It was all too morbid. Those people cleaning up the mass destruction, without remorse.

The sheriff understood the need for no conversation as they ambled, his arm around her and her arms around herself. He wasn't sure how he felt about the situation, let alone pretend to know what this young gal must be going through.

Paul was only going on the instructions he received once he called in. The FBI had told him to find this woman and that they had last been informed she was wanting to see her home. He drove straight there from Hayden. Worried about, well, just about everything. The people vacated, the people who weren't, the bombing of the snakes, the snakes in themselves, the FBI's ability to do whatever they wanted and Ann, whom he was escorting back to the hospital.

When the sheriff had arrived earlier at the Rocks, he saw the dead guy in the kitchen doorway. He became anxious to find Ann, but it seemed as if his instincts took over, leading him to her a few minutes ago. He was relieved she was alive, yet shocked by what she was engrossed watching. The sight and smell of the dead snakes was everywhere. It wasn't pretty. And the blood was nasty. He'd never seen so much in one place at a single time. Hoped he never would again either.

He was sad. This wasn't the same town he'd grown up in and he wondered how they would ever get back to normalcy here.

He opened the passenger side of the patrol car door for Ann. She thanked him in a whisper. He smiled, trying to comfort her, but knew nothing could. It would take time, he knew, for all of this to sink in, digest and be able to get over. For all of them, although he was sure he hadn't been through what Ann Rock had. The others too, he judged.

It was a quiet ride into the town, except for the dump trucks they passed every so often. They were loud. He wondered to himself how long it would take the Army to clean up this mess. They'd had his borough in their control so damn fast, he sort of figured it would probably be no time, before they were finished. Amazing, the power and strong-arm the government has.

They pulled up to the hospital a few minutes later and Paul escorted the woman to her husband's room. He was awake when they strolled in.

"Ann, where have you been?" Mitch asked, his deflated wife. She practically ran to him in her state of melancholy and immediately hugged him. He hugged her back. He didn't say anything else, automatically knowing she was upset and just needed comfort. He felt all the love he had for her, in the calm of this room, at that very moment.

The sheriff sat down in one of the chairs next to the couple. He stayed silent, waiting. When Ann finally did unwrap from her husband, she looked at him and said, "I appreciate you bringing me back here. Thank you."

"Your welcome. Do you need anything? Can I get you something?" She looked back to Mitch in a way that was asking him if he did.

"I know a lot is happening around here, but I'm starving," he said, right away. She looked lovingly at him. It broke the grim mood for her, temporarily.

"I guess we do want something, Paul. You mind?"

"Not at all. In fact, I can't remember when I ate last. I think I'm starved, too. Hell, its daybreak already. No wonder." He winked at the Rocks, hurrying back up, pleased he could do something, anything. Probably to make himself feel useful. And to avoid having to socialize with the feds and deal with what was taking place. He didn't think the killing of the reptiles was right, but he wasn't in command. Nothing he could do. And he had to accept that no matter what.

After he left the room, Ann told Mitch about her latest encounter. He was taken for a loop hearing everything she had to say. And angry, too. At himself. Again for being weak and unable to be the man. He hated the fact he was out cold, while his recently pregnant wife was out at their land witnessing something this unbelievable, the killing of the beasts, and also, she could have been in harm's way.

Mitch almost cried when she told him about the cruel manner in which the snakes were killed and then disregarded, in front of her very eyes. She shouldn't have had to go through that. Not alone. He could see how upsetting it was to her, but at the same time he was glad they were gone. Still, he sympathized with his wife.

Mitch couldn't help but think about everything she had been through, without him. He'd been run through the ringer, too, just not as much as what she had. He didn't like it. He had no idea if they would ever be unchanged from all this, especially since he was noticing an even different temperament in his wife right now. She spoke calmly, even though she was troubled, her once dramatic style was gone.

"It was horrible, Mitch. And I feel responsible. If I hadn't been so scared all along and kept forgetting things, then maybe I could have saved an entire race."

"Ann, don't do this to yourself. They were snakes, for Pete's sake. Not people. And they were dangerous and getting more and more so. If the government felt there was a need to kill them, then there was.

"You said there were a lot of them, right?" She nodded, looking at him, hoping he could say something to make her feel better.

"Well then, that's scary, Ann. And don't forget how scared we were of them. Fear is a survival instinct and you were right to be afraid. One almost killed Barbara, remember?"

"That's just it, Mitch. They never hurt me and if I could have been more mature, then that case scenario wouldn't have even happened. It's all my fault. Somehow I can't help but think I might have been able to communicate with them had I..."

"Stop it, Ann. It's over. Please. We can't change the past. No one can. All we can do is learn from all this. Okay?

"Look, let's give this a couple days. We'll go home for a visit. Think about things. See Meg and your mom. What do ya say? I don't want you feeling bad. We have a baby to think about now."

"I know, I know. But..."

"No, no buts," Mitch emphatically insisted. "Tell me what happened to Mark and Barbara, do you know?"

"The military came in an hour after we got here and asked Mark and Barbara to go with them. I don't know where they went.

"Have you looked outside?"

"No."

"Well Mitch, the entire United States Army is here, in Greenland. To kill those snakes. It's strange. Really strange. The people are gone and it happened so fast."

"Ann, everything is going to be okay."

Mitch didn't tell his wife one of the officials had been in to see him. He's actually the one who suggested they visit St. Louis for a few days, insisting it was best for them. And he made it clear, they wouldn't be allowed back on their property for the time being. It was best he got his wife out of here, until they had a chance to clean up the land.

He also emphasized the necessity to keep quiet about what they knew.

"All I could find in this joint were sandwiches. Hope its okay," the sheriff announced, coming back into the room, bringing an end to Ann and Mitch's conversation.

Chapter fifty nine

MARK WAS TALKING WITH DOUG this morning, while Barbara sat alone in the secured room, thinking. The general had been called out last night, but he never came back. The two had waited for him this whole time, before another man told them it was over, they could leave. That someone would be in contact with Barbara, soon.

When Mark had spotted the deputy through the plastic window, he took off, telling her he would be right back. It was fine. She needed to go over everything that had taken place and everything she'd been told, by herself. And she needed to reflect about the job offer. And about Mark's proposal. Shit.

All they talked about this entire time was how the government went about business and the reasoning behind their wanting to kill the large Colubrids. If they could believe all that was told to them, then they had both *guessed* they understood. It was a let down though, for them, especially Barbara, to not be able to study the novel breed. However, she could if she took the job. But did she want to work covertly for the feds?

How can my life be in such a state? What am I going to do?

If Barbara took the employment, she knew she couldn't marry Mark Gordon. She wouldn't be living here in Greenland. She'd be on the road, instead. And she imagined the work would be extensible and time consuming. No way could she have both. This torment wasn't fun.

Her whole adult life had been involved in what lived deep within the earth, and now, how could she give that up? She had a feeling the university would cut her off when they found out about her private laboratory. And they would once they realized she used them to intercept phone calls, keeping them secret for her own benefit. So if she wanted to continue her dreams, the only way it seemed it could happen, would be to say yes to the general. To completely start over on her own, seemed unrealistic.

But she loved Mark. Leaving him wouldn't be easy, if she wanted to. Did she? When that snake had almost destroyed her physical being and she came to, the first thought that swam through her mind was that she wanted nothing more than to spend eternity with the man. Maybe she should listen to that gut intuition?

About the time Barbara decided to give up this life altering decision and make it another day, Mark came back in through the door. He stopped short upon seeing her. He knew immediately she was mulling over what it was she wanted out of life. Odd how he knew her so well in such a short time, but he did.

His heart sank to his stomach as he realized she even had to think about it. The choice she would make. It meant to him, she couldn't possibly care enough for him if it was this hard, according to her expression she was giving him now. He hadn't expected this. It was a tough knock to deal with, on top of everything else.

They'd been so engulfed with the information from the general that he hadn't thought about her considering the other offer. He expected they would begin a new life together, along with a new research project. Possibly continue their own discoveries concerning the latest earth dwellers.

"Mark, what are you doing?" Barbara asked, curiously, seeing him stand in the doorway and stare at her.

"Why don't you tell me what you're doing?" came out, before he could help it. The tone in his voice was stale.

"I...just...I was just...thinking." He kind of scared her here. Her heart flipped a beat.

"Yeah, that's what I figured." Mark gazed down to the ground trying to come up with a way to say this tactfully. And a way to keep his hurt in tact. Although, he didn't feel like being tactful. The woman of his dreams was squeezing the life from him. Or so it felt these feelings were crushing his chest and the breath right out of him.

Gaining the strength to get this over with, he said, "If you have to *think*, then I don't see a future for us. Not together, anyhow." He looked her in the eyes.

Barbara was stunned, speechless. She could only sit there and gaze back at him. When she didn't say anything at all, he couldn't bare looking at her. He abruptly turned around and walked out of her life.

Unexpectedly, as Mark disappeared through the doorway, Doctor James had a flashback. To when she was ten. It was as clear as yesterday to her. However, not something she ever remembered, before this very minute. It was of her own father walking out the door that cold and dreary day in her youth.

Her mother and father had another long and drawn out yelling match, while she and her brother were sitting on the steps to the upstairs of her old house, listening. They both heard him say he didn't love her. That he was leaving. And he did. Almost as he said those words, they spied him at the front door. Without turning around, he strolled out of their lives. And there wasn't even so much as a care in the world for her, or her sibling. Not even a glance. It was more than devastating.

They never saw him again after that. And their mother never ever talked about the incident to them. In fact, none of them ever discussed the man again. He simply didn't exist anymore. Barbara didn't know why, but this shameful recollection brought tears to her eyes. She hadn't cried about it back then.

She also didn't know why this memory came to her now, in this predicament she faced at the age of forty-two. Or what it meant exactly. It was extremely painful, though. She knew that.

Barbara James got up and ran out of that place, to the exit door and on outside to the road. She kept going, too, until she reached town, never looking back at what could have been her world. She was mystified and dazed by the last seventy two hours and now this unexplained blast from the past was haunting her. All she could feel was the need to *run away.*

When she made it to the hospital, sweaty and worn, but still wound from the upset, she found a pay phone and tried to get it to work. It didn't. Frantic, she looked around desperately, wanting to find a means out of this situation. Emotions she hadn't experienced before filled her gut and she needed them to be gone. They were too hard to cope with. She wanted to go home, even though her lab was in reality her home and wasn't there any longer.

She quickly remembered she was employed with the Army, or would be soon. She could use that tidbit to get her a vehicle to get the hell out of here. She jogged back outside trying to find someone in charge. Her mind was in a jumble as she thought maybe she could go to Steve's. Surely he and Jim needed answers from her since she was responsible for taking away their lives, too. But hopefully they would understand and take her in. She didn't know. She just needed to leave Greenland, as soon as possible.

Mark never turned around after he gave the woman he loved the brush off. He was incredibly upset, but what was he going to do? He could only pick up the pieces of his world, help with the pieces of his town and get on with it. Even though he didn't feel like it. But he knew there was no other option for him.

He was feeling a heap of anger, too. He really thought the two of them would have made it. That there was no question. How dumb could he be? he wondered to himself. To think a woman like that could love him as much as he loved her.

Man, this hurt.

He made his way back to Doug, asking for a ride. The deputy was disturbed for the guy and obliged. He drove him back to Pine street, to his house as requested, which was another shocker for the men. The fissure had been completely fixed and paved. Both hopped out of the car to see if this could be real.

Mark in no way forgot what he was going through, but to see the repair done overnight like this was amazing. He had to get out and touch it. *How did they do that? In this amount of time? This is fantastic, yet unreal.*

Actually, all that had gone down was unreal. His whole life had changed, too, in a matter of a week. And he wasn't sure what he was going to do to fill the void inside of him. It was a feeling of intense loneliness tugging at his heart.

Doug had almost talked Mark's leg off on the drive. He still hadn't heard from the sheriff and he absolutely hated the FBI for taking over the town, practically destroying the place along with the reptilians. He knew Mark was distraught, but from the looks of him, he also knew he didn't want to talk about Miss James. So he didn't ask. He just ranted about how he felt.

The aloof attitude of the gents in charge of their so called *mission* here, really got his goat. He and the sheriff weren't used to not being in control and he repeated they could have handled the situation to Mark. Several times. He also wanted Mark to tell him everything he'd been told, after he finished with what he knew.

Mark invited him in. He did want to talk about the unusual. But not about Barbara James.

Chapter sixty

CLOSE TO TWO WEEKS LATER, Greenland, Kansas was back to almost normal. A few days after the annihilation, the town and surrounding country were practically *good as new*. All the holes were filled and except for the fill dirt looking fresh and several missing trees, it all seemed pretty regular. The Army was gone and the citizens were all working at their standard jobs. Except for the Jeffersons. They were on ten day cruise, suddenly coming into money.

The day the folk were let back into their domains was a day to celebrate. The sheriff and deputy had been at the roadsides, greeting each and every car, explaining. Charlotte was certainly glad to see them and couldn't wait to find out what in the heck was going on. When she first spotted the force, she was thankful, but asked the question as soon as she could.

"Why in God's name were we whisked out of here?"

Paul diligently told her about the chemical spill. How dangerous it was, the reason the town had to be evacuated so abruptly. They had to call the FBI in such a dire emergency. Of course, Charlotte remembered they were there before hand and how he hadn't liked it, making it clear she did know that and nothing sounded right to her.

The security had the answers, though. The sheriff told her the chemical was a new invention and the government was keeping a close eye on it, knowing the semi carrying a load was passing through Greenland ahead of time. They didn't really expect a problem per say with the chemical itself, but were watchful anyway. Something about how useful this type thing could be to the world, they were more worried about it being high jacked and getting into the wrong hands, then what actually did take place. However, there was no explanation pertaining to what it was. And they weren't willing to talk to the sheriff, until after the accident took place, the reason why he was perturbed by their presence, before he did know.

"Several deer crossed the road directly in front of the truck causing the wreck and the spill. Damn thing flipped over. Unfortunate, but lucky the feds were already here and could act with the speed they did. Everyone was okay and that's what should matter."

"What about the earthquake? Tell me why the state patrol took over. And what about them asking questions about Barbara James. In fact, Mark told me that was why they were here."

"Charlotte, the small rumbling down on Pine wasn't an actual earthquake, come to find out. It was a sink hole. It just reversed itself is all. Don't worry, it's been taken care of. The state officers were called in by a government party that watches these things. That was a totally different problem that just happened at the same time. Coincidence.

"And the FBI thought Doctor James could help. They were simply looking for her.

"Now, you're holding up traffic. I can get into more detail later."

Miss Charlotte went along with the charade as all the people did, but she expected there was more to this story. Only the sheriff and the deputy weren't budging in their stance. She knew a few people weren't made to leave, like the Rocks and Gordon, so she figured she'd find out what really happened, remaining suspicious.

But on this day, getting The Diner opened was more important. It was her entire life, so she let her inner rumblings go for the time being, glad to be home and wanting to help restore their town and the people's lives. She said she'd see the sheriff later and moved on.

Now, in the present, Charlotte still didn't have many answers and she and some of the folk were doing their damnest to find out why the land behind the Rocks looked like a mass grave site. Yeah, yeah. Paul kept telling her that's where they buried the newfound compound, she just wasn't buying it, was all.

Chapter sixty one

Mitch and Ann Rock spent a couple days in St. Louis, happy to be with family, getting over the short amount of time that had tainted their lives, probably forever. It was weird how it all went down. The doctor had come into Mitch's room shortly after the sheriff brought the food and dismissed him, never once mentioning the snakes. Or the invasion by the government. Or Mark Gordon and Barbara James. At this point they hadn't talked to the two biologists.

Actually, the sheriff never brought it up either. He'd been there with Ann and had seen the atrocity. The destruction wrecked upon the *innocent* – in her mind now. She couldn't understand why he only told them they'd visit soon. And that was it. He left after the doctor, practically right on his heels.

Anyway, they headed out of town that day and drove the entire route *home,* barely talking. It was dispiriting and a lot to take in; the whole new race thing. And there was really nothing else to talk about, anyway. They couldn't tell anyone. It was made clear by the guy who ushered them out of the hospital that day and amazingly had their car waiting on them, full of gas. Talk about not feeling welcome anymore.

So they stayed with her mother a couple days, until they got word the following Wednesday that Greenland High was open and the school was in session again. Mitch needed to get back to work. Ann did too, on the house. She was missing their new place and wanted to be settled, glad to get the phone call.

But the visit proved to do them good. Everyone was so excited about the good news, the baby that is, that virtually all they had a chance to discuss was the pregnancy. Meg couldn't wait to figure up the day it would be born, planning on clearing her schedule for that specific time, already. She was going to be a terrific aunt. In fact, Ann wondered if she wouldn't move to Kansas just to be near the new member of the family. She even took her to the doctor while she was there, insisting prenatal care be started ASAP. Ann went ahead and cancelled her appointment in Greenland since they were in St. Louis and rescheduled for the following month.

And she was glad she went. Turned out Ann was exactly one month along when the advanced ultra sound was used. She would give birth somewhere close to the first of December. It was ironic when the doctor told her, because it meant she'd gotten pregnant, before she ever forgot to take a pill, while on them. She decided God was certainly watching over her, willing her to miss those doses. They would have been bad for the baby's development. But the doctor assured her she and the little one were both fine.

Ann was relieved and happy her sister was with her during these first few days away from the abnormal living style she had grown accustomed. It's funny what you can get used to. And how hard any life change can be, good or bad. At first, living on the farm dealing with the daunting proved impossible and now, after understanding the perceived threat they dealt with were an advanced life form, she couldn't stop thinking about the possibility of communicating with them. Things could have been different.

Deep within, Ann did feel bad. She actually couldn't get the pictures of those dead snakes out of her head. She didn't tell anyone though, especially Mitch. He acted as if all was well again. Sort of like it never happened. Which caused Ann stress, but she never called him on it. She supposed he needed to be this way for a spell. Whatever he was going through, she didn't know. They only talked about the fact that Greenland was their home and they were going back.

Mitch knew Ann would never be the same person. He doubted he would be, but he was glad to be in St. Louis around family and friends. Around the regular. And away from all the upset and fright, the unimaginable and the ghastly. He was grateful it was over and that the creepy reptiles were gone, unable to terrorize them anymore. He wasn't trying to be insensitive to Ann's feelings about the matter or what she had seen, but she hadn't brought it up again, so he wasn't going to. He needed this reprieve from the chaotic lifestyle.

When at the doctor's office with Ann and her sister, he was ecstatic with the news. It made it all real to him. It was real before, but just having the man say he was going to be a father in eight months made him feel like one. He was relieved and ready to get on with life. He just needed these couple of days here, to let things soak in, or forget really. Not be responsible for anything, too.

Mitch decided when they did go back, it would be a fresh beginning for him and Ann. They would basically start over. Clean the house and get things done as they wanted to before...the nightmare. Get their life back to being planned and organized. Get ready for the baby. Live happily ever after.

Chapter sixty two

Mark Gordon stayed in his classroom after school, studying the anomalous rat snake, which was studying him. The two held eye contact. The damn thing had grown another foot and Mark pondered when it would reproduce.

It was unusual for him not be out in the field checking his crust sticks or looking for habitats, but that was pointless now. The downtown buildings were being refurbished as he sat here. By the government, disguised to be company workers from wherever and from whomever the made up employment was. Plus, the damage under his home was also being taken care of. He was amazed at the resources there actually was, to handle these kinds of *problems*. But supposedly there would be no worries about more earthquakes in Greenland. And insurance money was what the town folk were being told about the expenses. He didn't care anymore what people knew or didn't know.

Mark was still sad from losing the woman he loved, almost two whole weeks later, which would be tomorrow. He ambled back to his desk picking up the cat on the way. He sat long-faced in his chair petting the animal, deciding to open his mail. One thing he did have to be thankful for was the Rocks, he reflected. Ever since this *tragedy* of late, or whatever you want to call the snake's appearance and disappearance from Greenland, and his relationship with Barbara James, he'd relied on them for comfort. None of his family was among the living, his parents having passed on early in life, he had no siblings.

When all the uproar had come to an end, Mark realized he worked so damn much that he didn't really hang out with friends. Just his students for companionship. He had needed Mitch and Ann badly during this trial.

Fortunately, Ann wanted to discus the creatures with him. He had to talk about them. He needed closure on some level. If it wasn't with Barbara, then it would have to be his last year of research. Anyway, she wanted to listen to him and it made him feel better; however, he couldn't really feel that much better.

He kept quiet about the reptile he had contained. Mark thought it ironic the government knew so freaking much, but neglected to check out his classroom. It was obvious by now, Barbara hadn't told her new colleagues. That was something he guessed.

"You're a good baby kitty aren't you," he said to the cat, putting it down. In the summer time he took Charlie home with him, and some of the other critters. Mark made the trip to the school every day though, to take care of the others.

Down in the dumps, rummaging through the mess in front of him, Mark came across an envelope that wasn't post marked. There wasn't a return address either. His name was typed on the front. It was odd. He opened it without fanfare.

When he read the cursive writing that spelled out his name, Mark immediately knew who it was from. It was Barbara's handwriting, no doubt. He sat up forward, serious, anxious and leaned his elbows on his desk as he read this important letter. He had been slouching before.

It was as follows;

Dearest Mark,

I am so sorry for the way things ended. Please, I hope you believe that. I miss you terribly.

I want to explain whether it's too late or not. I don't in any way think you should forgive me, but this is vital for me to tell you this. I understand if you feel you never want to see me again. I don't like it, but do accept things the way they are. I can still see the hurt on your face, I caused, when you left me that day. I am pained by the reminiscence.

When you did walk out, I had a memory from my past as a child. I was ten the day my father walked out on me, for life. I hadn't ever thought about that very awful day, before this very troubling moment with you. I tried to run from the horribleness I felt in my gut. But it ended up being impossible, because it was from all those years of ignoring the deep wound my father caused.

I know you are not responsible for my mental health, but what I've realized since is what I want you to know about me. Remember when you said you knew nothing about me? Well, in all honesty, no one does. I've spent my entire life ignoring the hurt child in me, of course only to find out she wasn't really gone.

Seeing you walk out that door brought the same feelings front and foremost that the girl who watched her father leave felt. I can hear his words he told my mother plain as day ringing through my brain. He said he didn't love her. I think that's what frightened me the most. I grew up somehow believing I wasn't worthy of love, just like my mom.

I know it's not true, but it is seeded very deep inside of me. I guess at my ripe old age I'm going to have to learn how to love myself. The point is I was afraid of what we had. Crazy, isn't it? However, I want you to know that the love I felt, still do feel, for you is real. I made a mistake, not facing my grief. It interfered with my ability to make the right decision and I am truly sorry.

I wish you the best of the world, Mark. Be safe. If you have read this letter I hope you know I will always, until I die, miss you.

All my love, Barbara

That was all she wrote. Mark sat in his chair staring at the damn thing, a lone tear running down his face.

Chapter sixty three

Ann and Mitch Rock were back in the grove of their novel lives. It was Friday and they looked forward to the weekend and getting things done. She was fine. Mitch worked the rest of the week and everything seemed perfect in their world again. Ann wasn't scared to be alone anymore. Something inside of her had changed for good. She vowed to never be afraid of anything else ever again.

It was strange, sort of. When they had returned after the much needed change in scenery, the house was cleaned and the land was grated. All the newlyweds had to do was pick up where they left off.

Of course, they were sworn to secrecy about what really happened, but it wasn't a problem. Ann and Mitch agreed on the drive home that no one needed to know about the scary. On a certain level, they knew people had a right to live without fearing a serpent race that could actually take over the world. In fact, they talked a lot on the second trip, about everything and it really helped Ann.

And since they'd been home, Mark had discussed with them in great detail the impact people could have on the ecosystem, if they became nervous and started killing all Classes of snakes. Ann did not want that on her shoulders! The demise of the giant novel, yet scary beings was dreadful enough to bear.

Mark also explained the possibilities of the mutated race getting even bigger and stronger than they were, plus the fact of how easily and rapidly they multiplied. He told them the amount of food and space they would need in the future could certainly drown out the humans, along with all other species. And if their intelligence would have developed even more, it was probable an event such as this wouldn't be too far off. Of course, most of his hypotheses were just that.

Ann was beginning to see things worked out as God intended. She tried to believe that, anyway.

It was the beginning of April and foremost on her mind these two weeks later, was getting ready for the newest member of their family. Well, she tried to forget about the other, while making preparations and also continuing with the work on her house. One thing new she had decided to do was read the books she bought about all the wildlife in Kansas. She had every intention of learning about her roommates on this planet and then teaching her husband and child of them.

On this warm and breezy afternoon, Ann was outside planting some flowers. She had done so much inside that she needed to be out here, although this wasn't an important task. It was relaxing. Ann wanted to start enjoying what the good fortune their hard work had brought. She relished the sunshine and fresh air, making a point to enjoy her day.

Thinking about the steaks she was going to make for dinner, she smiled at the notion of how she and Mitch had no problem of getting a new list going. And they were making progress. They hadn't really changed, she thought. They were still planning out their lives as usual.

Out of nowhere, disrupting the peace and quiet, Ann heard a strange noise to the left of her, interrupting her speculations. She was kneeling on the front porch where she had already pulled the grass from the cracks facing the road. She turned her head casually to see what it was, without stopping her digging.

There, directly in her face was the monstrous beast she remembered all too well. The intimidation's neck was swaying side to side, the head of the living creature crept close to her face. The massive body of the novel ophiomorphous hung from the roof of her house. It's black hide ticked in beat. The eyes were unmistakable and focused on hers.

The noise was the familiar hissing the giant snake was making, only it wasn't as loud. Ann didn't flinch or bat an eye. She looked into the mesmerizing eyes of the overgrown reptile, calmly and paid attention.

Somewhere in Ann Rock's mind was the idea, she was thankful this large lizard-looking amphibian had survived. In another place lied her original fear, but she subconsciously suppressed it. The feeling of responsibility for killing off these things was stronger. She also felt sympathy in another part of her being for this one, knowing it lost its family, its race. She wished she could talk to it; however, she couldn't do anything. What she felt in her conscious mind was literally nothing.

The blackness of the skin against the underbelly crept as usual and she could see the fangs. Ann was aware of the powerful muscle the surreal had. She could feel its breath, while it maintained its scratchy murmur close to her eyes now. But Ann couldn't react physically to the ungodly, because deep within her intellect, it just wasn't possible.

Then she heard a car coming down the road freeing her from her illusory state.

The originally intimidating and unthinkable, abruptly slithered away from her. Just as quick as it had descended upon her.

Ann continued with her work as if this didn't just happen, because she didn't really remember in her cognizant mind.

Mitch came pulling into the drive a few short seconds later. He honked, seeing his wife enjoying her day and doing something she loved, for a change. He knew it was hard on her to let go what had come to pass. Hell, it was hard for him, too. But they had to. No reason to not live life to the fullest, while you have a chance.

All the things they discussed with Mark had helped some. Of course, they felt bad for the guy. He was so depressed over Barbara, he had hung out here since their return. They'd become good friends by now.

Mark had concluded a lot about the big snakes and kept working on figuring out everything about them. It was his way, Mitch thought, of coping.

One thing he'd deduced from the black, fast growing snake he still had, was that the skin's constant motion was a way the large were genetically changing. How he had it pegged, was that the snake's outer layer was adjusting on a cellular level, altering, to protect themselves from man's heat seeking technology. A survival mode metamorphosis due to the past generations being unable to endure the encounter. He wondered if Barbara had that figured out, but mostly he didn't talk about her.

In addition, Mitch and Ann almost had their book complete and decided to start working on getting a publisher. That helped take up their thoughts and nights, too. That and all the debate they had arguing about the baby's name. Mitch laughed to himself about this notion. He liked Jonathon Mitch and she wanted something like Jebb Adam. They both planned on a boy, although they hadn't decided to find out for sure ahead of time. Well, Mitch was trying to talk her into it.

Getting out of the car, happy to be home and spend time with Ann, Mitch unexpectedly looked to the roof. He thought he saw something move. He adjusted his glasses and blinked his eyes a couple of times, then searched the top of their house for a good long while. He didn't see anything out of the ordinary.

But he had that odd feeling in his gut again and began to get chary...

Oh... whoa...wow.

Mitch, buddy. Nothing is on the roof; it's just an old fear. Let it go. Come on, get a grip. Everything is fine. The snakes are long gone. New life, remember. You're being that dope again. Get over it.

Pulling himself together he continued to walk the short distance to his wife. "Hi honey, how's everything going?"

Ann smiled from ear to ear. "I'm fine," she sang. "I'm glad you're home. Hungry?"

Chapter sixty four

It took Mark a while to comprehend the unexpected surprise he was sitting there holding. After about five minutes of staring at it in silence, it finally dawned on him, Barbara would have had to of hand delivered this. Today.

When that concept hit him, he flew up out of his chair and stumbled out the door. He loved her and wanted her back. He'd been through hell the past two weeks without the woman of his dreams and this time he knew he would fight harder for the opportunity to love her forever, even though he knew he would no matter what.

So what if she had to think about things. He was the one who screwed up by not giving her the chance. He'd told himself over and over again what an egotistical-self-righteous-bastard he'd been to her. Kicking himself day and night for being so stupid.

And now, she believed he was so far into himself, she didn't even try to come back. Only an apology and explanation – that he didn't need or want. Mark battled down the hall and down the steps two at a time, racking his brain on when she could have possibly snuck the letter into his room, practically breaking his neck when he tripped on the last step outside. He was moving so fast.

But when he took a look around the school grounds, he didn't see anything. Her anyway. He let out a disheartened sigh and sat down. Most everyone was gone, so if her car would have been anywhere in the parking lot he would have seen it. He wiped the tear from his face. He wanted to just let lose and cry, but he knew he couldn't. Not here.

Mark lowered his head, his arms resting on his knees. It was a nice afternoon, but he really didn't notice. He'd already tried to find Barbara. But she was undercover according to the FBI when he talked to them a week after that horrible day. He had no idea of how to look for her. Or where to begin.

"Damn it, Mark, when did she place that letter on your desk? Think," he commanded, of himself, regret and despair swallowing him alive.

"Just a few minutes ago, Gordon, when you were staring at the defunct black snake no one knows you have." His head shot up. It was her. She was standing in front of him looking very much like an angel. But he was too stupefied to move. He wanted to get to her and grab hold, never let go, he just couldn't. He sat there like a fool gawking at the beautiful Barbara James.

"I love you, Mark Gordon."

She began crying. Tears welled in his eyes too, but he was still wordless.

In between blubber, she told him she didn't have her car anymore, because she didn't have a job. She quit. It was just her. That's all she could offer and she was afraid of that. The reason she hadn't shown up earlier.

"I decided the possible rejection you might show me wouldn't be near as bad as never trying. I was on my way a few minutes ago, after I left the note. But I had to turn around just to find out, Mark."

"Do we have a chance?" She stood there wishing he would say something, more scared right now than of any other time in her entire life.

It seemed like eons were speeding by, before Mark could comprehend his frozen state of utter shock. Finally, "Are you ever going to answer my question?" he choked out, speaking softly, his voice full of passion. She looked at him funny. Then slowly she remembered what he had asked her, in that room the day she found out her life, as she knew it, was over.

"Yes.

"Yes, Mark Gordon.

"I will marry you."

The Truth

THE LIVING ORGANISM THAT HAD just visited Ann Rock was on the move. The powerful, sizeable being was gliding through the earth, effortlessly and at an incredible rate. Three other outrageous reptiles were following.

It wasn't long before the snakes found their den, the same one seen on Barbara's camera, safe, unharmed. The many were waiting on the scouts. The unimaginable intertwined with the others, hissing as they went. The eye slits expanding.

These Squamata were certainly advanced genetically. It happened to be the latest generation of the novel breed of reptile stemming down the evolutionary branch of the government's experiment in genocide warfare. Twenty years ago the original offspring hadn't survived long. The mutated genes caused a short life span. But as with any other species, it *adapted* through the years.

Charles Darwin was the first to present this type of evidence of evolution. He provided the argument that all living things on earth today are descendants with modifications of earlier species. He also proposed a natural selection to explain how evolution takes place.

Over a course of time, a species modify their phenotypes in ways that permit them to succeed in their environment. Just as these newest members of Mother Nature have done. And it makes sense, the black rat snake, an easily adaptable reptile from the large family of Colubrids, would be the common ancestor in the history in making. Because a single species can give rise to two or more descendents the number of course multiplies.

All living things face a constant struggle for existence, including humans. Thus variation is inheritable; survival of the fittest very real. Adaptations are passed on to offspring, which are reflected deviations in genotype; genetic changes.

Because the rat population was already huge on earth and because they have no adult predators, besides people, it makes them the fittest Class of reptile, able to leave a large number of mature offspring, in which gives them mortality selection, along with reproductive success. (They did live in the dinosaur era.)

These newest carnivores' killing method is also a factor in being able to endure. The young are born able to feed, with already enhanced strength and ability to perform, each generation getting stronger, quicker and more intelligent. The mutated genes provided the ability to change faster than what's considered the norm. Instead of over a hundred years, it has taken place in twenty and it will continue to advance rapidly with each batch born.

The new and improved snake terrorizing Greenland and other parts of the world, will gain power in numbers soon. They will leave their normal living environment beneath the earth's surface, because eventually they will have to. When the creeping skin is able to adjust to man's machinery – able to be undistinguishable from heat sensitivity, which won't be a problem since they are ectothermic – then it will be time to surface for good.

The ones killed were of the second to last brood. The snake that had just been at the Rock's homestead was not one of them. The generation before weren't able to communicate as easily with one another as these most modern in fruition are. The reason for the different lairs. And the different behaviors the biologists noted.

The giant snake's environmental factors now are one reason the distributing traits they are passing are selected. Their food source is nearly depleted below. In order to maintain a healthy race, it will be imperative to operate above ground.

The government's interference in biological tampering with the natural has certainly changed ecology. Because the Kingdom of animal they chose had already been around for billions of years, the reptiles already had a proven capacity to perform.

A big mistake.

Earthquakes are being underreported by many agencies today. The volume and damage are being hidden from the average citizen, also the frequency and count. And think about the ones that aren't detected. It gets daunting.

Mark Gordon was correct in his theories regarding the cause; *perhaps a life force beneath our surface is the real underpinning of the earth's rumblings.*

About the Author

Diney DeRuy is the author of the series *i like ice cream in my coffee* and the novel *Tina Clay*. Born and raised in Pittsburg, Kansas, by businessman Gene Bicknell and tax professional Marie Brinkman, she is the second of five children.

Diney has the mind's eye to create an unnerving read. With her education from Pittsburg State University and by combining her life experiences, she is good at taking real events and twisting them into something frightening. Always engaging, madly ingenious and exceptionally creative, the reader loves her work.

DeRuy's home base is in Springfield, Missouri, and she writes with the encouragement of her three sons.

Printed in the United States
33775LVS00005B/122